the summer before the summer of love

Also by Marly Swick

Monogamy
(originally published under the title *A Hole in the Language*)

the summer
before
the summer
of love

stories by
Marly Swick

HarperCollins*Publishers*

These stories originally appeared in the following publications: "Moscow Nights," "The Shadow of the Cross," "The Other Widow," *The Atlantic Monthly*; "The Summer Before the Summer of Love," *The Gettysburg Review*; "The Ghost Mother," *Redbook*; "The Garage Sale of the Three Lindas," *Colorado Review*; "The Prodigal Father," *Sonora Review*; "Crete," *Indiana Review*.

HarperCollins books may be purchased for educational, business, or sales promotional use. For information please write: Special Markets Department, HarperCollins Publishers, Inc., 10 East 53rd Street, New York, NY 10022.

FIRST EDITION

Designed by Caitlin Daniels

Library of Congress Cataloging-in-Publication Data

Swick, Marly A., 1949–
   The summer before the summer of love : stories / by Marly Swick. —1st ed.
      p.   cm.
   ISBN 0-06-017254-1
   I. Title.
PS3569.W467S8   1995
813' .54—dc20   95-21750

95 96 97 98 99 ❖HC 10 9 8 7 6 5 4 3 2 1

acknowledgments

I would like to thank the Nebraska Arts Council, the Yaddo Corporation, the Helene Wurlitzer Foundation, the Breadloaf Writers' Conference, and the University of Nebraska Research Council. And special thanks to my editor, Robert Jones.

For Ray

contents

moscow nights

Sitting in the waiting room at Planned Parenthood, Jonathan and his mother made an odd couple. He could feel everyone's eyes on him, wondering. The young punk couple with the his-and-her studded motorcycle jackets. The stylish black woman with her gold leather attaché case. Two overweight semicomatose teenage girls. A yuppie-ish couple huddled over the Sunday *New York Times* crossword puzzle. Jonathan wondered if they had made a point of saving the puzzle all week for this purpose.

He wanted to be a good son but he couldn't help feeling that *this* was asking too much. Beyond the pale. Last week his mother had called and left a message on his machine: Could he possibly give her a ride to the doctor the following Friday afternoon? When he'd called her back to say okay, he thought she'd sounded weird. "What's wrong?" he'd asked her, against his better judgment, not really wanting to get into anything. During the past year or so since his parents' divorce his mother had started confiding in him things he did not particularly want to hear. Intimate things. Private feelings. Details about her sex life. Things he preferred not to think about—or picture. He had tried hinting that his sister, Debra, would be a more appropriate confidante, but his mother ignored the hints. His mother and sister had never really hit it off.

"I wasn't going to tell you," his mother sighed, "but since you asked—"

"You don't have to tell me if you don't want to," he'd interjected. "Really."

But of course she *had* gone ahead and told him. And just as he had known it would be, it was something he did not want to know. On the phone he had been shocked into silence for a moment. Then his automatic sympathy reflex had kicked in and he had mumbled all the appropriate comforting responses. Or at least he'd given it his best shot. But when he hung up, he'd found himself stalking around his living room, muttering curses and slamming drawers. When he calmed down, he had called Farrell.

Since Farrell had moved out, Jonathan had been rationing his calls to her—no more than one a week. They were "trying to be friends." Farrell had been skeptical at first, arguing that it would be better for both of them to quit the relationship cold turkey, but he had finally persuaded her to give peace a chance. Although he had sworn up and down that he harbored no secret hopes of a rapprochement, he still could not believe that it was over. *Kaput. Finito.* He had been in love with Farrell most of his adult life. They had met back east in college—Intro to Film Noir—and moved to LA to pursue film careers together. That was three years ago. Now Farrell was in UCLA law school and he was still writing screenplays during the day and driving an airport shuttle bus at night. They were moving in different directions, she'd said to him gently one night after dinner. Then, when he'd argued and balked, she'd said *she* was moving in a different direction; *he* was standing still—going nowhere. He was completely taken aback. He hadn't the faintest idea that's how she saw things. He said if it really bothered her, he'd change. But she didn't want to hear it. She had already rented a one-bedroom apartment in Palms, she informed him. Wait a minute, he'd said. But she was already packed and out the door. That was Farrell. Once she even so much as thought about leaving, she was as good as gone. "Bitch!" he'd shouted, running alongside her old VW. "Bitch!" Until she'd turned onto the highway and sped away.

Still, he loved her. He wanted her back.

When Farrell answered on the second ring, he was surprised. "It's Saturday night," he said. "I didn't think you'd be home."

"In law school there's no such thing as Saturday night." She sounded impatient. "I'm in the middle of *Palsgraf versus Long Island Railroad*. This better be good."

"It's good," he said, "in a bad way. It's my mother. I'm taking her to Planned Parenthood next Friday to get an abortion. This is a forty-seven-year-old woman we're talking about. Can you believe this?"

"Wow," Farrell said. "Your mother." He could tell she was picturing his mother with her matching handbag and shoes and hairdo that looked as if it had never been slept on.

"I don't think she should tell me these things. I'm her *son*, for chrissakes." He walked over to the tape player and inserted one of Farrell's favorite cassettes. "It gives me the creeps."

"Is that my Stephane Grappelli tape?" Farrell asked.

"I don't know. Maybe." He turned the volume up a notch.

"So why doesn't the guy go with her?" She was starting to sound impatient again and he imagined her flipping the pages of her casebook, neatly highlighting in yellow as they talked.

"You mean Re-Phil? Hah! What a joke. I told her the guy was a total loser. Not to mention physically repulsive. She says he couldn't handle it. She says he's quote emotionally fragile unquote. She refuses to tell him. Can you believe this?"

"Well," Farrell sighed, "I think it's kind of nice she's so open and that she trusts you. She's treating you like an adult."

"I'm not an adult! I'm her kid. It doesn't matter how old I am, she's still my *mother.*"

"She's also a woman."

"I don't *want* to think of her as a woman."

There was a silence in which he could see Farrell's suit-yourself shrug. He didn't want to push it. Just these past couple of weeks he thought he'd detected a gradual warming trend on her part. "Well, I'll let you go," he said, still half hoping she'd say it was all right, she'd rather talk to him than study.

"Okay," she said. "Hang in there."

"Right. Will do." He forced himself to hang up before he blew it by saying something insistently personal or pathetically sentimental. He marked a red F on his calendar and counted back, adding up all the other little red and blue F's. The blue F's were the times that Farrell had called him. The red F's were the times he had called her. Over the past two and a half months since she'd moved out there were only five blue F's as opposed to thirteen red F's. Not counting the times he'd got her answering machine and hung up. This depressed him. He looked at his watch. Lately, since Farrell moved out, he was always looking at his watch. Time moved more slowly, sluggishly. He felt like an old 45 being played at 33.

"They're already half an hour behind schedule," his mother fretted, blindly flipping the pages of a much manhandled *Newsweek*.

"I'm sorry," he said. He remembered Farrell's once pointing out to him that when he was nervous he tended to speak in non sequiturs. He got up and paced over to the window, waited a minute for the receptionist to get off the phone, then gave up and gravitated back to where his mother sat. "It can't be much longer."

"Oh well. It's all experience. Grist for the mill." As if to illustrate the point she pulled a fancy notebook from her handbag and jotted down a couple of phrases.

Peering over her shoulder he read, "like patient fish waiting to be gutted." A year or so before the divorce his mother had enrolled in an evening poetry workshop at Los Angeles Community College. The instructor—no doubt thrilled to find someone who knew how to use an apostrophe—had encouraged her to send out her work. The day after she received her first acceptance she announced she wanted a divorce. His father had been stunned. Whenever Jonathan visited him in his new studio apartment in the Marina, his father had seemed bewildered and woebegone, like a dog banished for bad behavior. Jonathan and his sister had held long worried telephone powwows about him—until he surprised them by promptly falling in love with a young woman in his building, a pretty divorcée with a six-year-old daughter. By Hanukkah he had himself a whole new family. So Jonathan and his sister shifted the focus of their worry back to their mother, who had joined a Singles Book Lovers Club and struck up a thing with some unprepossessing loser named Phil Kapischkey, or "Re-Phil" as Debra immediately dubbed him, since their father's name was also Phil.

"What on earth do you see in him?" Debra had protested while he was in the men's room. It was their mother's birthday dinner, the first time they had all met.

Taking offense, their mother had leapt to his defense, ranting on about how he had a Ph.D. from Harvard and had been a Russian Lit professor at USC before he retired, how cultured and refined he was. To drive home her point she said that they were reading *Anna Karenina* aloud to each other in bed—a chapter a night.

"Jesus," Debra had shuddered, "spare me the gory details." Their father at least had been tanned and fit—a weekend tennis player.

"*Anna Karenina*!" Jonathan had groaned, picturing the thick paperback with its thin pages and microscopic print. "You really think this thing's going to last that long?"

His mother was still busy scribbling notes in her little notebook when the nurse-practitioner called her name off the chart. "Evelyn Levitov."

When she didn't respond Jonathan poked her gently in the ribs. "That's you," he said.

She dropped her pen and clutched his arm. "I'm scared, Jono." She squeezed her eyelids shut, damming the tears.

His heart pounded. Even now—as an adult—it unnerved him to see one of his parents show any sign of weakness. "Come on now." He put his arm around her shoulders and steered her back toward the nurse. "It'll be over with in half an hour."

"She'll be just fine." The nurse smiled reassuringly.

His mother attempted a smile and handed him her alligator handbag. She was dressed in a gray knit suit and looked as if she were on her way to some ladies' luncheon. "Keep an eye on this," she said. "Buy yourself some lunch."

Listening to the forlorn click-click of her high heels down the ugly corridor, Jonathan suddenly wondered what Re-Phil was doing at that very moment. He imagined him hunched contentedly over a large bowl of steaming borscht. *Stupid bastard. Selfish wimp.* Jonathan stormed back through the waiting room and out onto the sidewalk and across the bright, busy street to a phone booth at a corner gas station. The phone book had been ripped off its chain, so he had to call information. *K* as in *kangaroo*, *a*, *p*, *i*, *s*, *c*, *h*, *k*, *e*, *y*. *Philip*. He scribbled the number on the back page of his mother's fancy little notebook, dropped in a quarter, and dialed. Re-Phil's "Hello?" sounded simultaneously suspicious and hopeful. For a moment, imagining his mother's possible outrage, Jonathan was tempted to hang up.

"Who is this?" Re-Phil demanded. "Speak up!"

The voice, professorial and testy, goaded Jonathan into speech.

"This is Jonathan Levitov," he said. "There's something I thought you might like to know."

His fury partially spent, Jonathan suddenly realized what he must look like walking down the sidewalk with his mother's alligator handbag. He tucked it under his arm and crossed the street to the coffee shop where he'd told Re-Phil he would meet him in twenty minutes. Re-Phil was taking medication for a nervous condition and could no longer drive, but he said he'd call a cab. He only lived ten minutes away, near LaBrea and Beverly. Jonathan ordered a cup of coffee and waited. Ever since Farrell had left him he felt conspicuous and pathetic sitting alone in restaurants, conspicuously pathetic, as if everyone were looking at him knowing he'd been dumped. He checked his watch, again, and glanced around for a discarded newspaper, a flier—anything to look busy and distract himself from wondering if he'd done a stupid thing calling Re-Phil. Maybe he should have minded his own business. Which he would have been more than happy to have done if his mother hadn't dragged him into this mess. All this new "openness" was highly overrated. When Debra had an abortion her sophomore year in college, she had at least been considerate enough to keep it a secret from their parents. He recognized one of the pudgy druggies from the clinic sitting at a nearby table, staring at him. She was gurgling the last inch of her Diet Pepsi and he had this terrible intuition that any second now she was going to come over and talk to him. Hurriedly fumbling with the clasp, he tore open his mother's handbag and fished out the little notebook and started furiously jotting down notes, his brow furrowed in mock concentration, as if he were trying to remember some complex mathematical equation. The girl got up and left. He relaxed and put down his pen. The notebook fell open to a poem-in-progress, with lines crossed out and cramped phrases squeezed in above them. His mother's handwriting was difficult to read, but the word "Kotex" leapt out at him. He sighed and slammed the notebook shut, signaling the waitress for a refill.

Two or three months after his father had moved out, his mother had dragged him to a group poetry reading in some little bookstore on Westwood Boulevard. The poetry was amateurish and he fidgeted in boredom until—at last—his mother got up there and started to read. Then his boredom turned to appalled embarrassment as she read one long confessional poem after another in some Amazonian voice he didn't even recognize. He'd expected maybe bad Emily Dickinson but this was more like bad Allen Ginsberg. She might as well have been standing naked at the podium. He wanted to stick his fingers in his ears. All manner of disgusting personal details—sagging breasts, hemorrhoids, flaccid penises, stretch marks, semen, tears, menstrual blood. There was even a poem about his birth, which she made a point of dedicating to him, smiling out at him in the second row, as she described the "wine dark slug of placenta" and the obstetrician "neatly darning the hole in the old worn sock of her vagina" until he was afraid he was going to be sick or faint. When it was over—at last—everyone had flocked around her, flapping excitedly, chirping their praise. Her cheeks were flushed, her dark eyes bright as she looked over at him as if to say "Well? So?" He had intended to tell her just what he thought—to really let her have it—but somehow, with all her admiring fans standing there awaiting his proud response, he had found himself smiling wanly and giving her the thumbs-up sign.

From across the restaurant Jonathan caught sight of Re-Phil heading toward him, breathless and unkempt, hair uncombed and shirt misbuttoned. In his white shirt and slacks with his thatch of bristly white hair he looked like an old polar bear. Not so much fat as massive. Jonathan looked pointedly at his watch.

"Sorry," Re-Phil wheezed. "The cab was late."

Jonathan plunked a dollar bill on the table and said, "Let's go. She might be done by now."

A tender stricken expression flitted across Re-Phil's face as he noticed the alligator handbag. "She didn't tell me," he said. "I didn't know a thing."

"Ignorance is bliss." Jonathan held the door open and waited for Re-Phil to pass through into the bright dazzle of sunshine. High noon. He felt like a bounty hunter bringing his man to justice.

The waiting room was more crowded than when he had left. Jonathan had to elbow his way to the front desk where he was told that his mother was in the recovery room. "She's feeling a bit woozy," the nurse-practitioner said. "It's not uncommon. We'll just let her rest a few minutes."

Jonathan squeezed himself in between Re-Phil and the yuppie husband and repeated what he had been told. Craning his neck, Jonathan could see that there was only one corner of the Sunday crossword puzzle still partially blank. On the table next to the vinyl couch was a wire rack full of pamphlets on various methods of birth control and diseases: herpes, gonorrhea, AIDS, PID. Re-Phil was engrossed in a pamphlet on the cervical cap. Jonathan suddenly remembered the time their apartment had been broken into when they were living in Dupont Circle. Predictably enough the thief had stolen a brand-new Nagra tape recorder, the stereo turntable, a broken Nikon, and some junk jewelry. But the thing that really got to them was the fact that the thief had taken Farrell's diaphragm out of its blue plastic case and stuck it to the bedroom wall with a hat pin from one of her vintage hats. Farrell, relatively calm and stoic up to that point, had screamed when she'd discovered it later that night. And Jonathan had felt the hairs rising on the back of his neck as she pointed speechlessly to the dead diaphragm skewered there like some voodoo sacrifice.

Re-Phil stood up abruptly, clumsily knocking over one of the pamphlet racks. "Here she is," he said. "I see her."

Jonathan looked up. From the other end of the hall, his mother gave him a limp wave and pale smile. Then she noticed Re-Phil. Her step faltered, the nurse gripped her arm more firmly. His mother looked confused for a moment, then angry. She shot Jonathan a dirty look. The nurse handed her a small vial of pills. "Just in case there's any discomfort." She patted her on the shoulder. "Be sure to call if you have any problems or questions."

The moment the nurse turned to go, Jonathan and Re-Phil both rushed up and claimed an arm. Evelyn shook them off. "I'm all right," she said irritably. "I can walk." She smiled at Re-Phil, pointedly ignoring Jonathan. "I'm sorry about this. It was sweet of you to come, Phil."

Sweet, Jonathan fumed. "Here." He handed Re-Phil the handbag. "I'll go bring the car around."

On the drive home his mother and Re-Phil huddled in the backseat. Jonathan felt like he was at work, driving the shuttle bus. He cranked up the radio and pretended to ignore them. In the rearview mirror he could see the top of his mother's silvery blonde head resting against Re-Phil's bearish shoulder. His huge hand cradled her skull, his fingertips tapping out the tempo of the music on her forehead. She didn't seem to mind. Jonathan remembered this game he used to play with his parents when he was little, just learning to read. The three of them would lie in bed together and trace letters on each other's backs, underneath their pajamas, and the tracee would have to guess the word. They called it Ticklegrams. He had tried it years later with Farrell but she was too ticklish, she could never hold still long enough.

They dropped Re-Phil off at his apartment on Sycamore at Evelyn's insistence over Re-Phil's protests. He wanted, he said, to come fuss over her—fluff her pillows and serve her hot soup and read aloud to her. Jonathan thought it was the least he could do, considering, but his mother held firm. "Not today," she said. "Maybe tomorrow."

"Promise?"

She nodded wearily. He kissed the back of her hand. *Christ,* Jonathan thought, *who does he think he is? Count Vronsky?* After Re-Phil got out, Jonathan turned to the backseat and said, "You want to come up front?"

His mother shook her head frostily. He shrugged and turned the radio back up. They rode the rest of the way in noisy silence.

At his mother's house, his old house, Jonathan busied himself making a pot of tea while his mother futzed around in the bathroom. When she emerged after what seemed like an alarmingly long interval during which he'd imagined her hemorrhaging to death on the tile floor, she walked silently past him into the den and flipped the TV on to "Oprah." He set the pot of tea on the end table next to the sofa and trotted off to the bedroom for a blanket and pillow. He was only gone a second, but when he returned, her eyes were closed and she appeared to be asleep. He tiptoed over and turned the volume on the set down and then collapsed into his father's old La-Z-Boy. Oprah was talking to obsessive-compulsives. One middle-aged Japanese man was explaining how he couldn't seal an envelope without first checking and rechecking to make sure his four-year-old daughter was not inside. Jonathan sighed. People were so crazy. He didn't know one person you could call really well adjusted. It was all just a matter of degrees, a continuum. Today it was red and blue F's on his calendar. Tomorrow—who knows? He got up and paced restlessly around the house. The hallway leading to the bedrooms was lined with framed family photographs. Mostly him and Debra, declining in cuteness with each passing year. There were a couple group portraits with his father, but his mother had removed their wedding picture, exposing an ugly nail hole surrounded by chipped plaster. In the dim light of the hallway he peered at his watch.

When he returned to the den, his mother's eyes were open. She had removed her suit jacket and was sitting up, sipping a cup of tea. Her hair was mussed, and in her satiny black slip it occurred to him that she exuded the mature sex appeal of, say, Lee Remick.

"You feeling okay? You want anything?" he asked.

"I'll be all right. You don't need to hang around."

"That's okay. I want to," he said, wiping up some spilled tea with a pot holder. This wasn't strictly true. What he wanted was to feel virtuous, beyond reproach. "Anyway, I don't have anything better to do." He meant to strike a jocular note but didn't quite make it.

His mother reached over and patted his hand, then modestly adjusted her slip straps. "You really need to let Farrell go," she said gently.

He shrugged. "She's gone." He swiped an old *New Yorker* off the coffee table and leafed through the cartoons. "We're just friends."

"Your father and I tried that—the friends bit." She paused to slosh more tea into her cup. "It didn't work. But then maybe your generation can handle these things better. Do you think?"

Jonathan shrugged. For some reason it irritated him whenever his mother tried to engage him in some discussion about men and women. Even though he was equally irritated whenever his father refused to discuss such personal issues, which was always. "In our generation an ex was an ex. Completely out of the picture. Of course we expected things to last forever," she sighed. "Whereas I don't suppose your generation ever really expects anything to last." His mother blew on the hot tea, musing. "There's some corollary or something there. Although I can't quite think what it is."

"If X equals expectation, and Y equals degree of friendliness with Ex, then more X results in less Y," he said, pleased with himself.

His mother laughed, spilling some tea on the blanket. Hearing her laugh, Jonathan suddenly felt something inside him relax and expand. For the first time all day he didn't feel like picking a fight with someone. "Hey!" He tossed the magazine aside. "I've got a great idea. How about some canasta?" He leapt up and grabbed the cards from the cupboard. "Jesus. I don't believe you still have these." He smiled at the worn, dog-eared faces of Lady Di and Prince Charles that he'd brought back as a joke from his junior year abroad. The summer of the royal wedding. He hummed as he dealt the cards, transported back to a simpler, more light-hearted time in his life. The summer he was twelve, with a broken leg, and his mother had sat by his bed playing canasta with him by the hour. The last time he'd played was right after he and Farrell had started sleeping together. She had come down with mono, and to help pass the time he'd taught her how to play canasta, but she thought it was a stupid game and insisted he learn how to play chess instead. Farrell was an impatient teacher and he was a slow pupil. They fought so much he finally flushed the chess pieces down the toilet. The evening of the ill-fated birthday dinner his mother had bragged that Re-Phil was a world-class chess champion, which was just one more black mark against him as far as Jonathan was concerned.

As if she had read his mind—it wouldn't be the first time—his mother suddenly stopped arranging her cards and said, "You know you really shouldn't have called Phil. He had nothing to do with it. You've just created an embarrassing situation. For everybody."

"What are you talking about?" He squinted at his cards, the setting sun shining directly in his eyes. "It takes two, you know. In my generation we males take responsibility. Fifty-fifty." He discarded the jack of clubs.

"What I'm talking about is that Phil Kapischkey and I have a platonic relationship, more or less. Prostate problems. And this medication he's on, well—" She shrugged and waved her free hand vaguely. "If you must know, your father was the one who—"

"Stop! Just stop right there. I don't want to hear this. Jesus!" He slapped his cards down on the tabletop, rattling the teacups. "You don't have to tell me this shit."

"And you don't have to shout." Frowning, lips pursed, his mother focused intently on her cards, fussily tweaking them into a perfectly symmetrical fan. Tweak, tweak, tweak. His arm shot out and knocked the cards out of her hand.

She sighed and glared at him—a cool, dispassionate, unmaternal glare. "Just what are you so angry about?"

The question surprised him, caught him off guard. He bent down and started picking the cards up off the floor. Lady Di's and Charles's royal smiles seemed to have frozen into aloof reproach. Hunched over in his chair, he could feel the blood rising to his face, his heart pounding in his ears, as if he were back in high school geometry and the teacher had asked him some question he didn't know the answer to. The loud silence. All those eyes trained on him. Then he heard Farrell's voice—he had broken down and called her in the middle of the night shortly after she had moved out. "You know what your problem is?" she'd asked. Lying there in the dark, alone, his heart pounding, he had said, "No. Do you?" And she had said, "Yes," and then heaved a big sigh and said, "Never mind," and hung up on him.

His first response was a sort of dizzying relief. Then, lying there in the dark silence, alone, he could hear the bees buzzing inside his brain. Curiosity propelled his arm out toward the phone and cowardice yanked it back under the covers. What you don't know won't hurt you, his mother always used to tell him.

He dumped the cards on the coffee table, looked at his watch and stood up. "Debra will be home in half an hour. If you need anything, you can call her." He zipped up his windbreaker. "Okay?"

"Fine." She shrugged.

At the door he hesitated. "Did he know about this?"

"Your father?"

He nodded.

"I thought you didn't want to know."

He walked back into the room and perched edgily on the arm of the sofa opposite his mother. "Just this one thing."

"It hurts," she said, picking up the vial of painkillers and prying off the lid. "Get me some water, would you?"

As he shut off the faucet in the kitchen the phone rang. It was Re-Phil. "How's she doing?" he whispered, as if he were in the same room.

"Fine," Jonathan said. Then, after an awkward pause—"Look. I'm sorry about all this. I shouldn't have called you."

"No, no. I'm glad you did. You did the right thing."

Jonathan could hear a piano rhapsodizing away in the background. Something tragically romantic. Russian. Full of doomed yearning. Rachmaninoff or Tchaikovsky. "Do you think she feels like talking to me?"

"Not right now," Jonathan said. "Now's not the right time."

"I understand." He cleared his throat. "You must wonder, I mean about your mother and me, and I just wanted to say, to ex—"

"Please," Jonathan cut in. "Please don't explain anything." He hung up and returned to the living room with the glass of water. As he set the glass on the table, he suddenly recognized the piano piece—"Moscow Nights." His sister had driven them all crazy practicing it over and over again for a recital.

"Who was that?"

"Count Vronsky, at your service." He clicked his heels.

"I thought you were leaving." She blipped the volume on the television set up, tuning him out.

"I am." He had to raise his voice to compete with the local newscaster's. "But first I want to know. Did he know?"

"Your father?"

"Yes!" He stomped his foot in frustration.

"It's really none of your business you know."

"I know! I *know* it's none of my business. That's what I've been telling you all along. But since you've *chosen* to make it my bus—"

"No," she said. "The answer to your question is no."

"No? He didn't know?"

She nodded. "It was just a silly accident. There was some financial stuff we needed to discuss and we decided why not try to make it pleasant, for a change—why not do it over dinner? Try to be friends. After all, twenty-six years—" She shrugged. "So it was pleasant enough. Kind of comforting really, you know?" Jonathan nodded. She paused for a sip of water. "Afterward he brought me back. I'd mentioned that the sliding glass door was off the track again and he volunteered to see if he could fix it. We had a couple of brandies." She sat up straighter and pressed her knees together primly. "Your father and I—well, sex was never our problem."

"You know what your problem is?" He could hear Farrell's voice again. He balled his fists in the pockets of his windbreaker and shook his head, as if to knock out her voice.

"You okay?" his mother asked. He nodded.

"You can imagine how foolish I felt when I found out—like some silly teenager, at my age. Your father has his own life now. With Jennifer." The name of his father's new Significant Other rolled off her lips effortlessly. No sign of jealousy. "There was no sense stirring up trouble."

"Trouble," Jonathan repeated tonelessly, suddenly recalling his father's one feeble attempt at a father-son talk. They were in the car. His father was giving him a ride home after a high school wrestling match. It was pouring rain and Jonathan was depressed and silent, having lost the match. His father, never noted for his sensitivity to mood, chose that occasion to caution his son about the risk of getting some girl "into trouble." He painted a gloomy scenario in which Jonathan dropped out of high school, married, moved in with the girl's parents, worked at a car wash during the day, took classes at a vocational school at night, and crawled home exhausted to a squalling baby and an even more exhausted wife. By the time the Lincoln had sailed into the garage, Jonathan felt like shooting himself to put himself out of this mythical misery. For months after that little chat, he couldn't even unhook a girl's bra without seeing himself dressed in sudsy coveralls, hosing down some car.

The painkiller must have contained some sort of sedative. His mother's head had fallen back onto the pillows and her eyelids drooped and fluttered. He tiptoed over, turned off the television, and shut the blinds. It was just getting dark out. He knelt down beside the sofa and whispered, "I'm going to take off now. I've got to go to work."

"You know why you're angry?" she murmured.

"Why?" He felt his pulse start to race. He held himself very still.

"You were always like this, always." A dreamy smile floated on her face.

"Like what?" he said.

But she was gone. Out like a light, as his parents used to say.

Outside it was dark and misty. He drove around aimlessly for a while trying to figure out what he felt like doing. He had lied to his mother about having to work; he had arranged for the night off just in case of any complications. His stomach rumbled. All he knew was that he didn't want to go home. He ran through a mental menu—hamburger, Thai, sushi, pizza—waiting for a nod from his belly. He was hungry but not really in the mood. Finally he just pulled into a Taco Bell that he happened to be passing. There was a newspaper lying on the table next to him. As he crunched on his taco, he skimmed through the movie listings although he wasn't really in the mood for that either. In the booth opposite him a fat bright-eyed baby held court, propped up in a carrier contraption on top of the table. A little boy about five or six tore off tiny pieces of tortilla and handed them to his baby brother, who squashed them in his fist and rammed them clumsily into his mouth. The boy's older sister was making a daisy chain out of straw wrappers, and the mother stared out the window dreamily as bits of shredded cheese and lettuce oozed out the end of her burrito. She was very pregnant. For the first time Jonathan thought about the aborted fetus and wondered if it had been a boy or a girl. Growing up he had lobbied tirelessly for a brother. A younger brother who couldn't run as fast or read as many big words. He had even had the name picked out: Duke. Duke Levitov. Finally they had bought him off with a dog. A German shepherd. His mother had automatically started calling the puppy "Duke," but he had said no, the dog's name was Major—just to let *them* know that *he* knew a dog was a poor substitute for a brother. The baby started to cry. The pregnant woman continued eating her burrito and staring out the window as if she were just some stranger who happened to be sitting at that table. The baby cried harder. Jonathan got up and left.

Instead of getting back on the freeway and heading for home, Jonathan cruised along Olympic Boulevard, listening to the radio, pretending that he didn't know that he was just stalling, just seeing how long he could put off giving into his worst instincts. He looked at his watch. Only six-thirty. He wished it were later, after midnight. For some reason he had this notion (fantasy) that things would go better if he woke Farrell up. Her defenses would be down and she would answer the door in her flannel nightgown all warm and fuzzy from sleep, a tender smile hovering on her lips from some pleasant dream—preferably about him—although he knew this was really pushing it. He also knew that Farrell was generally cold and crabby upon being awakened. By the time he pulled up in front of her building it was nearly seven. It was only the second time he had been to Farrell's place and he had taken a wrong turn. He slumped in his seat and looked up at her lighted window for a few minutes, trying to divine whether or not she was alone. Lights were burning in the front room. The bedroom was dark. He took this as a good sign, but as he walked up the front steps it suddenly occurred to him that maybe this was actually a bad sign. Twice he stretched his hand out to ring the bell and then snatched it back. His heart beat like a conga drum in his chest, some crazy savage arrhythmia, and he thought maybe he was going to have a heart attack right there on Farrell's front stoop. Then just as he was about to turn and flee, the front door flew open and there she was. In the momentary startled confusion he thought that she must have heard his heart pounding, like a knock at the door, but in the next instant he noticed that she was dressed up, dressed to go out.

"What are you doing here?" she gasped. "You nearly gave me a heart attack." She was wearing the dangly silver fish earrings he had bought for her in Taxco. As she spoke, they leapt and shimmied impatiently.

"I was just driving by and thought maybe you'd like to take a study break, go out for a cappuccino or something." Standing there in the dark Farrell smelled sweet and familiar. He had a sudden intense desire to lick her face, the way his dog, Major, used to greet him after a long absence. "I've had sort of a rough day."

"I'm sorry," she said. "One of my professors is having a party. I've got to go. In fact I'm already late. I promised him I'd be there by eight."

"No problem," he shrugged. "Just an impulse." He turned to go. "You look very pretty, by the way."

"Thanks." Farrell's voice softened a bit—relief that he wasn't going to create a scene?—and she slipped her arm through his as they walked down the flagstone path toward the street.

"So what's this guy teach?" he asked.

"Torts," she said casually, but somehow the word sounded sweet and gooey on her lips.

At his car they paused. It was cooler now, the marine layer. "How's your mother?" Farrell fished a Kleenex out of her jacket and wiped the thick film of moisture off the windshield so he could see. The gesture touched him.

"I don't know," he sighed. "Okay I guess. Considering."

"Frankly, I never knew your mother had it in her."

"You don't know the half of it, believe me." He was half hoping she would ask him what he meant and invite him inside to tell the whole story, but he knew she wouldn't. Somehow he knew that this torts professor was "the one"—the one he'd been dreading. And the reason Farrell was being halfway warm and affectionate was because she was happy.

"Let's have lunch sometime," she said as he opened the door of his car. "Give me a call."

"Sure. Okay." He nodded cordially. Lunch. It felt unreal. As she turned to go, his brain translated the action into screenplay directions—a little technique he had developed years ago, during a bad acid trip, to take the edge off reality—or unreality, depending how you looked at it. It gave him the comforting illusion that all this chaos was really under his direction:

> She leans over—through the open window—gives him a tender peck on the cheek, and runs off. He sits for a moment, watching her in the rearview mirror until she disappears out of his line of vision, and then, slowly, he turns the key in the ignition. Backing up cautiously, he maneuvers his beat-up car out of the tight parking space. Then suddenly, as if possessed—*Close-up of foot on accelerator*—he floors it and the car lunges forward. *Medium shot* of Farrell's crushed body. Something glimmers in the car's headlights near her outstretched arm. Camera *zooms* in. We recognize one of her silver fish earrings, lying there on the dark pavement like a beached mackerel. *Cut to exterior.* Mother's house. Night.

Jonathan did not know how long he had been sitting there in the driveway. The house was dark except for a light in the bedroom. He didn't really know what he was doing here. He had been half-tempted to follow Farrell to the party and to—do what? Punch the guy out? Kidnap her? He hadn't really even known where he was heading until he was almost here. In the dim light of the car's interior, he peered at his watch, surprised by how early it still was. Surprised that the night was still young when he felt so old and tired. And at the same time young—a small very old, very tired child in need of comfort.

He opened the car door and got out. The next-door neighbor's dog barked as he walked across the lawn toward the house. At the door he hesitated, wondering whether he should ring the bell so as not to startle her or whether that might only wake her up. He knocked softly. When he didn't hear anything, he opened the door with his key. It was pitch black in the entryway. He flicked on the light and kicked off his loafers. In his stocking feet he tiptoed down the hall and paused outside his mother's room. She was awake. Lying in bed watching an old movie on television, her hands resting lightly on her breasts in their flimsy nightgown. In the moment before she sensed his presence, he caught a private glimpse of her that made him catch his breath. A glimpse of her as a woman, a self, apart from him. But in the next instant she looked up and smiled and was his mother again.

"Hi, Mom. What're you watching?" he asked even though he had recognized the film at first glance.

"*Strangers on a Train.*" She yawned and patted the empty bed. "Join me?"

He was surprised that she didn't seem more surprised to see him. Almost as if she'd been expecting him. He padded across the room and stretched out on the other side of the king-size bed. "How you feeling?"

"Not bad, considering." She tugged her French conversational grammar book out from underneath him and slid it under the bed. Shortly after the divorce she had begun planning a trip to Paris. A commercial came on and she muted the sound. "How 'bout yourself?"

"Okay, I guess. Considering." He rolled over, his back to her, and sighed into the pillow. She picked up his hand and gave it a maternal squeeze. "I'm sorry I behaved like such a jerk," he said. His voice sounded small and wobbly. "I don't know what my problem was. Is."

"There's plenty of other fish in the sea." She slipped her cool, soft hand underneath his T-shirt. "*Il y a beaucoup des autres poissons dans la mer.*"

He flashed on a tight shot of Farrell's hand reaching up to unhook her dangly earrings and dropping them—plink, plink—onto the night table beside the professor's bed.

Outside it had begun to rain lightly. A gentle rat-a-tat-tat against the glass. He kept his eyes shut tight. His mother's feathery fingertips tickled as she traced the letters on his naked skin. He guessed the words aloud one by one. *SAD, MAD, BAD, DAD, GLAD*. The soft touch and simple words were soothing—*HOG, BOG, DOG, LOG, FOG*—so, so soothing—like rain, like heartbeats. *JOY, TOY, COY, BOY*. Her fingers froze.

"It was a boy," she whispered. "You always wanted a brother."

"No I didn't," he lied. "Not really."

She started to cry.

"Hey," he said. "Hey. It's not so bad." He patted her hand clumsily and handed her a Kleenex from the box on the night table.

"Look at us," she laughed and blew her nose. "Two real sad sacks, as your father used to say. It was one of his favorite expressions, remember?"

Jonathan nodded. On the television screen Bruno, the psychotic, had his hand down a sewer grate, straining and stretching to touch the cigarette lighter he had dropped. Close-up of the lighter with the crossed tennis racquets embossed in gold. The murder evidence. In college Jonathan had written a term paper on the crisscross imagery in *Strangers on a Train*. The professor had given him an A and said it was a "very mature" piece of work.

"You watching this?" his mother said.

He shook his head. "Not really."

"Then how about some canasta?" She tossed the used Kleenex into the trash basket beside the bed.

"Yeah, sure. Why not?" He picked up the remote and clicked off the television. "I'll get the cards."

He got up and walked through the dark house to the den. Next door the neighbor's dog was barking again. The cards were still out, sitting on the coffee table. He grabbed the cards and then made a quick detour to the kitchen, where he swiped a couple of beers from the refrigerator. He set the beers on the night table. His mother had put on a robe and smoothed out the bedspread. He handed her the double deck to shuffle. When he was little he used to love to watch his mother shuffle cards—so quick and graceful, like a magic trick. He practiced and practiced but never got to be much good. The barking next door had escalated into a frenzied lovelorn howling. A canine aria of outraged loss. Jonathan leapt up, walked over to the open window, and yelled, "Quiet!"

For a moment, there was a stunned silence. Then the dog started up again—a tentative whimper at first, then a yelp, then a full-fledged howl. Jonathan slammed the window shut and went back to the bed.

"You know"—his mother paused, cards in hand—"I still dream about Major sometimes."

"Really? So do I," he confessed. He had always felt a little stupid dreaming about a dog. "What do you dream?"

"I dream he's still alive." She handed him the deck. "That's what I dream, too," he said, and as he started to deal out the cards, he suddenly had an odd sensation, as if he were a ventriloquist and that dog out there were his dummy, whimpering and howling in the night.

the shadow of the cross

Lying in the unfamiliar bed beside his familiar sleeping wife, Evan tries to remember back to the time, not so impossibly long ago, when he did not love Delia, who is still awake, like him, in the adjacent hotel room. He can see the bright hem of light underneath the door dividing their two rooms. It seems, in the darkness, like some golden, electrified boundary: the line between right and wrong, the line between light and darkness. He imagines that she is propped up on a nest of pillows, reading herself to sleep. All day, in between sightseeing excursions, she has been reading *Death Comes for the Archbishop*. Unlike him, she reads very quickly and does not comment aloud on what she is reading. Her bright, dark, birdlike eyes seem to fly over the printed words. She makes fun of the ponderous way he pores over the travel guides, underlining and starring the important tidbits of information. She calls him "the graduate student." And his wife, Molly, laughs and nods her head.

The two women love to find him ridiculous. He understands the dynamic at work here and generally plays along with good humor. The silly but beloved castrato. That's his role. Meanwhile, Molly, the wife, must act unromantic and unpossessive so that Delia, the single friend, will not feel like a third wheel. And Delia, the loose cannon, must strike just the right balance so as to suggest that she finds her friend's husband attractive (otherwise both the friend and the husband might take offense) without actually being attracted to him.

Behind the closed door the light blinks off. Like Evan, Delia is an insomniac. And often, lying restlessly awake next to Molly, his brain grinding away in the darkness, he has thought that he should have married a fellow insomniac, instead of a woman whose eyelids seem to operate like an on-off switch to her brain. In the old days, in the early years of their marriage, it was different. Molly would stay awake, whispering with him in the darkness a kind of conversational lullaby until sometimes he drifted off to sleep before her. But ever since Aviva, their first daughter, was born, Molly has slept like a rock. An oblivious, complacent rock, he thinks, restlessly tossing off the blanket, although usually her soft, even breathing is a source of comfort and pleasure to him.

He slides gingerly out of bed, walks over to the window, and pulls back the drape. In the moonlight he can see the looming dark shape of Taos Mountain. He remembers snatches of Cather's description, which he skimmed earlier in the day, at the airport, when Delia left the paperback lying on the seat next to his while the two women went off to the ladies' room. In the deep, deep silence he can almost hear the faint clopping of Bishop Latour's horse as the bishop makes his way up the dusty path toward the house of Padre Martinez, that lusty, lackadaisical excuse for a man of God. In college ("The American Novel from Hawthorne to Hemingway") Evan had written a paper identifying Padre Martinez as the true hero of the novel. He remembers the novel only dimly and wonders if he would see it the same way now. Now that he is a husband and a father.

The dark, ancient immovability of the mountain calms him, and he thinks maybe he can sleep. The room is chilly. As he slides back underneath the covers, Molly's warm, soft, sleeping flesh seems like a gift, as fragrant and delicious as fresh-baked bread. He licks her shoulder and she stirs slightly, as if shrugging off a fly. He does it again and she does it again and he smiles to himself in the darkness, happy to have reminded himself that he does in fact love his wife. Almost as much as he loves their two daughters, Aviva and Chloe, who are staying with his parents, back in LA, for the weekend. With his eyes closed he can see them, clear as a home movie, lying in their twin beds, sleeping the deep sleep of the innocent. The thought of doing anything to lose them sends a shiver through him, and he nestles closer to his wife's inert yet receptive flesh. As he drifts off toward sleep, the ghost of Bishop Latour materializes in the empty chair by the window. Evan breathes easier as he senses the bishop's stern, unflinching eye gazing upon him, making certain that even in his dreams he does not cross that bright golden line.

The next morning the three of them meet in the hotel lobby and walk the four picturesque blocks to Michael's Kitchen, the description of which Evan has starred and underlined in his well-thumbed guidebook. The early morning light is so pure, so *lucid*, that he feels somehow relieved, as if this is not a place for murky, hidden entanglements. Only bright, primary relationships—wife, husband, friend—as in a children's book. A block from the restaurant the two women pause in front of a small gallery, their attention snagged by some unusual-looking rugs. He waits patiently for a few moments while the women debate whether a particular rug would look good in Delia's bedroom, and then, like a dance partner, he places his hand lightly in the small of his wife's back.

"Come on," she says, hooking her arm through Delia's. "We've got a starving man here."

Both women smile indulgently, as if his appetite were something sort of crude and silly and male, like a jockstrap. But once they are actually seated in the crowded restaurant, after a fifteen-minute wait, both women order larger breakfasts than he does. While he eats his modest scrambled eggs and toast, they wolf down Amazonian platters of *huevos rancheros*, refried beans, and tortillas. Between mouthfuls they negotiate the day's itinerary. The balance of power here is tricky. Delia, the outsider, insists on her total amenability to anything, while Molly and he gently butt heads. His wife is a great believer in spontaneity, hanging loose, what she calls "playing it by ear," a phrase he has come to detest over the nine years of their marriage. Having no talent for improvisation, he prefers the comfort of a set score. In the end, however, they generally end up doing whatever Delia wants to do. Because she refuses to state her preferences and because she is, in a sense, the guest in their relationship, they struggle to divine her true wishes and grant them. It is a form of hospitality, even though all three of them are away from home. By the time the bill finally arrives, they have agreed that they will spend the morning at the pueblo and then drive to the D. H. Lawrence ranch; the afternoon they will "play by ear."

Evan holds the restaurant door open for the two women. Every time he walks outside, he is amazed by the place, as if his amazement were a dog he had parked outside, to wait faithfully for him. After eleven years of Los Angeles smog he thinks of Taos as a sort of Shangri-la, except for the steady stream of traffic through the center of town, which woke him at dawn. He is a sound engineer for a recording company, and his acutely developed hearing is both a blessing and a curse. Of course, the traffic in Santa Monica, where they live, is much, much worse than the traffic here, but it has a different pitch and rhythm, so familiar to him by now that he never even hears it unless it suddenly shuts off, like the hum of a refrigerator. He notices Delia's pace slow down involuntarily as they pass by the shop with the rugs, and he can feel her wanting to ask if they can stop for a minute, now that the shop is open, and then deciding not to, probably because she thinks he won't want to.

"Let's duck in here for a second," he says, "and check out the prices."

Molly shrugs, surprised, and Delia looks away from him, as if aware that he is doing this for her. A faint smile flits across her face. Inside the shop the two women bend over a rug, examining it more closely in a businesslike way. Molly is a part-time interior decorator and Delia is a textile designer. They met about a year ago, when Molly "discovered" Delia, who was just breaking into the design scene in LA after several years in Honolulu. She has an ex-husband who doesn't get mentioned much, at least not in Evan's presence, still living in Hawaii. Evan glances at the price tags on a couple of the rugs and can't believe they're serious. Still, as he surreptitiously watches Delia's delicate fingers stroking the weave and hears her disappointed sigh, it is all he can do to keep himself from whisking out his Visa card and playing the indulgent father. What he feels for her, however, is not paternal.

"Isn't he being a model of patience?" Molly looks over at him and winks. The salesgirl laughs in a sisterly fashion. And he shrugs, a silly grin on his face, like some harmless husband in a sitcom.

"Let's go," Delia says abruptly, rescuing him.

Out behind the hotel, they are sitting in the car with the motor running, waiting for Molly, who has run back inside for the extra roll of film she suddenly remembered. He sits in the backseat of the rented Ford Taurus, conscious of his fuzzy bare legs stretched out on the seat. This morning, when he emerged in his khaki shorts, the women teased him about his gorgeous legs. To cover his embarrassed pleasure, he pointed out that no man these days would ever dare to make such a sexist remark about a woman. They agreed that this was true but appeared to feel no remorse.

Delia sits in the passenger seat, cleaning her sunglasses, which dangle from a shocking-pink cord around her neck. She holds them up close to her mouth and huffs hot breath onto the lenses, as if giving them mouth-to-mouth resuscitation; then she polishes each lens with the hem of her turquoise tank top. Each steamy little huff sends a shiver right through him.

Seating themselves in the car has become yet another covert exercise in diplomacy. When Delia makes a beeline for the backseat, Molly protests, offering various excuses to avoid ending up in the conventional gestalt: husband in driver's seat, wife in passenger seat, friend in backseat. "I feel like driving," Molly will say, or "Let Evan sit in the back so he can stretch his legs. Do you mind?"

The fierce sun beats down on the car and sweat starts to trickle inside his T-shirt, but he feels no real impatience for Molly to return. The radio plays Spanish pop music. Unlike the two women, who are fairly fluent, he doesn't understand a word of Spanish. He feels a vestigial flicker of anger from last night, the one time he has lost his cool thus far. Tired from the flight and the long drive up from Albuquerque, they were sitting out on the patio at Ogelvie's after dinner, drinking blue margaritas. They were all fairly smashed by this point, and the two women had started chattering away in Spanish, pretending to be talking about him, hamming it up, until he had stood up abruptly and stormed off to the men's room. When he returned, they apologized. The guilty look on their faces and their obvious desire to "behave" reminded him of his daughters, and he melted immediately.

"Would you like me to change the station?" Delia asks politely. Her hand dangles over the backseat, almost grazing his bare knee. All six feet and one inch of bodily sensation are abruptly focused in his right knee. He is hypnotized by the languid sway of her fingers. He feels as if he is back in high school. He hates it and loves it.

"No," he says. "It's fine."

Delia shrugs and nudges the air-conditioning up a notch.

The real agony is in not knowing what Delia feels. Sometimes he is certain that this madness is mutual, that they are both locked into a terrible frozen passion. What is so terrible, he thinks, besides the obvious guilt, is that it can last forever precisely because it *is* frozen: This passion, unlike most passions, cannot melt away or burn itself up. He remembers those rock stars in the sixties who used to have plaster casts made of their erections. He thinks he may be doomed to go through life with a permanent emotional, if not physical, erection.

Other times, he thinks the whole stupid, sick thing is all in his own mind and hormones. Delia is completely innocent, "clueless," as his older daughter would say. If Delia knew what he was thinking and feeling, she would be furious with him for ruining a lovely, lighthearted friendship. Sometimes he thinks maybe he should just get it off his chest, confess to her like a naughty little boy, and try to proceed as if this were just a silly adolescent crush, which in fact it may be. But something always stops him. He's not exactly sure what. He's not sure of anything anymore. It could be loyalty to Molly, he thinks, but more likely it is the fear that Delia will say she feels the same way he does. And then what?

Delia leans over and punches in a different radio station. He thinks about leaning forward and switching off the ignition to save gas, but he feels somehow safer with the motor running. The best evidence to support his theory that his passion is not totally unrequited is how silent they get whenever Molly leaves them alone for more than a minute. The joking drops away. Around Molly they are like two old friends, but alone together they become strangers. Their silence seems to expand inside him, the pressure building, until he thinks it might blow a hole through his chest. He rolls the window down, then back up, as if to let something in or out.

"Here she comes. Finally." Delia pats his knee as she waves to Molly running across the parking lot, her Nikon suspended from her neck like a third eye.

"Sorry, sorry, sorry." Molly slides in breathlessly behind the wheel. "Here." She yanks the camera strap over her head and hands Evan the Nikon.

As she puts the car in gear, they all start to talk at once.

Molly sails out of the parking lot and turns right, with no need to consult a map. After college she lived with her painter boyfriend in Santa Fe for a year, and she seems to remember her way around the area as if it were yesterday. It was she who suggested this trip, one evening at El Coyote, when somehow they got onto the subject of New Mexico and Delia confessed she had never been and had always wanted to go. "Evan's never been either," Molly said, unwrapping her steaming green corn tamale. "We should go. The three of us. Why not?"

And here they are.

Hearing conversation from the backseat is difficult, so Evan entertains himself by focusing the camera on one woman's face and then the other's, back and forth, as if he were filming a tennis match. The two women could be sisters. They are both dark, tanned, lean, not at all out of place in this geographical context. He suspects that some narcissistic attraction is at the basis of their friendship, since people often comment on the resemblance. He also suspects that this is part of *his* attraction to Delia: He feels that he already knows her but not quite. Looking at her, he sees many of the same obvious physical charms that drew him to Molly in the first place, without all the inevitable irritating little habits that start to grate on your nerves, day in and day out, over the years. Somehow Delia is more like the way Molly was before he got to know her so well. She is tuned in to him in the way Molly was before she got to know *him* so well. Sometimes he can *feel* her listening to him when he speaks; he can *feel* her watching him as he walks across the room. Whereas Molly has seen and heard it all before. Or at least that's the impression she gives. Oblivious complacency. He imagines that making love to Delia would be the best of both worlds: all the comforts of home plus the thrill of a foreign port. He sighs and puts the lens cap back on the camera.

"Here we are," Molly says, pointing to a dusty cluster of adobe buildings that he recognizes from countless paintings and post-cards. At the entrance is a sort of tollbooth. Molly stops the car and rolls down the window, smiling her irresistible smile.

An unsmiling Indian man says, "The entrance fee is five dol-lars."

Delia immediately grabs her wallet and pulls out a five, but Molly waves it away, taking instead the bill that Evan proffers from the backseat.

"It's another five if you want to take pictures," the man says, frowning at the Nikon.

Evan groans and Delia nods her head in agreement. Molly, a photo fanatic, hesitates—both Evan and Delia kid her about being part Japanese—and then reluctantly says, "We'll leave the camera in the car."

Delia gives her a supportive pat on the back and Evan lets out a sigh of relief. All along he has had this worry, probably com-pletely irrational, that when the snapshots are developed, they may reveal something to his wife that she has failed to pick up on. Since she is an avid photographer, most of the pictures tend to be of Delia and him. Delia and him in front of various scenic backdrops. Pictures don't lie, or so they say, and anyway, who can pore over real life with the same sharp-eyed scrutiny that, in the tranquillity of recollection, a photo album allows?

On the way back from the D. H. Lawrence ranch they all admit they are hungry, and Molly insists on stopping at a road-side café instead of driving a bit farther to a place that Evan has read about in one of his travel guides. This is part of the playing-it-by-ear portion of the afternoon. The place is grubby and the food turns out to be overpriced microwaved mush. Evan is sulky,

Molly defensive, and Delia withdrawn, trying for once not to take sides, Evan thinks, since Molly's side is so clearly insupportable in this instance.

"Come on, it's only lunch," Molly says, "not the end of the world."

After this tacit admission from Molly that she blew it, Evan nods his head agreeably and says the only complimentary thing he can think to say about the meal: "The beer is nice and cold." After all, it *is* only a meal, and he does not really care that much about the restaurant. He just resents his image as the uptight graduate student enslaved to Fodor and Frommer; he wants it duly noted that playing it by ear does not always get you what you want. The only memorable part of the meal, as far as he's concerned, was the moment when Delia reached across the table with her napkin and pulled a string of cheese off his beard. Molly was busy talking to a couple at the next table who had daughters about the same ages as Aviva and Chloe, and didn't see it. Although he was slightly embarrassed, the gesture struck him as very, very intimate.

Back in town they split up. The women go off to poke through the galleries, and he goes back to the hotel for a swim. The couple from the lousy restaurant are sitting out by the pool while their daughters splash around in the water. Seeing the little girls having such a good time, Evan suddenly misses his own daughters and feels a pang of guilt for not having brought them along, even though they adore staying with his parents, who spoil them rotten. His daughters are both blonde, like him, and so fresh and beautiful, like rosebuds, that Evan fears that he will walk into their room one morning and find nothing but two little piles of wilted petals lying on their twin beds.

When he comes in from swimming, the bed is littered with shopping bags and Molly is in the shower, singing old Linda Ronstadt songs. He nudges the packages to one side and stretches out on the bed. His muscles feel deeply relaxed from all the sun and swimming, but his mind feels tense, tight. He wishes he could reach inside his skull and massage his brain until his choppy brain waves flatten into gentle ripples. Through a cloud of steam he sees Delia standing in the shower spray, naked, beckoning him to join her. He forces his eyes open, flicks on the bright reading light like a splash of cold water and concentrates on the mandalalike sand painting hanging on the wall opposite the bed. The shower clunks off and Molly emerges from the steamy bathroom, patting herself dry with a white towel that makes her dark tan appear even darker.

"God, I'm beat." She sweeps some packages onto the floor and throws herself onto the bed next to him. "Did you have a nice swim?"

He nods.

"Delia went back to one of the galleries. I told her we'd meet her at Doc Martin's at eight." She rolls over and tugs his beard flirtatiously. "I even made reservations."

He pats her naked rump. "Good girl." He stares up at the ceiling, praying that he will be able to make it through this trip without doing something stupid, something everyone will regret.

"That really was a wretched dump we had lunch in." She reaches into a bag and pulls out two beaded belts that say TAOS and two T-shirts with coyotes howling at the moon. "I got these for the girls."

"Good." The sight of the little red and blue T-shirts seems to snap him back to himself. "Let's call the girls," he says, reaching for the phone. He knows that if he can just hear their voices, everything will be all right.

"We'll be home tomorrow, and I just called last night." She folds the T-shirts and stuffs them back in the bag. "Your mother will think we don't trust her."

"I just want to hear their voices," he insists. "Okay?"

Molly looks at him sharply, as if she is about to say something, and then shrugs. He reaches over and grabs the receiver and dials the number. Molly rests her wet head on his chest. Chloe, the five-year-old, answers on the second ring and launches into a shrill, breathless account of how Tuffy, his parents' old sheltie, dragged a dead bird into the living room while they were eating pizza. He can feel Molly's laughter tickling his chest hairs. When Chloe runs out of verbal steam, Molly tugs at the phone cord. "Let me say hello!"

He holds the receiver to her mouth. He suddenly feels very

companionable, lying in bed naked with his wife, talking to their offspring. "Wow," Molly gasps appreciatively, "that's amazing. Now may I please talk to your sister?" Evan winces as Chloe slams the receiver onto the counter and Molly says "Ouch!" He kisses the top of her head and runs his free hand along the smooth curve of her inner thigh, higher and higher, until she moans slightly and slaps his hand playfully away. "This is sick. I'm talking to your daughter."

"Hey, Vivi, how's it going?" Evan raises his voice so that his older daughter can hear.

"Fine," she replies, like the aloof, blasé eight-year-old she has just recently become. "I was watching a video. *Splash*. Tom Hanks sells fruit and vegetables and stuff. Daryl Hannah's a mermaid. And he—"

"We have to go, sweetie," Molly butts in, knowing that if she doesn't, Aviva will summarize the entire plot in excruciating detail, with much backtracking and editorializing. She wants to be a movie reviewer when she grows up. Her favorite game is playing Siskel and Ebert with her best friend, Sage.

"Phew," Molly sighs as she hands him the receiver to hang up. "I hope this is a passing phase. Otherwise she's going to be a real bore at cocktail parties."

He laughs and insinuates his hand back between her legs. For the first time since they left home, he feels relaxed, centered, like his old self.

"This looks serious," she says.

"Reach out and touch someone." He laughs and pulls her down on top of him.

The door next door opens and shuts. Both of them freeze. They listen to Delia moving around, rattling paper, sliding open drawers. Molly reaches over and turns on the clock radio. A weather report. She rotates the dial until she hits some music. Next door the shower blasts on. They both unfreeze and pick up where they left off, but not quite. The momentum is broken. Something has gone out of it. They are like dancers who have suddenly lost the beat.

Dinner at Doc Martin's is a leisurely affair. As far as they can tell, nothing happens in Taos at night. The one movie theater in the plaza is showing something they have already seen. So they eat slowly, noting how delicious it all is. When they trade bites, Evan notices, Molly and he trade, and Molly and Delia trade, but he and Delia do not trade, as if this would be too intimate. He can't tell whether Molly notices this or not. After dinner they order coffee. Then brandy. Mostly the two women keep the conversation gently afloat. Every so often he swims in with some comment and then swims away again. He notices a single man at a corner table watching them, the two women, like a dog with his nose pressed to the glass, his eyes full of naked longing. The man is about their age, not bad-looking, dressed in casual but expensive clothes. A lawyer or architect, maybe. Recently divorced.

For a moment, as he starts in on his second brandy, Evan toys masochistically with the idea of inviting the man to join them. Ever since he fell in love with Delia, he has spent a lot of time thinking about the possibility of her meeting some other man. Sometimes, lying in bed next to his wife, he wishes that Delia *would* fall for someone and soon. Before he has a chance to do something stupid. He knows, rationally, that this would be best for everyone. In his fantasy the four of them become the best of friends: tennis doubles, dinners at each other's houses, shared vacation condos in Aspen and Maui. But in his dreams all he feels is misery, rage, murder.

Delia yawns and sighs. She stretches, twisting to the right and then to the left. Her breasts rise and shine underneath the gauzy fabric of her dress. "I think I'll go read for a while and turn in early," she says. "I didn't get much sleep last night."

"Me neither," he says.

Her dark eyes lock with his for an instant and then quickly break away. She sighs again. She looks tired, unhappy, tired of being unhappy. This is part, maybe the main part, he thinks, of what attracts him to her. This shadow of unhappiness. He knows that a smarter man would take this as a warning. What you see is what you get: an unhappy woman. But he, of course, thinks he can be the one to ring the bell, as if this were one of those carnival games where men line up with sledgehammers and pound away with all their male might. He will be the one to smash her unhappiness to smithereens and walk off with the prize. He is the prince in disguise that the sleeping princess has been waiting for all these long years. Delia, Delia, let down your hair.

"Poor Delia," Molly says, watching Delia walk away from them.

Evan feels a lick of anger as it suddenly occurs to him, ungenerously, that Molly enjoys feeling sorry for Delia, enjoys going out of her way to appear so very sensitive, enjoys bending over backward so as not to rub in her advantage as the wife. If he were Delia, he would hate her. He thinks of all the times Molly has urged him to think of someone, one of his musician buddies or tennis partners, to "fix Delia up with," as if she were broken, in need of repair. Out of the corner of his eye he sees the single man at the corner table—the nice-looking, well-dressed one— slap some money down and head toward the front door. In a hurry, Evan thinks. And he has a sudden, terrible hunch that the man has a plan. As Molly chatters on about the schedule for tomorrow, their last day in New Mexico, Evan imagines the man waylaying Delia at the corner with some light, inconsequential pleasantry, falling into step with her, inviting her for a nightcap in the hotel bar.

"We have to stop in Rancho de Taos," Molly is saying. "You have to see the San Francisco de Asis Church, if nothing else."

Evan nods, not really listening. He is remembering the moment he realized that his feelings for Delia had changed. Molly had been after him for weeks to fix Delia up with his friend Jack. "Just invite him to dinner," Molly had said. "Don't say anything about Delia. We'll have the Narvesons over too, so it won't look so much like a setup. "

But when Evan finally got around to inviting Jack, a notorious womanizer, Jack, as if smelling a trap, asked if he could bring along a date. Thrown for a loop, Evan had thought about just saying yes but instead he spilled the beans to Jack about Delia. To hell with female subterfuge. Jack was skittish, dubious; he didn't want any part of it, and Evan found himself launching into a hard sell. When he had finished waxing eloquent about Delia's charms, Jack had laughed and said, "Maybe *you* should go out with her. You sound like you've got a bad case." "Don't be ridiculous," Evan had snapped back. Jack just smiled skeptically, eyebrows raised, and said, "Thanks, but I think I'll pass."

And suddenly Evan felt as if he had been granted a stay of execution. Later, as they were walking to their cars in the parking lot, Jack spanked Evan's rear with his racket and said, "Don't do anything I wouldn't do," and winked. After that Evan had avoided Jack, making excuses until Jack finally stopped calling.

Molly sets down her empty brandy glass and pats his hand on the white tablecloth. "Let's go," she says. "You seem tired. Are you all right?"

"Fine." He downs the last of his brandy. "Why wouldn't I be?" He stares at her, as if daring her to continue, his heart pounding. She looks across the table at him, her jaw set, eyes narrowed, her expression like a clenched fist ready to strike out. *Now*, he thinks, *now*, bracing himself for the first blow, *now*.

But her eyes slide away from his and her expression relaxes into a blank smile addressed to no one in particular. He feels simultaneously let off the hook and let down. She stands up and slings her handbag over her shoulder. "Coming?"

Outside, the evening air is surprisingly cool. Molly shivers and Evan puts his arm around her shoulder and pulls her toward him as they make their way back to the hotel. The stream of traffic has dwindled to a trickle, and the night seems almost peaceful. The dark shape of the mountain squats in the distance. The wine and the brandy have dulled his nerves; he thinks maybe he will be able to sleep tonight. But as they cross the hotel lobby, past the cocktail lounge, Molly nudges him in the ribs and says, "Look." He looks over, into the dim interior of the bar, and sees Delia sitting at a small round table with the man from the restaurant. Although Evan has imagined this very scenario, it comes now as a total shock, like a wave of icy water. Delia's back is to him, so he can't read her expression. She doesn't see them, although the man looks up, and Evan sees the click of recognition in his eyes. He waits for the man to say "There are your friends" and for Delia to turn and wave, but the man apparently says nothing of the sort.

"Want to join them?" Evan says.

Molly laughs. "I don't thinks she needs us." She links her arm through his, shepherding him toward their room.

In the darkness, lying next to Molly, who is out like a light,

Evan checks the luminous dial of his watch every few minutes, wondering what they are doing. Now the man is paying the bill. Now they are strolling toward his hotel room. Now he is ... Later he hears voices, male and female, murmuring in the hallway. Delia's muffled laugh. He has all he can do to keep himself from flinging open the door and ordering Delia inside like an angry father. Or a jealous husband. But what right does he have to do such a thing? So he just lies there, jaw clenched, not daring to breathe, until he hears a door open and shut and the thud of footsteps padding off down the hall. He imagines the sound of water running in the sink as Delia brushes her teeth, more musical than Handel's *Water Music*. In the hallway, right outside his door, the footsteps pause for a long moment and then continue on. Smiling to himself in the dark, Evan feels almost sorry for the guy.

The plan is to stop at San Francisco de Asis Church, in Rancho de Taos, drive down to Santa Fe for lunch, and continue on to the airport in Albuquerque. After a rushed breakfast in the hotel coffee shop, they settle their bill and load their bags into the trunk of the Ford. As usual, Molly drives and he sits in the backseat, skimming the guidebook. Delia's long hair is caught up in a neat ponytail, exposing her bare neck, which is paler than the rest of her, more vulnerable-looking. Evan dares to reach out and tuck in the label of her T-shirt, which is sticking up. The two women discuss a design project they are both going to be working on when they return home. Evan wants to ask about the man in the bar but doesn't trust himself to strike the appropriately casual, big-brotherly tone.

The ride to Rancho de Taos is short. When they pull into the dirt parking lot, the church takes him by surprise. Although he has thumbed through an entire book of paintings of the church in the hotel gift shop, its simple beauty seems fresh and pure in the early morning light. His spirits lift. As the three of them make their way across the dusty lot toward the church, Molly unscrews the lens cap of her camera and hands it to Evan to put in his pocket for safekeeping.

"I'd like to see the mystery painting," Evan says, pausing by the parish office. "I've read about it." They look at Delia, who nods agreeably. "They're supposed to have a little slide show and everything."

"Okay," Molly shrugs. "Why don't you two go see it and I'll meet you at the church?"

"You're not interested?" Delia asks.

"I've already seen it," Molly says. "But you two should go. It's definitely worth seeing."

Molly walks on ahead and the guide ushers Evan and Delia inside to a small viewing room with folding chairs lined up in rows. They are the only ones in the room. The guide asks them where they are from and whether they have any children. When Evan says, "Two daughters," the guide nods and smiles at Delia, assuming that she is the mother. After a couple of minutes of stiff small talk, the man glances at his watch and says it is time to begin. He walks over and switches off the lights. For a moment the room is pitch black. Then the first slide lights up the screen. The familiar voice of educational filmstrips tells them the history of the church as the slides click on and off, a tad too slowly, leaving just enough time between images for boredom to set in. They learn how adobe bricks are made. They learn who painted the *retablos* and that the parish has undertaken the arduous task of restoration. Like a little kid waiting for the magic act to begin, Evan shifts restlessly in his uncomfortable chair, anxious to get to the part about the mystery painting.

Finally, after what seems like hours, a slide of the painting flashes on the screen. Beside him, in the darkness, he can feel Delia snap to attention as the narrator launches into his droning explanation of the painting's mystery.

"What makes this painting so unusual," the narrator says, "is the fact that although in daylight it portrays the barefoot Christ on a shore in Galilee, in complete darkness the portrait becomes luminescent, the figure seems to become three-dimensional, and a cross appears over the left shoulder of Jesus." The narrator goes on to say that eminent scientists from all over the world have studied the painting, subjecting it to chemical analysis and Geiger counter tests, but no scientific explanation has ever been found for the portrait's marvelous luminosity.

At this point the slide show ends and the guide invites the two

of them to step forward to view the actual painting. In the darkness the guide's gentle, disembodied voice tells them to be
patient; their eyes will need a few minutes to adjust. He says that
although some people see the phenomenon very clearly, other
people have difficulty seeing it, which makes Evan strain his eyes
in the dark, as if this were some test that he is determined to pass.
The guide steps discreetly out of the room, leaving them to experience this religious miracle in privacy.

It feels eerie, spooky, standing there alone in the dark silence,
which both of them seem reluctant to break. Then, just as he is
convinced that nothing is going to happen, the background
begins to take on a strange glow, the figure seems to come forward, and he sees it: the dark shadow of the cross. He is surprised, considering how irreligious he is, to feel the hairs tingling
on the back of his neck, and at the same moment Delia reaches
for his hand. The image is not steady. It pulses in and out of
focus, teasingly. Delia rests her head against his chest and he
wraps his arms around her. When she presses against him, he
feels a glow spreading through him like the mysterious glow of
the painting.

"Oh, God," she says, miserably, "goddamn it. What the hell
are we going to do?"

As if rebuking her profanity, the guide bustles back into the
room and flicks on the overhead light. Heart pounding, palms
sweating, Evan blinks in the sudden bright glare. Delia takes a
circumspect step away from him and fishes her dark glasses out
of her purse. Standing there in front of the blank screen, he feels
as if they are characters in some corny old B movie. He can't
think of anything to say that doesn't sound like some hack wrote
it. Despite the fact that he still feels the glow burning inside him,
where it is dark and safe.

On the way out Evan drops a five-dollar bill into the offering
box. Blinking in the bright sunshine, they make their way slowly
across the dirt parking lot to the church, not saying anything,
threading their way through the handful of dusty cars with out-
of-state plates.

"There she is," Delia says, pointing.

Molly waves and smiles. She is standing in the courtyard of the church, in front of a tall wooden cross. "How was it?" she says, walking toward them. "Did you see it?" She hums the theme from "The Twilight Zone" and laughs.

"I saw it," Delia says. "Pretty weird."

Evan just nods.

"Really? You really saw it?" Molly's smile fades and she looks so wistful that Evan rests his hand lightly on her shoulder. "I never saw it," she says. "I couldn't see a damn thing."

"It was pretty fuzzy," Delia says consolingly. "It was probably all in our heads. Some sort of hypnotic suggestion."

Molly shrugs, squinting into the viewfinder, taking a couple of steps backward and adjusting the focus. "You two stand over there," she orders. "In front of the cross."

"Just what the world needs," Evan says with a sigh. "Another picture of this church." But he obediently trudges over and stands next to Delia.

"Such a martyr." Molly shakes her head at him through the viewfinder. "Move closer together."

Evan hesitates and then takes a step sideways and boldly puts his arm around Delia's waist. He feels her stiffen, and then, after a moment's hesitation, she puts her arm around his waist.

"That's good," Molly nods.

Beside him Delia lets out a sigh.

"Now, do you think you could manage a smile?"

Evan frowns and glares at Molly. For a moment he hates her for being so hopelessly dense, so willfully blind, and as the camera shutter clicks, he has a fantasy, a wild hope, that when the picture is developed, this passion that feels to him so palpable will miraculously have taken shape on the negative, some dark shadow of love that defies the scientists' explanations and his own fainthearted denials. *Now*, he thinks, bracing himself, *now*.

the other widow

In the past two months since David's sudden death, Lynne has stopped eating, started wearing nothing but black, and found herself a therapist in the yellow pages. She has never really had much faith in therapy—all that high-priced crying over spilt milk, but she has no choice: If she doesn't talk to someone about David, she is afraid she really will go crazy and wind up in some mental hospital shuffling around in bedroom slippers, zombied out on lithium, weaving pot holders while her six-year-old son, Kyle, gets shunted from one abusive foster home to the next, in training to be a mass murderer. As a lapsed Catholic, she knows that you pay for your sins, and she is paying ninety dollars an hour, which she can ill afford, in order to talk to someone, someone who has sworn a professional oath of confidentiality, about her clandestine affair with a married man who was about to leave his wife for her when he suddenly dropped dead of a heart attack during a game of racquetball at the age of thirty-eight.

Petaluma is a small town populated by people with big mouths—sometimes she can't even believe the intimate details she knows, through the grapevine, about some people she has barely even exchanged two words with—and she feels that she owes it to David to keep their secret. Even if it bankrupts and kills her. Which she thinks it might. The only thing more painful than grief, she has discovered, is hidden grief. She feels like a closed coffin. Every night she cries herself to sleep, muffling her mouth with a pillow so that her son in the next room won't hear

her. Frequently, after she has cried herself out, she takes her sod-
den pillow and crawls into bed with Kyle, eking some comfort
from his warm, restless little body. If it weren't for Kyle—feeding
him his Cheerios every morning and giving him his bath every
evening, the daily rituals of care and maintenance—she probably
would have killed herself by now.

Whenever the therapist, a woman about her own age named
Eleanor, tries to steer the talk back to Lynne's own parents—
doing her therapist thing—Lynne returns politely but firmly to
the topic of David. She figures that she can talk to anyone any
time for free about her parents, but she can only talk to Eleanor
about David. She is paying Eleanor to listen to her talk about
David, the intimate details of their private relationship, the way a
girlfriend would under other circumstances. She thinks of
Eleanor as a sort of overpaid, overqualified girlfriend.

A lot of the younger, hipper doctors in town have their offices
in renovated Victorians in the small downtown area, and
Eleanor's office happens to be just one block down from the
building in which David's wife, David's *widow*—the very word
gives Lynne the chills—has her office. Fortunately, Sonoma
Realty, where Lynne works, is located two blocks in the opposite
direction, so that when she walks from work to her therapy
appointment, she is not all that likely to run into Rachel. In fact,
in the five weeks she has been coming to Eleanor's office on
Thursday afternoons, she has never once so much as glimpsed
the back of Rachel's head or even her car, a cantaloupe-colored
Karmann-Ghia. Even so, every time she leaves or enters
Eleanor's office, she can not help glancing to her left, in the
direction of Rachel's building, half-hoping and half-dreading that
she will see her, even though she never has.

So it came as a complete heart-pounding shock to turn the
corner at Alpha-Beta this noon, shopping for a few essentials on
her lunch hour, and nearly ram right into Rachel with her cart.
They greeted each other like long-lost friends—Lynne had sold
David and Rachel their house when they moved up to Petaluma
from the city about this same time last year—and Lynne somehow managed to mumble her condolences, which she could not
very well *not* do under the circumstances. Rachel thanked her and

Lynne glanced at her watch and gasped, as if she were late for an appointment, and was about to make her getaway when Rachel suddenly reached out and rested a hand on Lynne's forearm and said, "This is actually a stroke of luck. I was going to call you later today anyway." She paused to sigh and rearrange the few items in her cart. Lynne noted that all the items in Rachel's cart were sophisticated and adult—yogurt, brie, a jar of olives, chutney, something leafy that could be cilantro or maybe watercress—while her own cart contained peanut butter, apple juice, Teddycrisps, and Popsicles. They were standing by the freezer case and Lynne felt a paralyzing stab of pain as Rachel opened the glass door and casually tossed into her cart a pint of ice cream that Lynne recognized as David's favorite: Häagen-Dazs Vanilla Swiss Almond. It was her favorite, too, but she had not been able to touch the stuff since his death.

"I need to put the house on the market," Rachel said as she slammed the freezer door. "I can't afford it now that—" She let the sentence trail off. Lynne nodded sympathetically, at a total loss for words. Finally she looked at her watch again and managed to stutter out something to the effect that she would give Rachel a call later that evening.

"Do you have the number?" Rachel called after her as she hurried down the aisle. Lynne turned and said, "I must have it at the office," feeling the color rise to her cheeks as she thought of all the times she had called David at home while Rachel was at work and how indelibly the number was imprinted in her brain. She imagined that she would be able to summon it from the recesses of her memory on her deathbed even if she lived to be a hundred and suffered from Alzheimer's: 763-3118. At the checkout counter Lynne's hands trembled so violently that she had difficulty writing a check, and she grabbed her bag and fled to her parked car and drove directly to a pay phone and called Eleanor and begged for an emergency appointment.

And now, an hour later, she is sitting across from Eleanor, crying into a Kleenex, recounting blow by blow the unsettling encounter in the supermarket, when she should be out showing the McNairs' split-level on Sunnyslope Road to the Shimonos, when she should be out trying to make money instead of spending a dollar and a half per minute talking to some woman who merely nods her head a lot and whom Lynne increasingly suspects is gay and therefore, despite all her advanced degrees, probably does not understand what Lynne is going through, has *been* through, as well as your average woman on the street.

"I don't believe this. It's so incredibly ironic." Lynne blows her nose and attempts a little laugh. "She actually wants me to sell their house." She shakes her head in disbelief. "Life is so weird."

When Lynne pauses to allow Eleanor to interject some psychological input, there is a long loud silence. Lynne hates it whenever there is a silence like this; it makes her feel as if she is paying for nothing, for air.

"Of course I'll tell her no," Lynne says anxiously when it seems apparent that Eleanor is just going to sit there like some sort of silent oracle. "I'll make up some excuse."

Eleanor nods. Most of her nods seem noncommittal, as in "I see," but this nod seems to convey a note of approval, as in "Good girl," and Lynne immediately feels relieved, like a conscientious student who has divined the right answer. She knows that Eleanor thinks she needs to put David behind her and get on with her life. She suspects that although outwardly Eleanor pretends to be neutrally sympathetic, inwardly she thinks that David was just another chauvinist schmuck, untrustworthy to the max, who would have broken her heart one way or the other, sooner or later, alive or dead, and she should consider herself well rid of him. And that when she is finally cured, her only regret will be that he died before she got the chance to kill him.

"Okay then," Lynne says, "that's what I'll do. I'll call her tonight and tell her. I'll say I'm just too busy and I'll refer her to Dwayne Higgins." She looks slyly at Eleanor who laughs on cue. Dwayne is this pathetic macho desperado who wears pointy cowboy boots and one of those Texas string ties made of Lucite with a dead scorpion trapped inside and is always coming on to her, making suggestive comments and brushing up against her in the office.

Eleanor looks pointedly at the little clock on the table beside her and Lynne obediently pops up out of her chair and says politely, "I appreciate your taking me on such short notice."

"No problem," Eleanor says. "See you Thursday." Then, as she does at the end of every session, she cradles Lynne's hand in both of hers for a moment, as if to pump sanity into her. Even though it's a bit awkward, Lynne always finds it oddly comforting and feels a pang when Eleanor lets go.

After David dropped dead, her body went into severe withdrawal at such sudden sensory deprivation, and she found herself going to the beauty parlor every afternoon just to get her hair washed, just for the feel of someone's fingers against her skin. She would call a different salon each time and tell them the same lie—she was having her bathroom remodeled—and just needed to get her hair washed. Her waist-length coppery hair was her glory. Sometimes after they made love and her hair was all tangled up, David would sit in bed and patiently, gently brush the snarls away. Once she started therapy, though, she had to economize and cut out the beauty parlor visits. A couple of times she tried bribing Kyle to brush her hair, but he got too bored and restless, and she was afraid that maybe it would warp him sexually in some way, so she abandoned that idea. Then, for the first time in her life, she started experiencing these keen urges to get her hair cut off. Like Mia Farrow did when her relationship with Frank Sinatra ended. It seemed fittingly symbolic somehow, like cutting your losses. Once, on the one-month anniversary of David's death, Lynne had even called the beauty parlor she liked best and made an appointment but had then chickened out and canceled it an hour later. "I'm sorry, but I'm just not ready," she had told the baffled receptionist. "It's just too soon."

The Shimonos, usually very punctual, were late showing up at the split-level on Sunnyslope. "We lose ourselves on the way," Mr. Shimono, some sort of computer genius, apologized gravely. As a result, Lynne was late getting to the elementary school and Kyle was sitting glumly alone in the fenced-in playground waiting for her when she pulled up. Under the most optimal conditions, he was not one of those children with a sunny disposition, and now he glowered in the seat next to her, manically punching the radio buttons, daring her to tell him to knock it off. From the time he was born he had this way of making her feel inadequate and apologetic, just as his father always had. And like his father, she felt closest to him in bed. She enjoyed the bedtime ritual of crawling under the covers and reading him a book or telling him a story until he was so punch-drunk that his long dark eyelashes would start to stagger shut and she could cautiously extract herself and tiptoe out of the room.

His father, Charlie, had left her to move back in with his widowed mother who had always doted on him, leaving a note for Lynne on the kitchen table detailing his reasons for this decision in perfect outline form, complete with Roman numerals and capital letters, major headings and subheadings, like you learn in the eighth grade. He was a hydroelectrical engineer. When his mother died a year later, he had called Lynne to see whether she was interested in a reconciliation and when she told him to forget it, he had accepted a transfer to Nigeria, where he had lived for the past four years, unmarried, with two servants to wait on him hand and foot. Lynne found it absolutely incredible that Kyle, who had spent so little time with Charlie, could have somehow learned to duplicate all of his absent father's idiosyncratic expressions and mannerisms so precisely. Apparently, Charlie's genes had elbowed her genes aside just as he had always pushed her needs aside in real life. It seemed unfair. Here she was the one who had taken care of Kyle day in and day out—hauled herself out of bed when he had nightmares or a stomachache, wiped his stinky little butt, cooked his meals, entertained him when she was dead tired—and yet her son, the flesh of her flesh, was not the least bit like her. Physically, intellectually, emotionally, he was his father's son. In fact, she would not be at all surprised to come home one of these days in the not-so-distant future and find Kyle's closet empty and a note for her on the kitchen table. *Dear Mom*, he would print neatly, *This just isn't working out.*

In an attempt to placate Kyle she shouts over the radio, "I thought we could stop and pick up a pizza," even though she had left some chicken breasts out to defrost.

"Okay," Kyle nods, as if he is merely being agreeable, but he reaches over and turns off the radio.

She reaches her hand out and ruffles his silky hair and her eyes blur with tears. For the past ten months, all during her relationship with David, she kept picturing the three of them together as a family, doing family-type things—picnics, softball games, camping, educational field trips to the city. She imagined David and Kyle assembling model airplanes or watching some sports event on TV. And David had always seemed so willing and eager to step into the role of stepdad, assuring her that he considered Kyle to be a bonus, not a liability. He and Rachel wanted children, he had told her that first time they met for coffee alone, and had tried everything—all the state-of-the-art conception methods—but with no luck. He had looked so sad sitting there smiling across the table at her. It suddenly struck her that he was really a very good-looking man. As well as very kind and sensitive. She had liked his wife. As a realtor, you got to see people at their worst—buying a house is a stressful undertaking and the women are generally the most impossible—but Rachel Bloch had always been pleasant, considerate, and reasonable. And although she was a hotshot child psychologist, she had never acted snobbish or superior toward Lynne, who had a completely useless BFA in painting in addition to a real estate license. But even though she had never found anything wrong with his wife, at that moment—looking into his sad, kind eyes looking into her own eyes—she suddenly felt protective of him, as she would of some little boy who was sent off to school with a scanty, unnourishing breakfast and a too-thin jacket on a cold day. And after that, she found herself avoiding Rachel.

As they pull into the parking lot of the pizza parlor, Kyle blesses her with one of his rare sunburst smiles of approval and says, "This was a good idea, Mom." Before she can respond, he ejects from his seat and races toward the front door. Trailing along behind him, she attempts to console herself with the thought that she should be glad now that Kyle never really got the chance to know David better, since she and David usually got together during the daytime when Rachel was at work and Kyle was at school. Fortunately, David was a freelance writer who worked at home, and she had found it not too difficult to juggle her own schedule. So on Monday-Wednesday-Friday mornings and occasionally on Tuesday-Thursday afternoons, depending on Rachel's client load, David would zip over to her apartment and they would spend a couple of hours in bed, making love and fantasizing about the future. The future. Lynne feels this hard lump lodge itself in her throat just as the clerk asks to take her order. She stands there mute, unable to utter a sound, until Kyle tugs impatiently on her shoulder bag. "Tell him we want a large sausage and mushroom," he says authoritatively. The clerk looks at Lynne who just nods and pulls out her wallet.

After they have eaten the pizza—or rather Kyle has eaten his pizza and Lynne has picked at hers—he takes off to ride his bike for a couple of hours before bedtime and Lynne sits at the breakfast nook and stares at the yellow wall phone, rehearsing what she is going to say. She feels sorry for Rachel having to sell the house, knowing how much work she put into restoring the place, but part of her also feels angry at Rachel for being so willing to relinquish this tangible shell of David's life, even if he was planning to move out anyway. Lynne knows that if she were in Rachel's position she would do whatever it took to hang on to the house, at least for the time being. One of the things which she cries about late at night is that she has been left with so few physical remnants of David's presence in her life. A pair of gym socks, a soft-pack of Carltons with one crushed cigarette, a half-eaten container of Vanilla Swiss Almond in the freezer, a purple gloxinia (now half-dead) and a gorgeous Soleri wind chime that he gave her for her birthday. Sometimes late at night, lying in bed, when she hears the deep, melodious chimes, she feels that he is speaking to her from some other realm. She has not washed her pillowcases since he died, but his scent is growing fainter and fainter. She spends a lot of time lying on the bed during the day trying to conjure certain memorable moments of passion, but although she can remember the details vividly, the actual physical sensations themselves remain stubbornly elusive. Except occasionally in dreams when she can actually feel the touch of his fingers on her breast or the rhythm of him moving inside her. When he died, she did not hear about it for three days. During which time she nearly went crazy wondering what was going on with him. When he didn't show up at her place on Friday morning, as planned, she had called his house and got the answering machine. She did not call that weekend because she knew Rachel might answer, and anyway, she was miffed and expected him to call her and apologize. But when he did not call Monday morning, her anger turned to worry. She called the house and Rachel answered and she hung up. The fact that Rachel was not at the office only made her more worried. She paced around her apartment for a while wondering what she could do and then, out of desperation more than anything else, decided to call the racquet club where she knew he went most every day. A young girl answered and Lynne asked for David Bloch. The girl didn't say anything for a moment and then said, "Just a minute, please," and a moment later an older man, obviously the boss, picked up the phone. And that's how she heard.

Outside, she hears a scraping crash and rushes to the window, adrenaline already pumping. Kyle is lying spread-eagled on top of his bike, on the scraggly burnt front lawn. Thank God he's not on the street, she thinks, as she rushes down the hallway and out the door. He is already sitting up with his back to her by the time she is down the front steps and she thinks he must be okay, but when he turns around, blood is pouring from his mouth. *Oh god, oh my god,* she screams inside, trying to remain outwardly calm but one look at her face and he starts to scream as if he is dying.

Driving home from the emergency room, Kyle slumps in his seat, nearly asleep, doped up on some painkiller. There is a gauze bandage, like a little white beard, covering most of his chin. Two of his bottom teeth went through his lip. She had nearly fainted at the sight. The doctor, a stunning Indian woman who looked like an actress playing a doctor, gave him six stitches and complimented him on being such a brave boy. Kyle wanted to know if he would have a scar and seemed disappointed when the doctor assured him it would be very, very faint. Lynne pulls into her parking space and peers at her watch in the dim light. It is after ten o'clock. She carries Kyle into the building, staggering a bit under his limp weight, and manages to make it into his bedroom and set him down on his bed before collapsing. When she recovers her strength, she tugs off his Velcro sneakers and jeans, pulls the covers up over him, kisses him lightly on the forehead, flicks off the light, and tiptoes out of his room. God, she thinks, what next? Feeling shaky, she pours herself a shot of Jack Daniel's and then goes outside and drags his bike up the steps to the vestibule. It's a nice night and she would like to sit outside for a few peaceful moments, but she goes back inside so that she will be sure to hear Kyle if he calls out to her.

The living room, like the rest of the apartment, is a wreck. Her bimonthly cleaning service was sacrificed, along with the beauty parlor, to pay for her therapy appointments. She kicks a fleet of Kyle's Matchbox cars into the corner, gathers up some old unread newspapers and dumps them into a basket under the glass coffee table, and sinks, exhausted, onto the couch. Every night after Kyle is in bed, Lynne lies on the couch, drinking and thinking. She feels terribly, terribly cheated. Like a child who has waited patiently in line for a cookie, not shoving or whining, only to discover that the kid in front of her got the last cookie. For months and months, she was understanding and uncomplaining, waiting for David to extricate himself from his marriage. Although Rachel had always seemed to Lynne to be an unusually strong and confident woman, David assured her that underneath, Rachel was a quivering puddle of insecurity and that her self-esteem, her sense of herself as a woman, had been severely undermined by her inability to conceive a child. If he just left abruptly, he said, Rachel would be devastated. He had to proceed slowly and gently, he said, so that she would see that their basic incompatibility had nothing to do with her infertility—although he did concede that her single-minded obsession with conception had, in fact, cast a pall on the marriage—a gray, hovering sense of failure—as if, together, they had embarked upon a doomed business venture. The fact that Lynne had a child, he said, would be like rubbing salt in the wound. She understood, didn't she? And Lynne would nod and agree to wait just a little longer—until after Christmas or Rachel's parents' visit or David's latest article was finished—even though she wanted to cry and whine that she, too, had insecurities, *huge gnawing* insecurities—in fact, she would bet that her insecurities could eat Rachel's insecurities for lunch—and just how long did he intend to drag this thing out?

How did she know he wasn't just stringing her along? I mean, after all, she was the classic Other Woman, wasn't she? *Just have faith*, he would say, looking into her eyes, *trust me*.

And despite herself she did. Even though, as Eleanor continues to point out to her, she has no way of knowing that he actually would have left his wife, or that even if he left his wife it actually would have worked out between them, she *knows*. She knows he would have and it would have. And she doesn't want anyone trying to reason her grief away by pointing out that there was no guarantee. There are never any guarantees in this life, no matter what. You just have to go on gut instinct. And deep in her gut she knows that David loved her more than any other man ever has or ever will and that they would have been happy together. Yes, *happy*, she repeats to herself defiantly as she pictures Eleanor's dubious expression.

Lying on the couch, the empty bourbon glass clutched loosely in her hand, she nods off to sleep. She dreams that David and she are living in a playhouse in David's backyard. Their playhouse is a perfect miniaturized version of the big Victorian house in which Rachel lives. During the day, David and she sleep. Their bed is suspended by chains from the ceiling, like a large swing. At night, she sneaks into the big house and steals whatever they need—food, clothing, books, records, pretty trinkets. As she tippytoes around the big house during these nightly forays, her heart pounds, she is terrified. She knows that if she disturbs her, Rachel's terrible fiery wrath—like some sleeping dragon suddenly roused from her long slumber—will reduce Lynne to a tiny pitiful pile of ashes. This particular night as Lynne is reaching for a silver hairbrush gleaming in the moonlight on Rachel's dresser, she clumsily knocks a bottle of perfume off onto the wood floor. She freezes in terror. And then she jolts wide awake, her heart hammering, her neck twisted at a painful angle, shivering slightly from the cold, and gets up and stumbles down the dark hallway and climbs into bed next to her warm, sleeping son.

But she cannot fall back to sleep. It is a windy night and she lies awake, hour after hour, listening to the wind chime in the backyard. And that's when she decides that despite what she told Eleanor, she will call Rachel in the morning and agree to list the house. As soon as she makes this decision, she relaxes and feels herself drifting off again. It is as if she has known all along that she would say yes, that she couldn't say no.

All the next morning as she is going about her business, Lynne feels anxious and impatient, waiting for two o'clock, when she has arranged to meet Rachel at the house, David's house. The closing at First Commercial Federal drags on and on. First the escrow officer is late and then he drones on and on in an excruciatingly slow and meticulous manner, repeating everything twice. "In other words," he says and goes on to rephrase what he has just said until Lynne has fantasies of reaching across the conference table and stuffing his loud, ugly tie in his mouth. When the closing finally ends, she has her weekly appointment to drive Marion Lawrence around, showing her two or three new listings. She happens to know, through the Petaluma grapevine, that Marion has terminal cancer—breast cancer that has metastasized to her lungs—and is not expected to live long. But for some reason, ever since the recurrence of the cancer, Marion has developed this passion for house hunting. They never speak of Marion's illness, have never even acknowledged it, and yet have become quite close in a certain odd way. Even though Lynne knows that Marion is never going to buy a house, she does not resent the hours she has spent driving her around town, showing her through dozens of houses. She figures that somehow this little weekly charade calms Marion and allows her to pretend, for an hour or two, that she has a future like everyone else. When David died, Marion was the first and only person Lynne considered calling, confiding in—not her sister, not her friends—just Marion. But, in the end, she decided against it. She knew somehow that although Marion would be understanding and sympathetic, it would break the magic spell of their little outings. And so, instead, she had plucked Eleanor's name from the yellow pages.

Today when Lynne drops her off at her daughter-in-law's house, Marion sits for a moment, rummaging around in her handbag and pulls out a small, beautifully wrapped gift. "I may not be able to come next week," she says, not elaborating as people normally do. "And I wanted to give you a little something as a token of my appreciation."

Lynne thanks her, protesting that Marion really shouldn't have, and then drives off quickly, afraid she might burst into tears, which would ruin everything. Lately, she feels like some character in a soap opera, only not as well dressed. Since David died she has not taken any interest in her appearance. Until this morning. Knowing that she was going to see Rachel, who always looked so exotically chic, Lynne had stood in front of her full-length mirror discarding one sad, crummy-looking outfit after another until Kyle complained that he was going to be late for school and dragged her out to the car.

"Do you like this dress?" she had asked him as they backed out of the carport.

"Very nice," he said, sounding just exactly like his father, engrossed in examining and critiquing the contents of his lunch box.

She took a hand off the steering wheel and reached over and covered his eyes. "What color is it?"

"Pink."

"Bzzz." She pressed his belly button. "Wrong answer. Try again."

He giggled and squirmed away and shouted, "Purple!"

"You peeked," she said.

"You forgot to put jelly on my sandwich." He frowned down at the Saran Wrapped sandwich.

"We were out of jelly," she said. "Sorry."

He heaved a big sigh and snapped on the radio.

"Come on, it's not the end of the world," she said, turning down the volume. "Give me a break."

"Maybe I'll go live with Dad," he said coolly, turning to look out the window. This was his new favorite ploy that never failed to get her goat.

"Go ahead," she snapped. "Be my guest. They probably don't even have Welch's grape jelly in Nigeria."

She turned the volume on the radio back up and they ignored each other for the rest of the ride. When they pulled up in front of the school, she asked him if he was sure he felt well enough to go today, after his big fall. "You can stay with Nana, you know," she told him.

"I'm okay," he said, leaning away when she leaned over to kiss him. Then, just as he was getting out of the car, he surprised her by turning around and saying, "You look pretty."

And for the first time in weeks she had actually felt pretty. But as soon as she turns the corner of D Street and sees Rachel's jazzy Karmann-Ghia parked in the driveway, her self-confidence deserts her. She knows this is a bad idea. Why put herself through this? What can she possibly hope to gain by it?

As she gets out of her car and walks up the cobblestone path leading to the front door, she considers turning around and driving off, but just then, as luck would have it, the dog catches sight of her and starts barking, and a second later Rachel flings open the front door and calls out a greeting, holding the rambunctious dog by his collar until Lynne is safely inside.

"This is Roscoe," Rachel says, letting go of the setter's collar. The dog makes a beeline for Lynne's crotch, sniffing at her through her thin cotton dress. Blushing, Lynne tries to push him gently but firmly away.

"He's still a puppy," Rachel apologizes, dragging the dog away from Lynne. "David was going to take him to obedience school." She sighs and motions for Lynne to take a seat on the sofa.

Shaken, Lynne sinks down into the black Italian leather couch and holds her clipboard primly over the wet spot on her dress. David had always been inordinately fond of oral sex, more so than any of her half dozen previous lovers, and she keeps glancing nervously over at the dog, as if somehow David's spirit has taken hold of the animal. She dimly remembers reading about such things during her Carlos Castanada period back in college.

"Would you like some iced tea or a Diet Coke?" Rachel asks graciously.

"A Diet Coke would be great," Lynne says.

Rachel gets up and heads toward the kitchen, her armload of silver bracelets tinkling faintly. She is wearing black stretch capris like Lynne's mother used to wear, but somehow they look nothing like they looked on her mother. And an oversize black T-shirt and a short, boyish haircut that somehow manages to look ultra-feminine. Lynne suddenly feels like some leftover from Woodstock in her gauzy sundress and long straight hair. She looks over at the dog, who seems to be staring at her with a terrible yearning desire in his soft brown eyes—eyes that actually do remind her of David's—and remembers the sound of his voice telling her she is beautiful. *You're beautiful*, he would say, *so, so beautiful*. Of course, usually she was naked when he said this, and it had never occurred to her until now to wonder if he liked the way she dressed. Or even cared.

The phone rings and Lynne hears Rachel pick it up in the kitchen. While Rachel is talking, Lynne gets up and paces around the room. She has not been back inside the house since shortly after they moved in when she stopped by to drop off a house-warming gift. A hibiscus bush, the same thing she gives to all her clients. She is both relieved and disappointed by how spare and impersonal the room seems to be. Just the usual thirtysomething decor—Persian rug, bookshelves, abstract paintings, glass coffee table, piano, two huge cacti, and a few exotic trinkets picked up on foreign junkets. There are no corny wedding photographs or vacation snapshots. She remembers David telling her that they were married on a sailboat.

Rachel hurries back into the living room with Lynne's Diet Coke in a beautiful handblown glass, apologizing for the delay. "That was David's mother," she sighs. "She's driving me crazy."

Lynne nods and feels her heart sink. The woman who would someday have been her own mother-in-law if David's heart had not given out. Now she would never even meet her. To keep herself from sinking any deeper, she pulls out her pen and says, "Why don't you show me all the improvements you've made and then I can go back to the office and come up with an asking price." This was called a market value analysis, a part of the job that Lynne usually enjoyed.

In an effort to keep emotionally detached, Lynne jots down lots of little notes as she follows Rachel from the living room to the dining room to the sun room to the kitchen and out onto the newly laid patio. "Wow. You've done wonders," Lynne marvels appreciatively. "Everything's perfect."

"David loved this house," Rachel sighs, sliding the glass door shut as they walk back inside. "I figured enough was enough, but he still had a million plans. He was going to rip up the linoleum in the kitchen and put down a wood floor."

He was, Lynne thought, *when?* She has always sort of assumed that Rachel had to suspect something was going on, not with Lynne specifically, but with someone. All that passion. How could she not sense something? But she sees now that Rachel does not have a clue. They are walking up the stairs now, Lynne trailing along silently, unnerved by the thought of seeing their bedroom, which she had spent so much time trying *not* to picture during all those nights she slept alone, waiting for him to leave, to be with her.

But first Rachel opens the door to a pleasant little guest room all done in Laura Ashley prints. "Nice," Lynne says. Next Rachel moves across the hall. "This was David's study," she says, opening the miniblinds. In the sudden brightness, Lynne's glance pounces on a photograph of Rachel in a silver filigree frame sitting beside the computer. A glamorous head shot, like some movie star PR photo. And a smaller snapshot of the two of them with their arms wrapped around each other on some travel poster–looking beach. "He was planning to remodel the attic for his study eventually," Rachel says, "but I always liked this room, don't you?"

Lynne nods, feeling light-headed and confused. A couple of times when she had expressed some alarm or doubt upon hearing about yet another major new home improvement project—asking him why he would be willing to spend so much time and money on a place he would be moving out of soon—David had always reassured her that the renovations were all Rachel's pet projects, something he just went along with under duress. He said that the house was Rachel's substitute baby. Lynne feels her palms start to sweat and her intestines knot up. When Rachel leads her into the newly remodeled bathroom with its shiny black porcelain and brass fixtures, she wants to slam the door shut and lock herself inside until the churning wave of nausea passes. She actually considers asking Rachel if she could use the bathroom for a moment, but Rachel is already ushering her out and down the hallway, with its tweedy industrial carpeting and track lighting, to the master bedroom.

"This was our room," Rachel says, and for the first time Lynne hears the catch in her voice and sees the dazed, slack expression of pain in her eyes as they both stand there looking around the huge empty-seeming room. Up until now Rachel has seemed to her to be extraordinarily cool and detached, hardly the picture of a grieving widow. For the first time Lynne feels a genuine stab of guilt. She almost acts upon a sudden weird urge to reach out and take Rachel's hand, but just then Rachel walks over and throws open a window. "It's stuffy in here," she says. "I've been sleeping in the guest room ever since—" The sentence hangs in the air.

It is a beautiful room. Spare and Japanese. Tranquil. Tatami mats on the bleached wood floor, a low king-size bed with a simple gray comforter. Two exquisite wood block prints hanging over the bed. Lynne can not remember ever seeing a more inviting, soothing room. Looking at the pristine lacquered dresser top, she pictures her own bedroom with its tacky floral wallpaper and her dresser top cluttered with miscellaneous junk, and she imagines, painfully, that David must have felt a sense of peaceful relief upon returning home to this room. Despite himself. Even if he did really love her. She knew this was a bad idea. She wishes she had never seen this room. But then, turning slightly, she is suddenly surprised and gratified to notice a glaring eyesore. Pointing to a boarded-up rectangle on the ceiling, she says, "Does the roof leak?"

"No," Rachel shakes her head. "David was putting in a skylight. He was doing it himself." She looks for a moment as if she might lose control, then gets a grip on herself and walks briskly out of the room, saying, "Of course, I'll go ahead and hire someone to finish the skylight before you start bringing people through."

Lynne thinks she might faint, but she forces herself to take deep breaths and to remain on her feet through a sheer act of will. Like the time she was holding Kyle who was just a baby and she accidentally slammed the car door on her fingers and the pain was so intense she thought she was going to pass out on the sidewalk, but through sheer superhuman maternal instinct she managed somehow to reach over and open the car door and deposit the baby safely on the front seat before blacking out.

"Are you all right?" Rachel asks her, turning back to look at her standing there alone in the room, staring up at the aborted skylight. Their eyes lock for a moment and Lynne feels her pulse rev. She hovers on the edge of saying something, something to shock her, something to release some of this anger she feels building inside her, anger that she now recognizes has been lurking there, undetected, all along, like radon in the basement. Even though she knows that none of this is Rachel's fault, that Rachel is, in fact, the innocent party in all this, she wants to hurt her. "We were in love," she says. "We were having an affair." Her voice sounds shrill but bold and defiant, too loud in the empty room.

Rachel stands there looking at her with a benign, puzzled expression on her face for an instant and then it seems to hit her. Somewhere behind the eyes. Lynne braces herself, but instead of the fiery blast of wrath from her nightmare, Rachel just walks back into the bedroom, sits down on the edge of the bed, and says, "I thought there was someone."

"He was going to leave you," Lynne says, too carried away now to stop herself, like some internal dam has burst and she is being dragged downriver on a flood of emotion. "He was going to leave you for me," she says again, only this time as she says it, she hears her voice waver and she knows that it isn't true, it was never true, and she bursts into a humiliating flood of tears. Rachel reaches over and hands her a peach-colored tissue from a lacquered dispenser beside the bed. "I'm glad you told me," she says. "It explains a lot. And it took real courage on your part."

Lynne stops blowing her nose and looks at her, wondering if she is crazy. "It wasn't courage," Lynne mumbles, abruptly appalled and ashamed by what's she's done.

"Well, whatever." Rachel shrugs.

"I have to go." Lynne stands up, not knowing what else she can say under the circumstances, and heads downstairs. She is relieved when Rachel doesn't follow her. At the foot of the stairs the dog rushes over and leaps on her, and she has to wrestle with him as she crosses the parquet foyer and lets herself out the front door.

In the car Lynne just sits for a few moments resting her forehead against the steering wheel, trying to collect herself. *Don't think about it now,* she tells herself. *You'll have plenty of time to think about it later.* She fishes a crumpled dingy Kleenex out of her purse and dabs at her eyes and yanks a brush quickly through her hair, attempting to look normal. Then she glances at her watch and heads over to Kyle's school, relieved to see that she is not yet late; in fact, she is early. As she sits out by the curb waiting for school to let out, she thinks about walking across the street to the pay phone and calling Eleanor to ask for a special appointment. But somehow she does not really feel like talking to Eleanor. Not now, maybe not ever. She knows that Eleanor is a big believer in "the handwriting on the wall." She suspects that Eleanor must think that she is a complete illiterate when it comes to reading men. Still, she knows that he did love her. She *knows* that. *Don't think about it now,* she reminds herself sternly as Kyle bursts through the door in a swarm of other kids laden with lunch boxes and construction paper masterpieces. She waves at him and glances at herself in the rearview mirror. She doesn't think she looks too bad, considering. But the minute Kyle climbs into the car he looks at her suspiciously and says, "What's wrong?"

"Nothing." She attempts a cheery, reassuring smile. "Just a tiring day." She rummages in her purse and hands him a pack of Juicy Fruit. "How was *your* day? Did your stitches hurt?"

He shrugs and shakes his head, intent upon unwrapping a stick of gum and cramming it into his mouth. "Let's stop at Burger King," he says, in between loud smacks.

"Okay," she agrees, too tired to argue, even though it is nowhere near dinnertime and the defrosted chicken breasts from yesterday are just going to spoil.

"What happened to your dress?" He points to the damp spot over her crotch.

"A big dog slobbered on it," she says.

"Really?" He finds this hilarious and snickers, on and off, the whole way to Burger King. His father's sick sense of humor exactly. As they pull into the parking lot, Kyle reaches underneath him and waves Marion's slightly squashed package under her nose. "What's this?" he asks. "Is it for me?"

She shakes her head. "Sorry, Charlie. It's just a little gift one of my clients gave me." She takes it from him and drops it into her purse.

Inside, they sit in a bright orange booth, eating silently. While Kyle chomps contentedly on his hamburger, Lynne nibbles away at some french fries that she swipes from Kyle's bag over his loud, outraged protests. "Why don't you order your own?" he scowls, even though she knows he will never finish what he's got.

She shrugs and hands him a dollar bill. "Here. Go order me some french fries," she says, "if it kills you so much to share."

He hops up and runs to the counter. Any sort of financial transaction fascinates him these days. She has a feeling he is going to be a banker or stockbroker when he grows up. While she is waiting for him to return, she opens her purse and takes out Marion's little gift, hoping to distract herself from the awful scene at David's house. She slips off the curly pink ribbon and tears open the wrapping paper and lifts the lid off the small white box. Nestled in a bed of cotton is a silver brooch that Lynne immediately recognizes as the one she once complimented Marion on, weeks ago. Shaped like a large hibiscus blossom. Deeply touched by Marion's thoughtfulness, she pins it on the breast of her sundress.

As she sits there alone in the booth, squinting into the late-afternoon sun, she thinks about Marion, who knows she is dying, sorting through her belongings, making little bequests such as this, putting her affairs in order. And she thinks about David driving to the racquetball club and being carried out on a stretcher. Having absolutely no inkling as he ate his breakfast and searched for a pair of clean socks or whatever that soon he would be dead. She wonders what his last words to Rachel were. She wonders if he was thinking about her, Lynne, thinking about driving over to her house after the game ended and making love to her. He could have been thinking about it as he reached for his last shot. It was not really all that unlikely. *On the other hand*, she hears Eleanor's voice butting in, *he could have been thinking about telling you it was over. You don't know. You can't ever know. Shut up*, Lynne tells her, *leave me alone. What do you know?* She sighs and wonders what he would have done differently had he known, like Marion, that he was going to die soon. He probably thought he had all the time in the world to figure things out. She sighs again and wonders what she would have done differently had she known. She looks down at the damp spot on her lap and traces it with her fingertips. It is almost dry now, almost invisible, she is both glad and sad to see.

sleeping dogs

The mothers are standing on the corners again. It is a raw, drizzly afternoon, and from his vantage point in the kitchen, Ben admires their zealous endurance as he pours himself another cup of coffee. His wife has told him that the mothers have two shifts, morning and afternoon, at the start and close of the school day. Patience has the two-thirty to three-thirty shift. He sees her across the street, pacing the sidewalk on the southeast corner, wearing a red down vest, jeans, and hiking boots, talking with one of the other mothers who is pushing a baby stroller. He waves but she doesn't see him. He is just as glad. He has been working at home now for a little over a month—ever since the money his mother left him enabled him to quit his job and convert the garage into an office—and he still finds it difficult to settle into a routine, to focus. He will be sitting at his desk, in front of his computer screen, and the next thing he knows he is out in the yard trimming a lopsided hedge or raking leaves or pouring himself another cup of coffee. He wishes he could walk outside and talk to his wife, but he feels somehow as if he would be intruding.

He glances at the clock. Any minute now Max and Alex will be bursting in the door, laden with their matching Day-Glo lunch boxes and knapsacks. He still savors the unfamiliar thrill of being at home to greet them, but his sons already seem to take his presence for granted. Max, who was in the same third-grade class as Jason, seems to be both fascinated and gravely impressed by his death, whereas Alex, in kindergarten, doesn't quite seem to get it. This morning at breakfast as their mother poured coffee into a large thermos to take across the street to the morning shift, Alex took a bite of cinnamon toast and asked, "Is Jason still dead?" Max choked on a swallow of orange juice and said, "Don't you know anything? Once you're dead you're dead *forever.* That's what dead means. Right, Dad?" Ben nodded reluctantly and Alex burst into tears—more, Ben thought, from the indignity of being corrected by his older brother than from any sudden intimation of mortality.

According to Patience, there was no formal organization. The morning after the little boy was killed—a hit-and-run—half a dozen mothers just spontaneously gravitated to the intersection and posted themselves on each corner. By the first afternoon their number had doubled, and that's when they decided to split into two shifts. One of the mothers, a graphic artist, passed out T-shirts with the face of the little dead boy on the front and his name, Jason Grayson, and his dates, 1984–1993. On warmer afternoons when the women don't need to wear coats, they are a chillingly somber sight standing vigil in their identical white T-shirts with the dead boy's face smiling out at the stream of drivers, which slows as it passes by them. They seem like some sort of silent Greek chorus out of Euripides or Aeschylus. He imagines the hit-and-run driver having to drive by them every day on his way to and from work, unable to change his route, the mothers' relentless energy creating a magnetic force field that draws him involuntarily. It is the beginning of the second week now. Ben has asked his wife exactly what it is that they hope to accomplish by their daily vigil. After all, the police have someone posted nearby, watching the spot. Patience said they don't know; it is just something they have to do.

The front door bangs open and shut and his sons charge through the house and into the kitchen with windblown hair and ruddy cheeks—a gust of fresh air. Max grabs the chocolate milk from the refrigerator while Alex climbs up on the footstool and scoops out a handful of Fig Newtons.

"Hi guys, how was school?" Ben asks.

Intent upon pouring the milk, Max ignores him. Alex mumbles

"fine" through a mouthful of cookie. Neither of his sons have yet to master the art of small talk. They are like little barbarians, grunting monosyllabic responses to questions, and then suddenly launching into some jet-propelled, incoherent summary of a movie they saw on TV or a pedantic recitation of some new set of facts acquired in school that day: dinosaurs, powwows, the ozone layer. Ben fantasizes about father-son camping trips, sitting around the campfire talking about all the things he never talked about with his own father—but he is beginning to wonder if they will ever get beyond Ninja Turtles.

The night after the little Grayson boy was killed, Ben sat his sons down in the living room and explained to them what had happened. They listened solemnly and nodded when he asked, "Do you understand?" They shook their heads silently when he asked, "Do you have any questions? Anything at all? You sure?" Then finally Max spoke up. Just a week earlier he had gone to a big birthday party for Jason at Pizza Circus and he wanted to know what was going to happen to all of Jason's birthday presents. "Will we get them back?" he asked hopefully. That night in bed Ben had sighed and said to his wife, "Do you think we're doing something wrong?"

He glances out the kitchen window and sees Patience bending over, talking intently to a woman in a new Toyota station wagon with temporary plates parked by the curb. The woman dabs at her eyes with a Kleenex and Ben recognizes her. Nancy Grayson. She must have sold her old VW just before the accident. He can't imagine her out car shopping since it happened. She is divorced; Jason was her only child. A couple of the other mothers walk over and group themselves protectively around the car, reaching through the open window to give her an awkward pat or peck. After a minute, the station wagon takes off. The other mothers look at each other and shake their heads.

"Hey, Dad," Max says, "it's Friday. Can we rent a video for tonight?"

"Yeah," Alex seconds, "and a pizza."

"You want to rent a pizza?" Ben jokes. "For how long?" Max snickers and Alex punches him in the arm. "Okay," Ben intervenes before the fight escalates. "We'll rent a movie."

"What about the pizza?" Max says.

Ben looks at the chicken breasts defrosting in a pink pool of blood on the counter. "Looks like your mother has other plans. Sorry, guys."

"I hate chicken," Alex whines. "It's boring."

"You're boring," Max says. "Boring, boring, bor—"

"That's enough." Ben clamps a hand over Max's mouth.

"What's boring?" Patience walks into the kitchen and shrugs off her down vest. The boys smile angelically and give her stereophonic kisses on each cheek. She holds them close, squeezing them hard, and Ben knows she is thinking of the little dead boy. He reaches out and massages her tense shoulders until she relaxes her stranglehold on the boys. They squirm out of her arms and race downstairs to the basement rec room. She covers his hands with hers, still chilly, and tucks her head under his chin.

"Any news?" he asks.

She shakes her head and sighs. "I invited Nancy Grayson to dinner tomorrow. She didn't want to come, but I insisted. She needs to get out."

"Maybe she's not ready," Ben says, turning to put the chocolate milk back in the refrigerator.

"That's what people say to let themselves off the hook," Patience says, "so they don't have to deal with it." She gets up and rinses the chicken breasts under the tap. "How can you ever be ready?"

"I don't know," Ben mumbles, gazing out the gray window at the endless litter of fallen leaves he can never seem to keep up with. Downstairs he can hear the boys bickering over something. Patience is intent upon yanking the rubbery skin off the chicken breasts. He feels a damp, heavy compost of sadness in his gut—*Is this all there is?*—and, at the same time, a terrible fear at having so much to lose. He locks his arms around his wife's waist and buries his face in her thick, damp, dark, earthy hair. His own hair is dry and thinning—a visible sign, he fears, of depleted mental topsoil. He slides his hands under her flannel shirt, over her silky bra. On the outside she is strictly L. L. Bean, but on the inside she is pure Victoria's Secret. He still remembers his surprised delight the first time they made love, excavating through all

those politically correct layers of flannel and denim to arrive suddenly at that frivolous, elitist, secret whisper of lace and satin.
The opposite of his mother, who was all ruffles and rhinestones
and Shalimar on the outside, and white cotton Fruit of the Loom
on the inside. He knew at once that this was the woman for
him—a woman nothing like his mother. Just as he was nothing
like his father. And their marriage would be nothing like his parents'. They would wear their happiness on the inside.

While the chicken is baking, Ben drives the boys to the video
store and turns them loose to pick out one movie apiece. As long
as he's there, Ben decides he might as well pick up a movie for
Patience and him to watch later, after the boys are in bed. Maybe
because Patience is not with him to assert herself, he tries hard to
imagine what she would be in the mood to watch. Somehow it
seems important that he make the right choice. He wants to be a
good husband, a better husband than his father was, and he
thinks, by and large, he has been.

Max marches up and announces that he and Alex are ready to
go. His sons hand him their two videos—*Under Siege* and
Homeward Bound—and Ben reaches into his wallet and hands
Max a five-dollar bill to go next door to Open Harvest for some
yogurt-covered peanuts and raisins while he continues wandering
up one aisle and down the next, skimming the titles of the
movies, most of which they have already seen or would never
want to. He pauses by *The French Lieutenant's Woman*, takes it off
the shelf, and reads the back of the box. He knows it is one of his
wife's favorite movies; she has a thing for Jeremy Irons. Like
most of the women he knows, it seems. He goes over to the
checkout counter and as he stands in line, he tries not to think
about that night he had more or less succeeded in repressing
until last week, when Jason Grayson was killed, and suddenly,
there it was again.

Two years ago. A Saturday night. Patience and the boys were
in Tucson visiting her mother, who was recovering from a
cataract operation. He had not been able to take the time off
from work to go with them, and feeling bored and bereft all
alone in the empty house, he walked over to the video store.
Reversal of Fortune had just been released, and as he scored the

last red-hot copy off the shelf—the others having already been checked out—he heard a voice behind him mutter "Shit!" He turned around and saw Nancy Grayson standing there looking depressed. "Oh sorry," she said and smiled as she recognized him. "You got the last copy." She brushed a long strand of unruly hair out of her eyes and sighed. "I'm a Jeremy Irons groupie. Guess I'll have to settle for Sam Shepard tonight." Before he could say anything, she hurried off down another aisle. He stood there for a moment looking at the box in his hand, hesitating, and then glanced around the store for her. She was wearing a man's old flannel shirt that made her look small and fragile. Ben wondered if it was an old shirt of Tom's. They had all known each other casually, two decades ago, in high school. He and Tom had played on the basketball team, and Nancy, a pretty cheer-leader, was Tom's girlfriend. Ben didn't have a girlfriend, not until he went off to Grinnell, and he had always envied Tom and been tongue-tied in Nancy's radiant blonde presence. Some time last fall he had bumped into Tom at Target, buying a cheap set of pots and pans and flatware, and Tom had told him they were get-ting a divorce.

Nancy was squatting down, skimming the lower shelf of videos. As Ben walked up she was reaching for a copy of *Days of Heaven*. Her knees cracked when she stood up without her for-mer cheerleader's agile buoyancy.

"Listen," Ben had said. "Why don't you take this?" He held his copy of *Reversal of Fortune* out to her. "I'd just as soon watch something else. I mean, it's not that big a deal."

"Really?" She looked touched, almost on the verge of tears. "No, that's okay. I couldn't. But it's sweet of you to offer."

"I insist," Ben said, holding the tape out until she was forced to take it.

"Well, thanks," she said hesitantly. "But won't Patience be dis-appointed?"

"No problem," he shrugged. "She and the boys are off in Tucson for the week, visiting her mother."

Nancy sighed and nodded. "Jason's with his father. Every Wednesday and Saturday."

"Enjoy the movie." Ben walked off before she could protest

again, grabbed some new Steve Martin comedy off the shelf, and headed for the checkout counter. Nancy was already standing in line in front of him. Three giggling teenage girls were flirting with the good-looking clerk. Ben noticed that Nancy had picked up a large Hershey bar from the candy and soda pop rack that Ben resented because he usually ended up in a big fight with Max and Alex over junk food whenever they came here. Somehow the candy bar touched him, the thought of her indulging herself alone in front of the TV.

"Listen." She had turned to him. "Why don't you just come over and watch this with me? I mean, it's only fair, right?"

"I don't know, I don't think—"

"No, really. I'll make some popcorn. I'd like the company." She sounded awkwardly shy and vulnerable, like a teenage girl.

"Okay," he had said. "Why not?"

It is pouring rain on the ride back home from the video store. Max opens the sack of yogurt candy and pops a handful into his mouth.

"Give me some!" Alex demands from the backseat.

"Put that away," Ben says, reaching for the sack. "You'll spoil your appetite." The car swerves on the slick street and Ben grips the steering wheel rigidly and concentrates on peering through the clouded windshield. The rain is turning to icy sleet. The boys start arguing about which movie to watch first and Alex attempts to lunge over the front seat to grab his video away from Max but is nearly strangled by his seat belt.

"Stop it!" Ben shouts. "I'm driving. It's dangerous."

The boys simmer down and sulk. As a layer of thin ice forms on the windshield, reducing the visibility until he is hunched tensely over the wheel, driving half-blind, Ben feels the anxiety inside him building to a heart-pounding attack of panic. He keeps seeing things out of the corner of his eye and imagining himself skidding to a sudden stop—not in time—the sickening thud of a small body against the car's bumper—and that horrible, irrevocable, instantaneous realization that your life, as you knew it, is over and you have just entered some endless loop of night-mare and are now living the kind of life that happens to someone else, not you. Not me. Abruptly he pulls the car over to the side of the road and sits there, taking deep breaths.

"What's wrong?" Max asks.

"Nothing. I just have to scrape the windshield," Ben says. He fishes the scraper out from under the seat and gets out of the car. After he has scraped the glass clean, he gets back inside the car and sits there for a moment, reluctant to put the car in gear. Max and Alex stare at him, seemingly afraid to complain for once.

"You feel okay, Daddy?" Alex asks quietly.

Ben nods and manages a shaky smile, waits for a break in the traffic, and pulls back out onto the street. They are only three blocks from home. He creeps along at twenty miles per hour, like an old lady, like the way his mother used to drive him crazy driving well below the speed limit. His father and he used to joke about her driving in their rare moments of macho rapport. One of the few things they shared in common was their love of driving, of getting behind the wheel and cruising for miles and miles with no particular destination. They were not reckless driv-ers but prided themselves on a certain instinctual grace and agility behind the wheel. The closest Ben ever felt toward his father was during those driving lessons his father gave him just before his sixteenth birthday.

After the boys are finally in bed, Ben rebuilds the dying fire in the fireplace and pours them each a snifter of brandy while Patience changes into her purple plush bathrobe. They snuggle under one of the many afghans his mother crocheted for them and settle in to watch the movie. Patience yawns open-mouthed, like a sleepy child, and Ben strokes her hair. She kisses his ear and murmurs, "Thanks for getting this movie. It's just what I'm in the mood for."

Lulled by the warmth of the fire and the brandy, Ben finds himself nodding off, drifting in and out. The image of Meryl Streep standing all alone at the end of the pier, swaddled in black, looking out to sea, somehow reminds him of Nancy Grayson. He wonders if she and Tom have been able to offer each other any comfort. He hopes so but doubts it. He knows that Tom has settled into something with another woman—Ben has run into them a couple of times at the movies or the supermarket. The new woman is a younger but less pretty version of Nancy. He thinks how terrible it must be to grieve separately over your dead child. He can't imagine anything worse. Patience hits the Pause button on the remote and shuffles off to the bathroom in the ridiculous bunny slippers that Alex gave her last Christmas. In the few seconds she is gone, he can feel the empty space cooling next to him. When she comes back, he slips his hand underneath her robe and cups his palm around her warm breast.

By the time the movie ends, he is asleep. Patience tickles him awake—teary-eyed from the movie—and they stumble off to bed. As they pass by the boys' room, they pause in the doorway and watch them sleep. Alex sleeps peacefully, as if in suspended animation for eight hours while Max practices a kind of nocturnal gymnastics, sometimes thudding onto the floor in the middle of the night. Ben thinks of his panic attack driving home from the video store. He doesn't know which would be worse: losing a child or having to live with the knowledge that you inflicted the loss on some other parents, the guilt you would feel whenever you hugged your own child, knowing that you didn't really deserve him. Even if the accident were not your fault. An inattentive child simply darts out in front of you; the best driver on earth could not have avoided hitting him. Still, the guilt is there, it's yours. Every morning when you open your eyes, every night when you shut your eyes. It's there. As unavoidable as the accident itself.

Once in bed with the lights out, Patience conks right out while Ben, perversely, cannot seem to fall asleep. He lies there in the dark with his brain revving like the motor of a parked car. Although the house is set back, secluded by huge old fir trees, they live on a busy corner and every few minutes he can hear the whisper of tires passing by.

He wonders, as he often does, where these drivers could be going in Lincoln, Nebraska, in the middle of the night. He remembers driving through Utah with his parents, to California, the summer he turned thirteen. It was late and dark, a vast unbroken expanse of night. He was lying on a nest of pillows in the backseat; his father had the radio playing softly; his mother had fallen asleep, her head crooked at an awkward angle against the car window with Lichee (the second in what would be a long series of small, yappy, bug-eyed dogs) curled snugly in her lap. Suddenly the car swerved, followed by a dull thud. Ben sat up and said, "What was that?" His father slowed, hesitated—looking over at his wife, still sound asleep—and then speeded up again. "A dog," he said. "Damn thing came out of nowhere." He punched in the cigarette lighter, tweezed a Camel out of his shirt pocket, and held the tip of the cigarette against the glowing red coils. Ben twisted around, kneeling on the seat, and stared at the dark highway behind them, wondering if the dog were really dead. What if it were just injured, lying there all alone, in pain, whimpering? He couldn't see anything, but he felt sick anyway.

"Don't tell your mother," his father said. "It's just between us guys. Okay?" Ben didn't say anything. Lichee suddenly roused herself and bristled to attention. Ben could see her bug-eyes staring accusatorially at his father, who blew a big puff of smoke into her face. The dog let out a shrill, aggrieved yap. Ben's mother yawned and stretched and petted the dog. "What's up?" she asked groggily. "Nothing," his father answered, fiddling with the radio tuner. Ben pretended to be asleep.

The next morning when Ben looks out the kitchen window the corners are empty, "unmanned." The mothers have agreed to take the weekend off. The boys are eating pop-up waffles drowned in maple syrup. Patience sits across from them, making out a grocery list for the evening's dinner, leafing through a couple of cookbooks.

"Let's have spaghetti," Alex suggests hopefully.

Patience smiles, reaches out and smooths his bangs, sticky with maple syrup. Max leans over and reads the shopping list upside down. "Lamb," he wrinkles his nose. "We're having *lamb*." Alex pretends to gag and then makes pitiful baa-ing sounds.

"Moussaka," Patience says. "You'll like it. It's like Greek macaroni and cheese, sort of."

The boys look at each other dubiously.

Ben pours himself another cup of coffee "to go," slips on his
jacket and announces, "I'm going to try to get some work done."
They ignore him. At the back door he pauses and asks, "What
time's the dinner?"

"Seven," Patience says, engrossed in her cookbook. "I told her
to come around seven."

Out in his office Ben turns on his computer and stares uncom-
prehendingly at the glowing letters on the screen as if they are in
some foreign language. He closes his eyes. He wonders how
Nancy feels about this little get-together this evening, this obvious act of concerned kindness on Patience's part. He imagines
that his wife's well-meaning solicitude must make Nancy feel
even worse if, under the circumstances, she has any emotion left
over to expend on smaller regrets. He feels irritated and resentful
toward his wife—why couldn't she leave well enough alone?—
even though he knows that he is being unfair to her. This is the
way Patience is; this is part of what he loves about her. She
doesn't know how to look the other way. One year, in exchange
for mostly illusory household chores, she "rented" the spare bedroom (before Alex arrived) to a lonely Indonesian graduate student so shy and tongue-tied that no one else but Patience had the
patience to deal with him. Malik, now an engineer back in
Surabaya, still writes her adoring letters once a month. Another
time she organized an ad hoc hospice detail to help a woman she
barely knew from the day care center whose husband was dying
of cancer. A sort of suburban Mother Teresa who swears and
wears sexy underwear. And so it was only inevitable that Nancy
Grayson would fall victim to his wife's big heart. He should have
known.

It was only that one night. His one and only night of infidelity
in twelve years of marriage. He imagines that some other man, a
more adulterous sort, would dismiss it as altogether insignificant.
Ironically enough, it is his otherwise unblemished record of

fidelity that endows that one night—twelve hours out of twelve years—with such indelible intensity. He knows that, in its own right, it was not such a big deal. She made popcorn. They watched the movie and drank gin and tonics—a hot summer night. He said he better go, but somehow he kept staying, enjoying the strange but comfortable intimacy of sitting beside her on the couch, talking. More than ten years since he had talked alone like this to a woman other than his wife. Nancy told him that she had always liked him, even back in high school, how she thought he was different from Tom and his buddies—more sensitive and vulnerable. How, after Jason was born, Tom ignored her sexually and started to cheat on her. She was still a very pretty woman with an easy sort of sensuality and openness, no pretensions, no bitterness. Somehow the gin and the heat and the memories of Nancy's sweet blonde popularity and Tom's subsequent shoddy treatment of her alchemically combusted to awaken both a boozy sense of chivalry and lust. They went to bed. He awakened just after dawn, exhausted and hung over, and said he had to get home. A quick good-bye kiss, already tainted with guilt on his part. She said she wished she had been smarter back then and waited for someone like him. A Jeremy Irons instead of a Clint Eastwood. "At the moment," he had joked lamely, "I feel more like Claus von Bülow."

"Don't be too hard on yourself," she had said, which he had found an oddly generous remark from a cheated-on ex-wife. "I'd feel bad." On the short drive home the early-morning air was pure and cool after the stuffy bedroom. He drove with the windows rolled down. Sunday morning, too early for church. The tree-shaded streets were deserted. When he got to his own street, he kept on driving, out into the open countryside, the green fields. He drove fast, trying to clear his head, soothed by the sense of motion. He remembered when Max was a colicky baby, how—at their wits' end—they would strap him in his car seat and drive around aimlessly until he fell asleep, lulled by the car's steady rhythm. He thought how ironic it was that while he was betraying his own wife's trust, Nancy would perceive him as the husband she should have waited for. And yet he knew, despite the apparent irony, that there was some truth in what she had said.

He hears the boys shouting outside and opens his eyes. It has started to snow, the first early snowfall of the season. Max and Alex are scooping the skimpy wet frosting off the frozen lawn and attempting, unsuccessfully, to make snowballs. Ben waves at them and they wave back. He focuses on the blank computer screen, his fingers resting mindlessly on the keyboard.

They never "saw" each other again, except for the few times he bumped into her over the next couple years at school functions or chauffeuring Max to some event to which Jason was also invited. Usually they had their sons with them; it was safe and not so terribly awkward, polite and friendly with no undercurrent of smoldering looks or double entendres. Outside of the boys' school, they did not orbit the same social circle. Nancy never tried to get in touch with him or remind him of the incident. This was no *Fatal Attraction*. She was a nice woman, a sensible woman. Once they ran into her at Imperial Palace—he with his family, she with a pleasant-enough-looking man who covered her hand with his from time to time and smiled. Ben was glad for her. He wished her well. The last thing she had said to him that morning was, "Don't tell Patience." She took hold of his hand and gave him a steady look as if to say *Trust me.* "It's not necessary," she had said. He had nodded uncertainly, eager to leave. But he did trust her. And, for better or for worse, he had taken her advice.

His stomach growls. He looks at his watch—almost noon— and admits to himself that he is not going to get any work done today. The snow is falling more heavily now, a white blanket covers the lawn. He feels disoriented, as if he has missed something. It was autumn when he entered his office and now suddenly it is winter. He shuts off the computer and heads back to the house.

He is standing in the kitchen fixing himself a bologna and cheese sandwich when Patience appears, fresh from a shower, a towel wrapped around her wet hair.

"Nancy called," she says, sliding the cookbook back on the shelf. "She's got the flu and her sister's flying in from Denver this evening, so the dinner's off."

"Oh." Ben rummages around in the refrigerator. He holds up a bright yellow plastic squeeze-bottle of mustard, the kind the boys insist upon. "Are we out of adult mustard?"

"I guess so." Patience crumples up the moussaka shopping list and starts a new one, scribbling "Dijon" at the top. "We might as well have spaghetti. At least Alex will be happy."

"I'll go to the store," Ben volunteers. "It's snowing pretty hard." He knows that Patience, who grew up in Arizona, doesn't like to drive in snow. He sits down at the table and starts in on his sandwich.

"Thanks," Patience says and slides the shopping list across the table toward him. She gets up and goes upstairs. A minute later he hears the blow dryer buzzing overhead. He feels both relieved and strangely let down at the news that the dinner is off. The way he felt when his lottery number came up 298 after he had spent weeks studying maps and books on Canada. As if his whole life he has been waiting for some ax to fall that never falls. It just hovers in the air above him.

When he goes outside, he finds Alex busily shoveling the driveway with the miniature shovel they bought him for his last birthday. The snow is still falling, but he shovels away valiantly like some pint-size Sisyphus.

"You want to go to the store with me?" Ben asks him. "You've done a great job on the driveway."

"Okay," Alex says, pleased with himself, tossing aside the shovel as he climbs into the car.

Ben backs slowly out of the new carport. "Guess what?"

"What?" Alex looks up expectantly as he struggles with his seat belt.

"We're having spaghetti for dinner after all."

Alex beams and claps his hands. Ben thinks how great it is to be that age.

They skid to a fishtail stop at the corner, the corner where the little boy was killed. Inside his gloves Ben's fingers clamp the steering wheel in a deathlike grip. His heart pounds. He breaks out into a sweat. Alex obliviously sorts through the cassettes in the glove compartment. The street is already ugly with brown slush. Patience has always wanted to move back to the Southwest, and Ben thinks maybe it's not such a bad idea. Sunshine, swimming pools. He remembers visiting his parents shortly after they had moved down to Florida, to one of those retirement communities. They were sitting around the swimming pool after dinner when his father suddenly leaned over and pointed to a handsome silver-haired woman in huge dark glasses sitting off by herself, leafing through a copy of *The New Yorker.* "See her?" his father whispered loudly. "Her husband had a heart attack at the wheel last year, drove his Cadillac right into a taco stand and killed two little girls, sisters."

"Shhh!" his mother had hissed. "She'll hear you." His mother had turned to Ben and murmured, "He was really a very nice man, a retired pediatrician. They were a lovely couple." His mother sighed. "He took his own life a month later. A lethal injection."

"What did she say?" his father asked suspiciously. His hearing was going and he was becoming more paranoid, always imagining everyone was contradicting him. "He was a doctor," he said. "Imagine."

During the three days that Ben spent with them, his father had alluded to the unfortunate pediatrician's accident several more times, a bit obsessively, Ben thought. And not long after he got back home to Nebraska, his mother wrote and told him that his father had gone down to the Motor Vehicle Department to renew his license, which was about to expire on his seventy-sixth birthday, and had failed the eye exam. *Just between you and me*, she wrote, *I think he failed that test on purpose because he's afraid, lost his nerve. He sees better than I do.* It had been years since Ben had experienced any tender feeling for his father, whom he had long ago written off, but suddenly he had felt a lump in his throat. *He came home acting fit to be tied, cursing and slamming around the place, you know how he is, but he can't fool me. I know he's relieved.* She had gone on to talk about their health and the weather and at the end of the letter she had scrawled a hasty P.S. *Don't mention anything about the license to him.* And he never had. Six months later his father had suffered a massive stroke on the putting green and was rushed in an ambulance to the hospital, which he never left.

After his father's death, his mother and the pediatrician's widow, Sylvia, became inseparable, like sisters. They went on cruises and ate dinner together every night. They even bought two cockapoos, sisters, from the same litter and named them Zsa

Zsa and Eva. Ben had never seen his mother so relaxed and happy, almost lighthearted. He sensed that those five years after his father's death were the best years of her life.

They pull into the slushy parking lot at the supermarket, filled with people stocking up in case the storm worsens. Inside, they get a cart and divide up the list. Alex speeds off in search of spaghetti and hamburger as if he is on a scavenger hunt, while Ben plods toward the feminine hygiene section and tosses in the brand of tampons that is on the shopping list, then makes his way toward the produce counter. Alex races up behind him with the hamburger and spaghetti, and Ben sends him off to hunt for Parmesan cheese. As he debates about what type of let-tuce to buy, he wonders if Nancy really has the flu. He wonders if maybe he shouldn't just tell Patience and get the whole thing off his chest, out in the open, once and for all. After all, it is over and done with and never really went anywhere in the first place. But the timing seems bad. It would put Patience in an emotional bind. How could she resent Nancy, who has just lost her only child? He knows that, under the circumstances, his wife would feel compelled to rise above it, and somehow this would make his confession seem like an act of cowardice rather than courage. He remembers one of his mother's favorite homi-lies and can hear her voice: *Why stir things up? Better to let sleep-ing dogs lie.*

On his deathbed, in one of his rare lucid intervals, his father had turned to Ben's mother and said, "There's something I never told you, Betty. That trip we took to California?" His mother nods. "I hit a dog, killed it. You were asleep."

Ben looked at his father, utterly astonished. He could not believe that a man as emotionally detached and insensitive as his father would even have remembered the incident for three decades, let alone brooded over it.

"I'm sorry," his father said. "I should have stopped."

Ben's mother sat there stiff and silent for a moment, then looked over at Ben. "Did you know about this?" she asked him.

Before he could answer, his father caught his eye and shook his head.

"No," Ben said. "I must have been asleep."

His mother smiled and relaxed and reached over and patted his hand.

Alex materializes, out of breath, with the Parmesan cheese and a package of Oreos. "Can we get these too?"

"Okay," Ben says, even though he knows that Patience will disapprove. He wants his sons to like him, to remember him kindly, to miss him when he is gone.

At the last minute, as they are waiting in the checkout line, Ben sprints off and brings back some fresh orange juice and a pot of yellow mums with dark, shiny leaves—the green and gold of their old high school colors. Alex has opened the package of cookies and is eating one, licking the frosting off each side, the way Ben used to do as a boy. Ben reaches over and takes one for himself.

On the way back home, the snow has let up, and the streets have started to clear. Alex punches an old Bruce Springsteen cassette into the tape player. Ben takes a short detour, a couple of blocks out of their way, and pulls up in front of Nancy's house. The new white station wagon is parked in the driveway. "I'll just be a minute," he says, leaving the engine running.

"Where are we?" Alex frowns.

"Jason's mother's house." Before Alex can say anything else, Ben grabs the orange juice and flowers and rings the doorbell.

Nancy peers through the window and then opens the door, wrapping her old bathrobe more securely around herself. Her hair looks stringy and she's clutching a wad of Kleenex. Perversely, Ben feels better knowing that she really is sick, that she hadn't lied on his account. "I brought you these," he says.

She takes them and thanks him. "Tell Patience I'm sorry about dinner. Your wife's a very nice woman."

Ben nods. Nancy sneezes and closes the door as Ben turns to go. Her walk is unshoveled. He wonders what happened to the man she was with that time at the Imperial Palace, the one who kept squeezing her hand on the red tablecloth.

When they get back home, Patience is talking on the phone to her mother in Tucson. Her mother has developed diabetes and high blood pressure, and Patience worries about her out there even though her father's health is still pretty good. He still plays a set of tennis every morning. Ben puts the groceries away and starts working on the spaghetti sauce, chopping onions and garlic. He puts Alex to work frying up the hamburger. Patience smiles at them. The kitchen smells great. The windows steam up, warm and cozy. Patience hangs up the phone and sighs. "She's going into the hospital for some tests."

Ben walks over and gives her a hug. This is the stage they are going through now. They have been through the birth stage—their two sons—and now they are going through the death stage—two parents down, two to go. Patience helped him through his loss and he knows soon it will be his turn to help her through hers.

"We've got things under control here," Ben says. "Why don't you go relax for a while?"

Patience nods, gives Alex a love pat on his skinny butt, and goes off into the family room. Alex is standing on the little red footstool Ben's mother bought for Max when he was a toddler. Until her grandsons came along, those small fluffy dogs had always seemed to be the main source of love in his mother's life: She lavished affection on them and they ardently returned her devotion. Ben and his father had always resented the little dogs, sensing somehow that they gave her something which she found lacking in her husband and son. When he was a teenager his mother would occasionally ask him to walk the dog if she wasn't feeling well and he hated it. He hated being seen with such a sissy little dog; he felt he might as well be dragging along a box of Kotex on a leash. His friends all had German shepherds or black Labs.

But after his mother died, a sudden heart attack last spring, he had flown down to Sarasota for the funeral and to take care of things, only to find out that Sylvia, the pediatrician's widow, his mother's inseparable companion, had made all the arrangements and even packed up his mother's personal belongings for him. He was grateful, of course, but felt a bit useless sitting out by the swimming pool feeling more sad and lost than he would have expected himself to feel. Zsa Zsa, his mother's last dog, took a

liking to him, perhaps smelling a family resemblance, and followed him everywhere. When it was time for Ben to leave, he
had wanted to take the dog back home with him. He broached
the subject to Sylvia, who was clearly devastated by his mother's
death, and she looked so stricken that he quickly retracted the
suggestion. After all, the dogs were sisters, and he knew in his
heart that his mother would have wanted Sylvia to keep them
together. Still, it hurt him to leave the dog behind, and he
thought about it and missed it for a surprisingly long while after
he got back home to his wife and sons.

Patience walks back into the kitchen, fills the teakettle, and
sets it on the stove burner. "Smells good," she says. "Need any
help?"

"Nope," Ben says.

"Hamburger's done," Alex announces. "I'm going to go watch
TV." The wooden spoon clatters on the countertop and he takes
off as if he is suffering from sudden video withdrawal.

The teakettle whistles. Patience drops a jasmine tea bag into
the cup and pours in the steaming water. She sits down at the
table and takes small, gingerly sips of the hot tea.

"I stopped by Nancy's house and dropped off some orange
juice and flowers," Ben says. "She was in her bathrobe, looked
pretty miserable."

"Poor woman," Patience sighs. "That was thoughtful of you."

"Not really," he shrugs and concentrates on mincing the garlic
with surgical precision.

Patience stands up and carries her tea into the family room
where Alex is watching the *Homeward Bound* video for the third
or fourth time.

The kitchen suddenly feels quiet and empty. He remembers
how alone he felt that time Patience took the boys to visit her parents. How left out. How he wandered from room to room like a
ghost. He finds the babble of the TV through the wall both
annoying and comforting. Any minute now Max should be coming
home from his friend's house. Ben wipes a clear space in the
kitchen window with the sleeve of his shirt to see what the weather
is doing. It seems to be clearing. He looks across the street at the
corner and knows that the mothers will be out there bright and

early on Monday morning. He wonders how long they will keep up the vigil. He decides that he will ask if he can join them. If they ask why, he will say that it is just something he has to do.

The back door bangs open and Max bursts in, stamping snow off his boots. He sniffs the air. "Is that spaghetti?" he asks.

Ben nods his head.

"Cool," Max says and grabs an Oreo from the bag on the counter and stuffs it in his mouth before Ben has a chance to say a word. "When's dinner?" he mumbles, spraying cookie crumbs. "I'm starved."

"Soon," Ben says. "Think you'll make it?"

Max mutters something unintelligible and is gone. Ben frowns at the small drift of snow, already melting, that Max stamped off his boots. His own mother would have scolded him and made him wipe it up. Unless her current little dog had darted over and licked the puddle clean before she had a chance to spot it. His father rarely set foot in the kitchen, except to swipe a beer out of the refrigerator. Ben can't remember ever seeing his father so much as make a sandwich for himself—not once in nearly half a century of marriage. But Ben supposes that in his own way he was a faithful husband, if not a good husband. Or father. Ben takes a stack of Fiestaware dishes from the cupboard and sets them on the butcher-block table. He thinks about calling Max, then grabs a wad of paper towels, kneels down, and wipes up the gray puddle of snow. As he straightens up, catching a glimpse of his blurry reflection in the darkening window of the back door, he hears a dog whimper, faint but distinct, in the distance. And in that moment before he realizes that it is only the video, the muffled soundtrack from the family room, he stares out, as if staring down some long dark highway, and stops breathing, his heart pounding, his breath clouding the glass as he cups his palms against the cold window for a better look.

the summer
before
the summer
of love

The three of us were sitting on the muggy screen porch pushing the food around on our plates in silence. Meat loaf, Rice-A-Roni, and frozen peas. My older sister and I had just returned from spending the weekend at our father's small brown apartment in a huge new complex on the other side of town. It had only been a couple of months since he moved out, but it already seemed as if we had never lived any other way. Johanna and I were still full from the butterscotch beanies our father had bought for us at the Dairy Queen on the way back home. It was a muggy August night and the little girls next door were galloping back and forth through the sprinkler in matching pink polka dot bathing suits that had once belonged to my sister and me. The DiBernard girls were four years apart, like Johanna and I, so my mother gave Mrs. DiBernard all our old clothes. It was like watching old home movies of ourselves, of some dumber and happier time, and as we sat there pretending to eat our dinner in the steamy heat, I wished that Johanna and I were back inside those hideous bathing suits, splashing and shouting away.

"You're not eating anything," our mother reproached us, although she wasn't eating anything herself. She seemed twitchy and impatient.

"We had a big lunch," I said. "At China Palace."

Our mother frowned and pursed her lips. She thought our father was trying to buy our loyalty with Chinese food, Big Macs, and ice cream. I had heard them arguing about this on the phone the week before.

"Good meat loaf," I said, dutifully shoving a forkful into my mouth.

Johanna sighed and pelted peas at a couple of birds in the backyard.

Before the separation our mother had been a lazy, absentminded cook. Our father would come home from work and the still-frozen roast would be sitting there on the counter. He would jab a fork into it, then sigh and frown down at it, as if all of our mother's sins and flaws were neatly consolidated in this icy lump. "So what's the big deal?" our mother would say, picking up the telephone. "No one's going to starve." Half an hour later a pizza would arrive. The neighborhood kids always envied us when they spied the large indestructible pizza box sitting on the curb by the trash.

In those days, at least in Ohio where we lived, divorce was still something mostly associated with other people—movie stars or trashy types, people with winter tans or criminal records. All of our friends had two parents, and after our father moved out, the same kids who used to drool with envy at our empty pizza boxes suddenly looked down on us, as if we'd had to sell one of our cars or something.

Our mother seemed to take to the kitchen in a desperate attempt to salvage our respectability. For the past two months she had been serving us these dull, well-balanced meals. "You are what you eat," she'd say, smiling her new fake Betty Crocker smile. As if eating these boring all-American meals would make us just another boring all-American family.

"Are you finished, Suzanne honey?" She hovered over me and when I nodded, my mouth full of Rice-A-Roni, she whisked my plate away, whistling.

"What's her problem?" Johanna said as soon as the kitchen doors swung shut. "She's acting like a weirdo."

I shrugged.

A second later our mother returned with three bowls of sliced strawberries and bananas. Johanna sighed.

"Whoops," our mother said. "Almost forgot." She bustled back into the kitchen.

Johanna wrinkled her nose. "She knows I *detest* brown bananas." She picked out the offensive banana slices and stacked them like poker chips beside her bowl.

Our mother hurried back out with a plate of graham crackers. She seemed wound up, chattering away about nothing while Johanna and I dutifully moved our spoons back and forth between our bowls and our mouths. Every so often she'd give the graham cracker plate a little nervous nudge closer to Johanna or me, but neither of us showed any interest. In the old days we would have had Mallomars. Finally her patience snapped and she shoved the plate in Johanna's face. "Take a cookie!" she ordered. "You, too," she said, turning to me.

Surprised into obedience, we each automatically grabbed a graham cracker and bit into it as she plunked the saucer back down on the table. Then we saw it, or rather them—the surprise—hidden under the boring graham crackers. Four tickets. Johanna's eyes widened and she seemed to stop breathing as she reached out and picked one up and read aloud what was printed on it: "The Beatles. Crosley Field. August 20, 1966." Then she screamed so loud the DiBernard girls froze in their tracks and looked over at us in alarm. I smiled and waved and shouted, "It's okay, she's just going to the Beatles concert!"

Johanna had her arms wrapped around our mother's neck, jumping up and down, half strangling her, shouting, "You're the greatest, you're the greatest, thank you, thank you, thank you, thank you!"

"It's your birthday present," our mother laughed. "Happy Sweet Sixteen."

I picked up the rest of the tickets and stared down at them, not daring to ask. On the one hand, I wasn't as besotted with the Beatles as my sister and her friends, but, on the other hand, I didn't want to be left out of any major excursion. Crosley Field was in Cincinnati, over a hundred miles away.

"We're all going," my mother said, coming up for air and winking at me. "The three of us, plus Sharon." Sharon Dinsmore was Johanna's best friend.

"Oh my *God!*" Johanna screamed again even louder. "Does Sharon know? I have to go call her."

My mother shook her head, pleased and gratified to have broken, for once, through Johanna's new usual air of cool disdain. "I asked Mrs. Dinsmore's permission, of course, but I told her to keep it a secret."

"Oh my God, I don't believe it! Wait till she hears! Oh my God." Johanna raced off to the telephone. The air around us seemed to quiver for a moment in her wake, and then her shrill, thrilled voice floated down to us from the open window upstairs.

Flushed from all the big excitement, my mother smiled across the table at me. "So, what do *you* think?"

"Are we going to stay in a hotel?" I asked. The one time we had driven to Cincinnati for a cousin's wedding we had stayed overnight at a fancy hotel where the maid left chocolate mints on our pillowcases.

"I made reservations at the Holiday Inn," she said. "It has a swimming pool."

"Wow, that's great." I dipped my graham cracker into my lukewarm glass of milk and nibbled on it. I was thinking that even *my* friends were going to be impressed by this and wishing that Johanna would get off the phone with Sharon so that I could call my best friend, Lisa.

As if reading my mind, my mother paused in clearing the table and said, "Suzanne honey, I hope you don't mind that I didn't get a ticket for Lisa. It's just that the tickets were expensive and you know how crazy Johanna and Sharon are about the Beatles."

I nodded. This was an understatement. Our father couldn't afford to buy himself a new stereo yet, so every weekend Johanna spent most of her time lying in the front seat of his Camaro, punching the radio buttons to find Beatles songs. Her favorite was "Norwegian Wood." She practically fainted every time she heard it.

The screen door banged open and shut as my mother carried our dessert bowls into the kitchen. I reached over and ate Johanna's stack of mushy banana slices. Inside the house I could hear Johanna's squealing and my mother's humming as she ran water in the sink. She was humming "Can't Buy Me Love." Next door Mr. DiBernard came out and shut off the sprinkler. All he had on was some thin pale pajama bottoms that you could almost see through. The DiBernard girls started to whine in protest. He picked them up, one under each arm, and whirled them around in circles until they started to laugh and squeal. I got up and went inside.

Sitting in a booth at China Palace the following Saturday evening, Johanna smothered her egg roll in plum sauce, passed me the empty bowl, and announced to our father that we wouldn't be seeing him the weekend of the twentieth because we were going to Cincinnati to see the Beatles.

He frowned into his glass of beer, and I could see the objections ringing up in his mind, one after another, like prices in a cash register. One of our mother's big complaints against our father was that every time she got the spark of an idea, he dumped cold water all over it. "The thing you girls have to understand about your father is that he is essentially a very negative person," she told us as we were packing for the weekend. "Don't expect him to greet this plan with any enthusiasm."

"Well, I'm going," Johanna declared as she snapped the buckles on her suitcase shut. "No matter what he says."

"Me too," I said.

"Your father's not going to like you missing your weekend with him. He's a stickler for the rules." She picked some stray clothes up off the floor and tossed them into our closet. "Just be diplomatic."

Our father set down his beer and said, "She should have discussed this with me first. That's a long drive and those front tires are practically bald. Not to mention your mother's lousy driving. And the expense. It's not as if we have money to throw away."

"Oh, Daddy," Johanna sighed. "You know you are essentially a very negative person."

I kicked her under the table, but I could tell from his expression it was already too late. He was really mad now.

"For your information, young lady, just because a person has a little common sense does not mean he's negative. Your mother has always considered common sense to be one of the seven deadly sins. If it was up to your mo—" He broke off as the cheerful waitress appeared and asked us if we wanted anything else. "We're fine," he answered brusquely, not sounding at all fine.

"We wish we were going with *you*," I said as the waitress was walking away, before he could start up again. "Don't we, Johanna?" I kicked her under the table again. "It would be so much more fun."

She nodded, catching on. "She drives so slow and you know how she always gets lost."

"No sense of direction," our father agreed.

"And you know how she is in restaurants," I said. "The waitress has to come back about a million times because she can never make up her mind."

"And then she always wants to eat off everyone else's plate anyway." Johanna reached over and swiped a fried wonton off my plate by way of illustration. "And then she drinks all that iced tea and has to go to the rest room about every five miles."

"World's smallest bladder." Our father was nodding, half-smiling, starting to forget he was mad at us.

For a moment I felt a twinge of guilt as we continued to assassinate our mother's character, but I knew she would understand and, what's more, approve. "Remember, the key to your father," she had said just as his car pulled up out in front of our house, "is that he likes to think he's smarter than me." Then she'd laughed, as if this were the funniest thing she'd heard in ages.

"So, how *is* your mother anyway?" our father asked, momentarily mollified, taking a casual sip of his beer.

Johanna and I shrugged and looked down at our plates. It seemed that our father was much more interested in our mother since "the separation," as they called it, than he ever was before. Before the separation, he never seemed to pay any attention when she talked. He never asked about her day. But now suddenly he was all ears.

"Forget I asked," he said, signaling the waitress for the check.

The night before the concert Sharon slept over at our house so that we could get an early start in the morning. Normally the moment Sharon stepped through the front door, Johanna would whisk her upstairs to our room and lock me out. The two of them would spend hours up there whispering and giggling, ignoring my mother and me, walking by us as if we didn't exist on their way to the kitchen for Cokes and Fritos. But the night before the Beatles concert, the four of us sat around the table on the back porch chatting like four best friends, our age differences magically leveled by the general spirit of anticipation. In the soft summer twilight our mother looked prettier and more girlish, like the girl in the old snapshots of herself from the time before she'd married our father. In those snapshots she was always in a crowd of girlfriends, all dressed up, smiling expectantly.

It was late, past our bedtime, and our mother was talking about how during the war she had worked as a nurse in the WAVES, and Sharon, who wanted to be a doctor, was asking a lot of questions and listening intently, as if our mother were the most fascinating woman on earth. I yawned. I was tired and ready for bed, but it was a point of honor not to go to bed until I was ordered to do so. Johanna, bored and peeved, was pelting me with Jiffy Pop kernels. No matter what you did, there were always a whole bunch of kernels left unpopped in the bottom of the flimsy tin pan.

"Come on," Johanna said pointedly, "let's go watch Johnny Carson. Coming?" she asked Sharon, who nodded vaguely and said she'd be there in a minute. My sister and I stomped off to the den and turned on the TV.

"Sharon's just grateful because Mom convinced Mrs. Dinsmore to let her go," Johanna said to me, as if feeling some necessity to account for her best friend's sudden perverse interest in our mother. "Her mother wasn't going to let her go because John Lennon said the Beatles were more popular than Jesus Christ. But Mom called her up and said John had apologized at a public press conference and all, so finally Mrs. Dinsmore said it was okay." Johanna turned up the volume on the TV. Johnny was talking with Zsa Zsa Gabor.

Our mother and Sharon appeared in the doorway. "I'm going to bed," our mother said. "And you girls should be hitting the hay too."

"As soon as this part's over," Johanna said, not looking up.

"Well, good night. See you bright and early." Our mother turned and walked upstairs. Johanna and I shot each other surprised, suspicious looks. She *always* made us go to bed first. Sharon wriggled in between the two of us on her stomach. "Your Mom's really neat," she said.

"Shhh," Johanna glared at her. "I want to hear this." It was a commercial for Alka-Seltzer. Sharon gave her a weird look. Johanna reached up and snapped off the TV. "Let's go to bed."

"God," Johanna sighed and slapped down her discard, "I really don't believe this."

The three of us were sitting at a little round table in our hotel room at the Holiday Inn playing hearts. Outside it was pouring rain—not your gentle summer shower but a torrential downpour. When we checked into the hotel, the desk clerk had greeted us with the tragic news bulletin: The Beatles' Saturday evening concert had been canceled due to rain and rescheduled for noon on Sunday.

"It's a stupid idea to hold a concert outside anyway," Johanna muttered. "What do they think this is—California?"

Sharon pulled back the drape and stared out into the flooded parking lot. "Maybe God's showing them who's boss. You know, after what John said about how they're more popular than Jesus Christ and all."

"That's ridiculous," Johanna snapped. "Why would He pick Cincinnati? I mean they've just been in Chicago, for chrissakes. You think God would pick a more important city if He were trying to make a point. Anyway, John apologized in front of the whole world, on TV and everything."

Our mother was lying on the bed nearest the door with a washcloth draped over her forehead. At dinner in the coffee shop, she had taken two Bufferin for her headache. Johanna was mad because she'd wanted to at least go to a movie and our mother had refused to drive around a strange city in the pouring rain. She was acting as if somehow our mother were to blame for the concert being canceled.

"I'm bored with this game." Johanna tossed her cards onto the table and turned the TV on full blast. She flipped through all the channels twice and finally settled on a Western with a lot of loud shouting and shooting.

Our mother propped herself up on one elbow and lifted the edge of her washcloth blindfold in order to glare at Johanna, who ignored her. I could tell she was debating whether to ask Johanna to turn the volume down. After a second she just sighed and got up and slipped her dress back on over her black slip. Without even looking in the mirror, she ran a brush through her hair, slapped on some lipstick, and said she was going down to the lounge for a while. She emptied all the coins out of her wallet. "For the vending machines," she said, "in case you girls get thirsty."

As soon as our mother had shut the door behind her, Johanna leapt up and rummaged around on the dresser top.

"What are you looking for?" I asked.

"Car keys."

Sharon and I looked at each other apprehensively. Johanna had just gotten her driver's license the previous month after flunking the driving part the first time out.

"Damn." Johanna threw herself back onto the bed by the window. "They must be in her purse. Figures."

Sharon and I breathed a joint sigh of relief.

"This movie is boring." Johanna snapped off the TV. She looked at her watch and sighed. "What a drag. Right now if it weren't for this crappy rain we'd be listening to 'Norwegian Wood.'" She banged her head against the pillow a few times in frustration.

"We're going to see them tomorrow," I said. "If you saw them tonight, it would all be over with tomorrow. This way you have something to look forward to."

Johanna shot me a withering, scornful look. Sharon was busy searching her long dark hair for split ends. My mother's lipstick had rolled off the dresser onto the carpet next to my chair. I picked it up and drew a little dash on the top of my hand like I'd seen my mother do in the drugstore. Then I held my hand up to the light to see how this particular shade, Primrose, complemented my skin tone.

"Hey, I've got an idea," Johanna said. "Let's do makeovers, like in the magazines." She leapt up and dumped the contents of our mother's daisy-covered cosmetic case onto the bed. Most of the makeup looked new and shiny, purchased since the separation.

"You first," Johanna said to me.

I sat down in the swivel chair and Johanna draped a white towel around my neck. Then she yanked all my hair into a pony-tail and skewered it to the back of my head with a couple of sharp bobby pins. "Ouch! Be careful," I protested.

"This is Sharon of New York City," Johanna said haughtily, ignoring my outburst. "And I am Johanna of Paris." She tilted my head this way and that, squinting at me in the bright lamp light. Finally she shook her head and sighed theatrically. "Have you ever considered plastic surgery?"

"Cut it out," Sharon said, elbowing Johanna aside, and kneel-ing in front of me with the mascara wand. "Just close your eyes," she said soothingly, "and think of something nice." I thought of the DiBernard girls running through the sprinkler in our old pink bathing suits.

"I wonder what the Beatles are doing right now," Johanna said as she dabbed the powder puff over my face. The feathery little pats felt good. "I mean, really, what's there to do in Cincinnati, for chrissakes?" She sounded just like some jaded jet-setter, even though Cincinnati was the biggest city we'd ever been in outside of one trip to Chicago.

"I bet John and Cynthia are drinking champagne and doing It in a sunken bathtub," Sharon said.

"Doing what?" I said, opening my eyes.

Johanna and Sharon laughed.

"God, I'm making a real mess." Sharon spit on a Kleenex and rubbed underneath my eyes. "She looks like a raccoon."

"She's supposed to keep her eyes *open* when you do that." Johanna opened her eyes really wide and pantomimed applying mascara. She looked like an old silent film star pretending to be scared out of her wits.

Sharon tossed the blackened Kleenex onto the bed and took a step backward to assess the damage. "Look. She looks like your mother."

"Wow," Johanna nodded. "That's really weird."

I turned my head and stared at myself in the mirror on the wall opposite me and immediately turned my head away again. I had the sense that I was looking into the future, that some future me was staring back at me.

We were sound asleep when the key fumbled in the lock and a slice of bright light from the hallway slashed the dark room as my mother slipped inside and hurriedly rebolted the door. I was going to ask her what time it was, but before I could whisper anything, she tiptoed into the bathroom and shut the door. The water faucet blasted on and then I heard another sound that took me a minute to identify—the sound of my mother crying. I felt scared suddenly all alone in the queen-size bed and rolled over to see if Johanna or Sharon were awake. They were both breathing deeply and evenly in perfect unison. My mother's sobs were punctuated by low moans that scared me worse than the crying. Maybe she was sick. Appendicitis or something. I could hear her thrashing around in the tub. Maybe she was drowning.

"Johanna," I whispered into the dark space between the beds. "Wake up, Johanna."

Nothing. I climbed out of my bed and walked over to the other bed and shook my sister's shoulder.

"What?" she mumbled groggily. "What is it?" She opened her eyes and saw me standing over her. "What's your problem? What time is it, for chrissakes?"

"It's Mom," I said. "Listen."

Johanna heaved a sigh and sat up in bed. Silence except for the gentle splashing of water in the tub. She snapped on the light and squinted up at me, annoyed. "So?"

"What's the matter?" Sharon mumbled, flinging an arm over her eyes to block out the light.

Before I could say anything, defend myself, there was a loud knock on the door. In the bathroom our mother had turned the water faucet on full blast again.

"See who's at the door," Johanna commanded.

I walked over to the door and said, "Who's there?" Our

mother had repeatedly warned us never to open the door until we knew who it was.

"I have something you left," a deep male voice answered.

I hesitated and looked back at Johanna.

"Come on, Alice," he said. "I'm not such a bad guy. What did you expect?"

Alice was our mother's name. Johanna shrugged. I slid back the chain lock and opened the door a couple of inches. He was crouching down, setting a paper sack on the floor by the door. There was a little bald spot the size of a Necco wafer that glinted in the light. He started when he saw me.

"Oh," he said, running his hand through his hair. "I thought you were her. I didn't realize." When he stood up, he was tall and handsome like our father, but I didn't like him. "What's your name?" he said.

"Suzanne." I bent down and picked up the paper sack. He was barefoot and his toenails were clear and smooth unlike our father's, which were thick and yellow from some kind of fungus he'd picked up in the army.

As I was straightening up, he cupped a hand under my chin and frowned down into my face. "You look like her. Anybody ever tell you that?"

I shook my head.

He bent over and moved his face in close to mine. His breath smelled of liquor. "Promise me something, Susie Q."

I hugged the paper sack tighter to my chest. I was staring down at his bare toes, but I felt him pulling my eyes up into his until I was looking right at him. I thought maybe he was going to kiss me. I thought maybe I even wanted him to. Something about his eyes. "What?" I said.

"Don't grow up to be a cockteaser like your mother." He winked at me, then let go of my chin, and sauntered unsteadily down the bright hall.

I slammed the door shut and looked at Johanna and Sharon, who were sitting bolt upright in bed, staring at me as if they'd been electrocuted. No one said anything for a minute. We listened to the soft splashing in the bathroom.

"Give me the sack," Sharon said suddenly, breaking the spell.

I handed it over and she opened it.

"What is it?" Johanna said as if she didn't really want to know.

Sharon pulled out a black slip. Johanna and I looked at each other. Our mother's slip.

"Jesus," Johanna muttered. "I don't believe it."

I was standing there trying to figure out how a strange man could have got hold of our mother's slip when something in my sister's expression told me not to think about it too hard. Then Johanna yanked the slip out of Sharon's hands and tried to rip it in half.

"Don't!" Sharon tugged the slip away from her and shoved it back into the paper bag and slid the bag in between the mattress and the box spring, then threw herself back on top of the bed. "Now here's the deal," she said. "We never saw it. Nothing happened. We've been sound asleep the whole time." She leaned across Johanna and snapped off the lamp. "Okay?"

Johanna and I nodded silently in the sudden darkness. Then the three of us lay there wide awake, hearts pounding, pretending to sleep, until, a few moments later, we heard the bathwater draining away in loud gurgling gasps, the bathroom door stealthily opening and shutting, and my mother—smelling sweet and fresh, like soap and talcum—tiptoeing gingerly across the carpet and easing herself gently into bed, careful not to disturb us.

The next day the weather cleared up. We had breakfast in the hotel coffee shop, my sister silently glowering, my mother nursing a hangover. "What's with your sister?" my mother asked me when Johanna stalked back to our room to pack. I stared down at my waffle until Sharon kicked me under the table, and then I mumbled something about Johanna just being disappointed that the concert was postponed. My mother sighed and said something about my sister having a lot to learn about life. "There's not much in this world that doesn't disappoint you sooner or later," she said. Then she forced a little smile and said, "Listen to me. I sound like your father. Gloomy Gus. We're on vacation. Let's have fun."

Sharon swallowed a bite of French toast and said, "I'm having fun."

"Me too," I lied.

My mother kept darting nervous glances at the doorway, as if afraid that at any moment the strange man from last night would walk in. I thought about the black slip hidden underneath the mattress and wondered what the maid would think when she found it. Suddenly my mother excused herself and walked over to the cigarette machine and returned with a pack of Lucky Strikes. She had quit smoking—a major big deal—about three years earlier, but I didn't say anything. Her fingers fumbled as she unwrapped the pack, and her eyes slid away from mine, guiltily, as she lit a cigarette and exhaled. After a few minutes of desultory conversation, mostly initiated by Sharon, my mother looked at her watch and said we might as well get an early start, since there would be a lot of traffic. We nodded agreeably. She stubbed out her cigarette.

It was as if my sister never made the long trip home with us. As if that afternoon of the Beatles concert she vanished into some other dimension. Within a matter of days after our return from Cincinnati, Johanna got herself a job working afternoons and weekends at World Records, which was located in the mall within walking distance of our father's apartment complex, on the other side of town, and casually announced one night at dinner that she had decided that it would be more convenient if she lived with our father from now on. Our mother set down her glass of iced tea and said, "Over my dead body. You belong here, with your sister and me." My sister got up and left the dinner table without finishing her dinner. My mother sighed and looked across the table at me. "Don't worry," she said. "Your sister's not going anywhere."

That weekend she was gone. Moved out. My mother and I came back from the grocery store and found Johanna's side of the room stripped bare. Lying on the center of her bed, neatly made for a change, was a crumpled paper sack, which I recognized right away even though it looked pretty much like any other paper sack. I was about to snatch it up and hide it somewhere when my mother walked up behind me and said, "What's this?"

I didn't watch her face as she opened the bag. I busied myself pulling my sweater off over my head. All I heard was a quick intake of breath. My mother was sitting on the edge of the bed staring at the black slip as if it were a snake.

"What's that?" I said, heart pounding, trying to sound a little bored, impatient, innocent.

My mother gave me a long complicated look and then shrugged. "Ask your sister," she said, as if it were no concern of hers.

It was the night before school started, a couple of days after Labor Day. My mother, Sharon, and I were eating Eskimo Pies on the back porch. At dusk it was still sweltering. Vanilla ice cream streamed down my wrist and my tongue worked double-time. A large pizza box gaped open on the table. My mother flicked a fly away from the one remaining slice of congealed pizza. After Johanna defected to my father's apartment, my mother had seemed to lose interest in the four basic food groups and we quickly drifted back into our old diet.

After I'd polished off my Eskimo Pie, I picked up the luke-warm slice of pizza and nibbled at the stringy cheese. Sharon and my mother were looking at college catalogs that Sharon had brought over. My sister and Sharon would both be going away to college the following year.

"I want to go to Berkeley," Sharon sighed, "but you know my mother. Not to mention my father."

My mother nodded and blew out a smoke ring. Ever since Cincinnati my mother had been smoking like a house afire. "Maybe you could get a scholarship. Or loans."

I had told Sharon all about how Johanna had left the slip on the bed and how my mother had found it. Sharon had called Johanna and they'd had a big fight. Since the blowup, Sharon had started spending less and less time with Johanna and more and more time at our house, just hanging out with my mother and me. It was as if Johanna had left this vacancy and Sharon had decided to fill it.

*   *   *

It was Saturday night and I was sitting in front of the TV alone at my father's apartment. After dinner, Johanna had taken off to the record store, which stayed open until 10 P.M. even on Saturdays, and my father had gone off to some party at his new girlfriend's place. She was a widow with a three-year-old son named Stowe, which my mother, Sharon, and I all agreed was a stupid-sounding name. He said he wouldn't stay long and asked me if I minded being left alone for a couple of hours. I said no. He rumpled my hair and promised to buy me the new sneakers I'd mentioned I wanted. I really didn't mind his going. It all felt weird now anyway, ever since Johanna had permanently installed herself at my father's. It wasn't at all the way it used to be when the two of us visited him. My sister treated me like a not-so-welcome guest. She acted like my mother—or not *my* mother but *a* mother. She had taken to doing the grocery shopping and cooking for my father. Instead of going to China Palace, we had to eat what she cooked. Revolting recipes she got out of vegetarian health food cookbooks. Things with brown rice and tofu. She was dating some guy named Josh from the record store who played folk guitar, and now suddenly the Beatles were history. Instead she listened to Bob Dylan, Joan Baez, Judy Collins. My father had finally bought himself a new stereo, and when she wasn't working, my sister sat cross-legged on the living room floor next to the stereo, strumming the fancy new guitar that my father had bought for her, trying to pick out the chords to "Subterranean Homesick Blues."

The following Friday I called my father and gave him some excuse about why I couldn't come stay at his place that weekend. I had a big report due in social studies, I said, and I needed to use the *Encyclopedia Britannica*, which was at our house. I expected him to argue, but he didn't. He just said, "Okay. See you next weekend," and that was that. The next night my mother, Sharon, and I went to Mona Lisa's for dinner to celebrate my mother's new job as a receptionist at an ob-gyn clinic. We ate spaghetti with clam sauce and my mother poured red wine in Sharon's and my empty water glasses. After dinner, we drove over to the mall to see a movie. In the dark my mother unwrapped a giant-size Nestlé Crunch bar and passed big squares to Sharon and me. I broke off little pieces and held each one in my mouth until all the chocolate melted and then I ate the Rice Krispies part. When the movie was over, we walked out of the dark theater, blinking in the bright lights of the lobby, and practically bumped right into my father and Johanna waiting in line for the nine o'clock show. We all paused for an awkward moment in which nobody seemed to be able to think of anything to say. I felt a silly smile fade from my face. The look on my sister's face was hard to read. I wanted to say something. We were standing on either side of a thick blue velvet rope. My father was holding a large tub of popcorn in one hand and a Coke in the other, and I had the feeling that maybe if his hands had been free he would have done something, but as it was, all he could do was stand there. Then the lines started to move, rumbling and impatient, like two trains headed in opposite directions, passing in the night. My mother stood there for a moment, looking back at them, then she said, "The thing you have to remember about your sister is that essentially she's a lot like your father."

"She likes to think she's smarter than I am," I said, "but she's not."

"Are you sure?" My mother stopped and cupped my chin in her fingers and looked right at me.

"Positive," I lied.

When we pulled into the driveway, the DiBernard girls were chasing each other on their front lawn in some baby-doll pajamas printed with butterflies that I recognized as having belonged to my sister and me. I walked over to them and said, "Those pajamas used to be my sister's and mine."

The little girls stopped running around and flopped down on the grass, looking up at me expectantly, as if they were waiting for me to tell them something really important. But I couldn't think of anything else to say to them—they looked so young and trusting—so I just cut across the lawn in a big hurry, as if I had suddenly heard the phone ringing or my mother calling my name.

the ghost mother

The first night the girl is in the house I don't sleep at all. In the morning she sleeps late, still tired from the flight, I assume, even though we are two hours ahead of her time. Clifford tippy-toes around the bedroom and bathroom as he shaves and dresses for a 10 A.M. meeting at Paramount. His exaggerated effort not to disturb her—probably sound asleep in the guest room down the hall—irritates me. I want to say "Knock it off. She's only a knocked-up teenager, not some visiting dignitary." But I know how awful that will sound. When he swoops over for his good-luck kiss, I pretend to have fallen back asleep.

As soon as I hear his car back out of the driveway, I haul myself out of bed, down the hall past her closed door, and into the bright sunny kitchen. Another cloudless day in Southern California. The girl is from Wahoo, Nebraska. Too perfect.

Our best friends, Buddy and Eleanor, fellow Hollywood hacks, went berserk when we told them and accused Clifford of making it up. "We've got dibs on it," Clifford had said sternly. "After all, it's *our* life."

When the girl contacted us in response to our ad in the local newspaper, she said she had always wanted to live in California. She wanted to know if we had a swimming pool. She wanted to know if we were involved in "show business," as she called it, rather quaintly. She seemed pleased when we answered yes on both counts but still said she needed a week to think it over. She said she was also considering couples in Tampa and Santa Rosa.

That night we FedExed her Polaroids of our kidney-shaped pool with the sun sparkling on the blue, blue water, along with a picture of the two of us in what would be the baby's room, and two video cassettes—an episode of "The Waltons" I'd worked on and an ill-fated TV pilot about a farm family in Iowa Clifford had written. We figured we'd cover all the bases: the glamour of Hollywood coupled with the wholesomeness of the heartland. The whole time she was making up her mind I held my breath. I dreamed about her. She had long wheaty hair and teeth as strong and even as a row of corn kernels. Halfway through the week she called once to ask if it would be okay if she brought her cat. I hesitated for a moment—Clifford is allergic to cats—and then said sure, fine, we'd be honored to have her cat. The next night she called and said she had reached her decision: We were the ones.

Pouring myself a second cup of coffee, I frown at the clock on the stove. Ten-thirty-five. Twelve-thirty-five Nebraska time. Clifford and I have always been early risers, high-energy over-achievers. Now, instead of the sleepless nights everyone warns you about, I picture us standing over the crib of a sluggish, complacent baby, tapping our fingers, waiting impatiently for it to wake up. I don't know what's suddenly come over me. I don't know where all these nasty, negative thoughts are coming from. Like any good liberal, I have always championed the nurture side of the nature-versus-nurture debate, but the moment the girl stepped off the plane I found myself harshly scrutinizing her for possible undesirable genes: stringy hair, bitten-down nails, bad grammar. In the car during the ride home from LAX, I sat silent as a judge while Clifford made amiable conversation with the girl. From time to time, he would look over at me and smile encouragingly, probably thinking I was struck dumb with shyness or choked up with emotion, while the girl exclaimed over all the Mercedeses and Jaguars and the palm trees and the balmy temperature. She said it had been five below with the windchill factor in Nebraska that morning. She stuck her head out the window like a dog. Clifford chuckled, seemingly enchanted, even though his eyes were already starting to water and itch in reaction to the cat, which she had immediately released from its carrier. Doped up as it was on tranquilizers, the cat managed a feeble hiss as I reached back to pet it. I sighed and popped an aspirin, without water—a trick I had learned while sitting bumper-to-bumper in freeway traffic jams.

Everything about her annoyed me. After three years of fertility specialists—tests, drugs, inseminations, in vitro—it had come down to this: some gum-chewing, wide-eyed teenager in fake pink Reeboks. A domestic import from Norman Rockwell country. *Midwestward ho!* is the cry of all of us prospective baby buyers from the coasts. You go to Hong Kong for silk, Italy for leather, Switzerland for watches, and the prairie for private adoptions. All this talk about crack babies and fetal alcohol syndrome has us running scared. Buying a baby brings out all your most embarrassing retro instincts, straight out of Laura Ingalls Wilder and "The Mary Tyler Moore Show."

"Where's the beach?" the girl had asked—frowning suspiciously, as if the entire state of California had perpetrated a huge media hoax—and even though we were only a couple of blocks from our house, Clifford had indulgently swung the car around and headed off in the opposite direction, toward the Pacific Coast Highway. We drove a couple of miles up the coast and then pulled off into one of the deserted parking lots. It was dark already, but you could see the white ruffle of surf and hear the waves swooshing and thudding. The girl got out of the car and kicked off her shoes. As she scuffled across the sand toward the water, Clifford reached over and put his arm around me. "It's going to be fine," he said, squeezing my hand for emphasis. "She's not going to change her mind."

I nodded but didn't squeeze back. For the past month, ever since she had chosen us over the couples in Tampa and Santa Rosa, I had been scared to death she would change her mind. I sighed and pulled my hand away. "But what if I change *my* mind?"

He laughed, as if I had made a joke. "All sales are final. No refunds or exchanges."

I forced a little laugh even though it wasn't so funny. We had paid ten thousand dollars to a private adoption broker. Less than a Honda Civic, Clifford had pointed out philosophically. When we told Buddy and Eleanor, Buddy said why not pay fifteen and get ourselves a Buick? Who wanted an economy baby?

As the girl waded in the surf, the cat in the backseat suddenly seemed to sense her absence and sprang to life, scratching and yowling at the upholstery. At the sound of the cat, Clifford started to sneeze in violent little arpeggios. I got out of the car and hollered for the girl, waving my arms until she finally looked up. She sprinted back up the beach. She was wearing a baggy, drop-waist dress—the kind that all the young girls were wearing—and you couldn't really tell for certain that she was pregnant unless you already knew. The baby wasn't due for another ten weeks. That was part of the deal. She wanted a place to stay. She didn't want to stick around Wahoo once she really started to show. And we were only too eager to oblige. We wanted, we said, to be involved. We wanted everyone to get to know and like each other.

The instant she climbed back into the car the cat calmed down.

"Your cat was upset," I said.

"Poor baby," she crooned, scratching behind his ears. The cat purred mechanically, as if she had flicked some switch. "I've had Bobbie since I was six years old," she said. "Her full name is Bobbie Sox." The cat was jet black except for its paws, which looked like they had been dunked in a can of paint.

"You got any Kleenex?" Clifford asked me.

I rummaged in my purse and handed him a wad of tissues. He blew his nose and wiped his red, runny eyes as we pulled back out onto the highway.

"Look, there's the ocean!" the girl said, holding the cat up to the window and pointing. The cat sniffed the ocean breeze indifferently. "Wow, I really love it here." She sighed in starry-eyed contentment and settled back in her seat.

"Good!" Clifford handed me his soggy Kleenex to dispose of and beamed at her in the rearview mirror.

"Do you have a cold?" she asked. "Want me to roll up the window?"

"No, no," he shook his head. "I'm fine. Just a touch of hay fever."

The girl leaned forward and gave Clifford a spontaneous hug, then looked at me uncertainly, like a dog waiting for you to reach out your hand and pet it. "This must be hard for you," she said.

I was surprised, caught off guard, embarrassed. "Harder on you," I mumbled. Which was true enough, although somehow I didn't really believe it. The only thing in my whole life I had ever failed at was getting pregnant, and here was this semiliterate pom-pom girl who had succeeded without even trying.

Down the hall, at last, I hear the water pipes groaning to life in the bathroom. Ten-fifty-five. From the clock, my glance shifts downward to her purse, slumped there on the kitchen counter. A gaudy striped woven bag that looks like a deflated beach ball. The shower blasts on and the shower curtain screeches shut. The purse draws me like a magnet. The zipper is half-open and I can't help myself. I don't know what I expect to find, but what I find is just what you would expect to find in a teenage girl's purse: lipstick, mascara, Dentyne, a couple of movie ticket stubs, an old hairbrush with a rat's nest of cornsilk hair entwined in the stubby bristles, a couple of packets of honey-roasted peanuts from the airplane—one of which has split open. At the bottom of the purse, loose sticky peanuts are glommed onto shreds of Kleenex and a couple of stray bobby pins and tobacco flakes. When I see the tobacco flakes, I have to restrain myself from marching down the hall and demanding to know whether she has been smoking during the pregnancy. The adoption broker assured us repeatedly that the girl did not do drugs, drink, or smoke. If he was wrong about the smoking, who knew what else he was wrong about?

As the shower continues to run, I pull a fat shabby pink wallet out of the bag and study her driver's license. Giselle Marie Nelson. *Height* 5'5", *Weight* 115, *Eyes* blue, *Hair* blonde. *Birth date* 7/5/74. It is not a flattering picture. The camera has caught her with her eyes half-closed and a self-conscious twitch of a smile. It looks as if her hair is growing out of a bad perm, half-straight and half-frizzy, like the fur of some mythical hybrid beast. I flip to a picture of her family, a posed studio portrait. Straight out of central casting. The parents, Giselle, two younger brothers, and a dog. All blond, even the dog. In the bathroom down the hall I hear the shower clunk off, and I flip quickly through the other cloudy plastic windows, thinking maybe there will be a picture of the boy, the father, but all I find are some grandparents and a couple of girlfriends' class photos. The girlfriends are also blonde, blue-eyed, and pert-nosed; they could all be sisters. Disappointed and vaguely relieved, I slide the wallet back into the purse.

An instant later the girl appears in the doorway clad in an oversize hot-pink T-shirt and rubber thongs. "Hi," she says. "I thought I'd lie out by the pool. I mean if that's okay." Her long wet hair drips down the front of her T-shirt, her inflated breasts. She twists a strand nervously, then reaches into her purse for the hairbrush.

"Great," I nod and smile. "How about some breakfast?"

She shakes her head. I wince as she yanks the cheap wire bristles through her hair. Something brushes against my ankles. The cat mews once experimentally and then again, more peremptorily. "Looks like someone wants breakfast," I say brightly. Glad for something to do, I walk over and open the cupboard where I have stocked up on a variety of gourmet cat food. "I didn't know what she likes." I start pulling cans out—"Chicken, liver, seafood"—as the cat continues to kvetch at my feet.

The girl seems stunned and befuddled by the selection. "Usually she just eats dry food."

"I'll pick up some dry food later," I say, vaguely miffed, "but for now, how about seafood?" I open the can briskly and scoop its smelly contents into a bowl. The cat lunges for the bowl before it even touches down.

"Now. How about you? Are you sure you don't want something to eat? You must be starved. We've got eggs, cereal, English muffins." I laugh. "You've heard about Jewish mothers?"

The girl looks at the cat greedily smacking away at its bowl. "Maybe an English muffin," she says meekly. "But I can fix it myself."

"It's your first morning." I pull out a chair and gesture for her to take a seat. "Just relax."

As I cut and toast a muffin, she says, "I've never known any Jewish people before. At first I was sort of worried about the baby not celebrating Christmas and all, but then my friend

Leslie, who used to live on Long Island, said you get presents for eight days and that seems okay. I mean, it might even be better, spacing it out and all like that." She pulls a wad of hair out of the brush bristles and shoves it into her purse, then falls abruptly silent, as if afraid she might have said something to offend me.

I smile to show that I am completely unoffended. The cat, having licked the bowl clean, starts acting weird, pacing and circling the kitchen. "Does she need to go out?" I set the toasted muffin on the table along with a jar of marmalade.

"She's an indoor cat. She's been declawed." The girl spreads a thick layer of marmalade on the muffin and takes a huge bite. "Do you have a kitty litter box?"

I shake my head. Great, I think, a smelly cat box. But I smile stoically and say, "No problem. I'll just zip out to the store and get something." Happy for an excuse to get off by myself for a few minutes, I grab my car keys off the counter. "Do you want anything while I'm out?"

The girl is holding the cat on her lap, nuzzling her face in its fur like a little girl with a stuffed animal. It occurs to me how alone and scared she must feel. I pause on my way out the door and attempt a reassuring motherly smile. "How about a matinee later?"

She shrugs and nods. "Sure, if you want to."

"Good. Back in a flash. There's beach towels in the linen closet."

I head out to the carport and then think of something else. When I duck my head back into the kitchen, she is down on her hands and knees with a wad of paper towels, cleaning up a mess the cat has made the minute my back was turned. When she sees me, she jumps guiltily.

"I'm sorry. She never does this," she says. "It's just that she doesn't have her box."

"No problem. It's my fault. I should have thought of it myself." I sniff the air and walk over and take a charred English muffin out of the toaster oven.

"I'm sorry," she says again. She looks about ready to burst into tears as I toss the muffin into the trash. "Don't be silly. There's plenty." I hand her the pack of muffins. "I just wanted to tell you there's suntan lotion in the medicine chest. Be sure to use something strong. You don't want to get burned your first day out."

My little bit of motherly advice seems to relax her some. "You think maybe you could pick up some Canfield's diet chocolate soda?" she asks timidly as I'm heading out the door for the second time.

"Sure," I say. "Anything else?"

She shakes her head, then says, "Well, maybe some potato chips. Pringles, you know, the kind in the can. I'm sort of addicted to them."

I fish a little notepad out of my purse and dutifully jot this down, inwardly moaning at such trashy prenatal nutrition. The phone rings. I don't bother to pick it up. It's only Eleanor wanting to know how it's going so far with "The Incubator," as she has taken to referring to the girl. I cringe and blush, but the girl, intent upon buttering her second muffin, seems oblivious. To cover my embarrassment, I adopt a businesslike tone and ask the girl if she knows how to work the answering machine. She shakes her head, her mouth full of muffin. "Just let it ring for now," I sigh. "I'll show you later."

On the way back out to the carport, I sneak a glance in at her through the window. She is eating ravenously, as if she has not eaten for days, and talking to the cat in between mouthfuls. I can't quite make out the words, but it sounds like some sort of pep talk. When I get back from the store, the girl is floating on the raft in the pool and the cat is sunning itself next to a bowl of fruit on the dining room table. I chase the cat onto the floor and lead her to the utility room to acquaint her with her new kitty litter box. She blinks up at me unimpressed. It is a hot day, high eighties, and I imagine the girl must be thirsty. I watch her through the window as I pour some Canfield's diet chocolate soda into a glass of ice. The stuff looks revolting and I had to go to three stores to find it, but when I take a sip I have to admit it's not bad. The girl has on a tropical print bikini and is lying on her back, trailing her hands in the water. My gaze lingers on her naked belly, hovering above the water like a pale moon. As my eyes trace the smooth warm curve of it, I grip the icy glass so tight it almost slips out of my hand. How weird life is, I think as I trot outside: some sixteen-year-old girl in Nebraska gets carried away in the backseat of some boy's car after some prom or other and now here she is, floating in my backyard, our baby floating inside of her. If our newspaper ad had appeared a couple of months earlier or later, it would be some other girl, some other baby. Somehow, this thought depresses me. I prefer to think of this as fate, destiny, a thread in some grand design. According to some celestial, all-wise and knowing weaver, *this* baby was meant for Clifford and me.

"Hi," I say, then realize she's wearing a Walkman and can't hear me. I shudder to think what sort of musical education the fetus is receiving. Kneeling down, I make waves in the water until she raises her head and sees me. "Want a drink?" I hold up the glass. "Canfield's."

She paddles herself over toward the edge of the pool and I hand her the glass. "Thanks," she says. "It's so great here I can't believe it. I feel like a movie star."

"Your nose looks pink. Did you use the sunscreen?"

She nods.

"Well, I think maybe you should put some more on. The sun's very strong here."

"Okay." She shrugs and drains the dregs of her soda. She hands me her glass and I hand her the Bain de Soleil 15 in lieu of the Hawaiian cocoa butter she must have brought with her.

"You want any lunch?" I glance at my watch. "It's twelve-thirty. I can make you a sandwich."

She shakes her head. "I'm fine."

"Tuna? Ham and cheese?" I bend down and check the thermometer attached to the aluminum ladder. "Or I could make a salad."

"Okay. Tuna sounds good. Thanks. But I don't want to be any trouble."

"It's no trouble. I'm hungry, too," I assure her, although I generally skip lunch.

"You're going to be a good mother," she jokes as I walk back toward the house. For some reason the joke irritates me. Although I am glad to see that she has some sort of sense of humor. Of irony, even. Clifford and I would hate to have a baby with no sense of humor.

The instant I open the can of tuna the cat materializes at my feet. Through the window I can see the girl turn over onto her stomach, a painstakingly clumsy maneuver, and I bet she hasn't put any sunscreen on her back. As I mince the onion, I glance irritably at my watch. I should be at the computer, working on the revised treatment I'd promised Al Denker at NBC by the end of the month. And the afternoon was shot, too, since I'd promised to take her to a matinee. Still, it was her first day here, two thousand miles from home, and I couldn't very well just ignore her. It was just typical somehow that Clifford was all booked up for the day so that taking care of the girl was my responsibility. Long ago, when I had first decided to have a baby, I had come to terms with the fact that no matter how noble Clifford's intentions, I had better be prepared to take on the bulk of the grunt work. But that was the baby, not the baby's mother, which was a different matter altogether.

The cat was whining pitifully. I set the tuna can on the floor by its water dish to shut it up and then got the mayonnaise and pickles out of the refrigerator. As I scooped out the last of the Hellmann's, I recalled Eleanor joking that I had better stock up on Miracle Whip—everyone, she claimed, was addicted to Miracle Whip in the Midwest. The girl's eyes were closed. She looked blissfully peaceful floating out there. Her long hair shone like silver in the bright sun. I had to admit she was a pretty girl. And seemed to be polite and considerate. There was nothing about her, really, to account for the sudden wave of hostility—so intense I'd actually felt nauseated—that seemed to hit me the moment I saw her walk off the plane. I had recognized her at once, from the picture she'd sent us; she looked just like how I'd imagined she would look, no surprises there. The only surprise was my reaction.

For weeks, I had been waiting impatiently for her arrival. She was all I talked about: "Giselle this, Giselle that . . ." I had called and asked her what her favorite color was (purple) and redecorated the guest room in various shades of lavender. I put a tape player in the room and gave Zoe, Buddy and Eleanor's teenage daughter, a hundred dollars to buy some cassettes she thought Giselle would like. "How do I know what someone from Nebraska would like?" Zoe had protested, but she had done it, secretly pleased—Eleanor assured me—to have been called in as a consultant. Before falling asleep at night, I would create little scenarios—like scenes from one of my family sitcoms—about how it would be when she finally arrived. I pictured us shopping, going to the gym, making dinner, wandering through museums, eating club sandwiches at the Bullock's Wilshire Tea Room. Girl stuff. Growing up with two brothers, I had always wanted a sister. That I was, in fact, old enough to be her mother, I didn't like to think about. Somehow in my fantasy script I saw us more like two teenage girls whispering and giggling while Clifford brought us dishes of ice cream and smiled indulgently.

A couple of times my best friend, Eleanor, never known for her tact, tried to hint at some darker, more complicated picture. *Don't you worry she'll get too attached?* she had asked. *What about afterward? Are you going to stay in touch? Send her photos? Let her visit?* I could tell Eleanor thought it was a bad idea letting Giselle come live with us. She thought the whole transaction should be quick and businesslike, like a drug deal in the middle of the night in some deserted parking lot. But Clifford argued that it was better this way, our all getting to know each other. It was more humane and personal. In the long run, he felt, it would be healthier for all of us. Eleanor said she just hoped we knew what we were doing. I assured her we did.

But now, as I cut the sandwich in half and dump a handful of Pringles onto the plate, I am not so sure. When I glance outside, the raft is empty. A quick check reveals that the girl is not in the water or anywhere in the yard. Guiltily I imagine her in her room packing her suitcase while I look helplessly on.

Me: What are you doing? You aren't leaving?
Her: I can't take this hostility. (She dumps a handful of underwear into her open suitcase.) I know you're trying to act nice, but I can feel it. It's not my fault you couldn't get pregnant. (The cat sets itself down on a pile of clothes in the middle of the suitcase and she shoos him away.) I wish *I* couldn't get pregnant.
Me: I don't know what you mean. Clifford and I are overjoyed to have you here.

Her: Maybe *he* is. But you've got a problem. I may be from
     Nebraska, but I'm not completely insensitive.
Me:

As I am trying to think what to say, something that will change
her mind so that I won't have to explain to Clifford why she suddenly up and left, I hear the toilet flush and the thud of her bare
feet tramping down the hall toward the kitchen.

"You were right," she says. "My nose is completely fried." She
sits down at the table and I slide the sandwich over to her. "I
want to get some postcards when we go out later." She breaks off
a little glob of tuna and feeds it to the cat. "Leslie, my best
friend, said she was almost jealous. I promised to write to her
every day."

Leaning casually against the sink, I tear the foil off a yogurt
container and eat a couple of spoonfuls. "What about the boy—
you know—the father?"

"Oh, him." She shrugs and frowns down at her thigh, pressing
a finger into her flesh to see if she's sunburned. "Forget him."

She seems suddenly to have lost her appetite. She continues
feeding globs of tuna to the cat. If she were my own daughter I
would make her stop. Don't feed the cat from the table, I'd say.
And, no doubt, my daughter would frown and sigh and keep
right on doing what she was doing. Suddenly the thought of
being anyone's mother seems way beyond me, a task for which I
am monumentally unprepared and unsuited. Whatever made me
think I was cut out for this line of work? "Listen—" I say.

"Wait!" She grabs my hand and places it on her belly. "It's
kicking. Feel it?"

I nod solemnly, feeling the tears pushing against my closed
eyelids, the tightening in my throat. This whole thing is too, too
weird. Crazy. I snatch my hand away.

"Do you have names picked out?" she asks.

I shake my head, toss my yogurt carton into the trash, and
hand her the Calendar section of the *Times*. "Pick a movie you'd
like to see. I'll be back in a minute. I've got a load of laundry to
put in."

Trembling all over, I lock myself in our bedroom and fling

myself down onto the unmade king-size bed. I look at the digital clock on the night table. Clifford should be home by the time we get back from the matinee. While the girl is changing for dinner—Clifford promised to take her to a real Hollywood restaurant—I will take him aside and say, "This is an impossible situation. It's creepy. It's like something out of *The Handmaid's Tale*. Believe me, it's never going to work, so let's just call it quits right now. She can call those couples in Tampa and Santa Rosa back. Or we can help her to find someone else. She can keep the money."

Eyes closed, I can see the look on Clifford's face, confused and concerned.

Him: If you really feel that way, then I guess— (He shrugs.) But I don't get it. You were the one who wanted it so much. You couldn't wait for her to get here. (He loosens his tie and sighs.) Who's going to tell her? I just don't get it. What happened? (He sighs again and glances at his watch.) We've got reservations at Musso and Frank's at seven-thirty. (He whisks his tie off and rolls up the sleeves of his shirt.) I don't believe this. This isn't like you. (He brushes my bangs away from my eyes and holds my face steady between his hands.) Are you sure?

Me: I don't know.

Him: You don't know if you're sure?

Me: (I nod.)

Him: Great. (He leaps up and paces the room.) This is just great. (Stops pacing.) What if you were pregnant? You couldn't change your mind then.

Me: But I'm not. (I start to cry.) Don't you see? That's the point. I'm not.

On the way to the movie theater in Century City, the girl asks me if I have seen *Terms of Endearment*. When I say yes, she says that it was filmed in Lincoln, Nebraska, not far from her hometown. She was just a kid, but she still remembers her mother driv-

ing them to the campus to watch the filming. She asks me if I
have read the recent issue of *Vanity Fair* with Debra Winger on
the cover. When I say no, she fills me in on the semiintimate
details of Debra's affair with Bob Kerrey, the senator from
Nebraska. As we pull into the underground parking structure,
she whips out her hairbrush, turns her head upside down,
brushes her lank hair vigorously, and then shakes it loose. For a
glorious moment, until gravity takes its toll, she looks like any
young blonde Hollywood starlet. Riding the crowded escalator
up to the theaters, she says, "Is your hair naturally curly?" When
I nod, she sighs and says in an indiscreet tone of voice, "Too bad
the baby can't inherit your hair." If the girl were my daughter, I
would tell her to lower her voice, but since she is just a stranger
who will be gone soon, I shrug and smile and say, "But your hair
is such a pretty color."

Once the movie starts, the girl does not utter a sound. As she
sits quietly in the darkness raptly staring up at the screen, I begin
to feel more kindly disposed toward her than I have since the
moment I laid eyes on her at the airport. The evening she was
due to arrive—it seems longer ago than just yesterday—Clifford
and I went out to eat at a hole-in-the-wall Italian place near the
airport we had discovered years ago when we had first moved to
Los Angeles and were dirt poor. I was too excited to eat. I sipped
my glass of cheap burgundy and waited for Clifford to polish off
his ravioli so we could be on our way to the airport.

We got to the gate twenty minutes early and the flight was due
to arrive a half an hour late, so we had almost an hour to kill.
Clifford bought us a couple of magazines to read while we
waited, but I couldn't concentrate. We had stopped by Conroy's
and bought a bouquet of pink sweetheart roses and I was worried
they would wilt before her plane arrived. I had this image in my
mind of how it would be. She would straggle off the plane, one of
the last passengers to disembark, tired and shy. I would walk up
and say, "Giselle?" and when she nodded, I would give her a big
welcoming hug. There wouldn't be a dry eye in the house.

In fact, it all went pretty much according to my mental script
right up until the moment where I give her the big welcoming
hug and suddenly I couldn't do it. Suddenly there she was in the

flesh, the embodiment of my own body's failure. A ghost mother
hired to author a child under my own name. I felt like throwing a
tantrum right there in the airport, pounding my fists and kicking
my heels. It isn't fair! It isn't fair! But instead, I traipsed along
silently to the baggage claim.

After the movie ends, the girl and I ride the escalator back
down to the parking garage and drive home without saying much
of anything. It was that kind of movie, the kind that sends you
out of the theater wrapped in a dark, brooding cloud that dissi-
pates slowly. When we pull into the driveway, I exclaim,
"Clifford's home!" She seems almost as relieved as I am.

While Clifford and I drink vodka tonics, the girl decides to
take a nap before it is time to leave for the restaurant. We sit outside by the pool because the cat dander, in just one day, seems to
have permeated the house, and Clifford is looking weepy-eyed
although his mood is aggressively upbeat. "So how was your
day?" he asks me, eager to hear all the details. "Fine, great," I say,
giving him a breezy treatment of the day's activities and then
deftly switch the topic to business. The deal at Paramount looks
good, he says. Demi wants to do it, he says. "Great," I say, "that's
great." I think of her on the cover of *Vanity Fair*, naked and pregnant. "I'll have another drink," I say, holding out my empty glass.

Just before it is time to leave for the restaurant, I beg off,
pleading a headache and fatigue. Clifford assumes I am just done
in from overexcitement and says they will be back early and will
pick up a couple of videos on the way home. Great, I think, anything but *The Baby Maker*. "I'll make the popcorn," I say. I stand
in the doorway waving to them as they back out of the driveway
in Clifford's silver VW, waving until they have disappeared.

In the abrupt quiet aftermath of their departure, I can't think
what to do, what it is that I would usually be doing. I go into the
kitchen and open a Canfield's diet chocolate soda and grab a
handful of Pringles and gravitate down the hall to the girl's room.
The door is closed, and when I push it open, I am surprised by
how neat the room is. The bed is crisply made and all her clothes
are hanging in the closet. It occurs to me that she must be on her
best behavior. The cat is curled up on the pillow. She watches me
suspiciously with narrowed yellow eyes and then beats a hasty

retreat under the bed. On the night table there is a little stack of paperbacks and magazines, which I sort through. *Mademoiselle*, *People*, a dog-eared copy of Rosamunde Pilcher's *The Shell Seekers*, an oversize paperback entitled *Your Pregnancy: The First Nine Months*, complete with pictures. Sitting on the pale yellow dresser scarf, next to the ratty hairbrush, is a small bottle of cologne, Chantilly—a flash from my high school past. I spray my wrists with the cologne and run the brush through my hair a few strokes. The sweet, familiar scent disorients me. Suddenly I feel tired— terribly, terribly tired, more tired than I can ever remember feeling, as if I have been dragging around an extra thirty pounds. A little nap, I think. I fold back the covers and sink into the bed.

Breathing deeply, I close my eyes, and for the first time all day I feel relaxed. Peaceful. There is a soft thud at the foot of the bed. I open my eyes and see the cat sitting there, watching me. I stretch out my arm to pet her as she makes her way cautiously closer. Across the room, the gauzy golden curtains ripple gently in the evening breeze. I think of wheat, miles and miles of golden wheat swaying in the wind. The cat hesitates for a moment and then nestles up against me. I think of autumn. The harvest. I think of my bedroom back home, the brown leaves falling outside, and me inside, warm and snug, playing with my dolls, bundling them up against the cold, kissing and scolding, pretending to be a mommy. In the moonlit darkness the cat purrs—low and steady, like a finely tuned motor—beside me. Calm and content. As if she has known me forever.

the garage sale of
the three lindas

There are calligraphied signs stapled to every telephone pole within a two-mile radius and ads in all the local throwaways. The Saturday of the garage sale dawns bright and hot. We had first conceived it, a couple of weeks earlier at Beau Thai, as a kind of joke when Linda Bellman suddenly set down her chopsticks, overcome with exhaustion at the thought of schlepping all her stuff from Hollywood out to the beach. She was moving to a thousand-dollar-a-month dollhouse on the Venice canals, getting divorced again. As an art director on low-budget films, she was forever rescuing huge weird objects from trash cans. Her latest find was a shadeless ceramic lamp, the base of which was a cape-waving matador whose leg had been amputated above the knee.

"You should have a garage sale," Linda Wu told her, expertly tweezing the last straw mushroom with her chopsticks. "Get rid of some of that junk. In fact, I've got all that shit that Sonia left behind. All that lousy wood she was going to use for her framing business." She slammed down her Sapporo. "Manipulative bitch."

"I never really liked her," Linda B. confided belatedly, munching on a sticky handful of *mee krob*.

I sat there peeling the damp label on my beer, mentally sorting through my cupboards and closets. "You know, I have boxes of Kelvin's old records that are just taking up space, I guess." He had celebrated our breakup by buying a CD player.

"We can call it The Garage Sale of the Three Lindas," Linda B. laughed.

"Sounds like some Mexican festival," I'd said. "The Day of the Dead Stuff."

The three of us were born within a year of each other—1950 and 1951—and it seems that our mothers—Bernadette, Ruth, and Dolly—had each chosen the name Linda with the same hopes in mind, the same image of the same pretty, popular, modern sort of girl: treasurer of her class, runner-up for Homecoming Queen, Candy Striper, solid B student with a nice steady boyfriend. They chose the name—the future "us"—to be in step with the fashion of the time. Like beige wall-to-wall carpeting. Nothing too extreme. Not for them those fusty dark Persian rugs of their own mothers or those dusty biblical names of the girls they went to school with—the Marys, Naomis, Esthers, and Miriams. All those pretampon names as bulky and passé as old Kotex swaddled in layers of toilet tissue in our mothers' wastebaskets. They must have looked into our pudgy red baby faces and envisioned us as something sleek and stylish—the latest female technology. Linda Corvette. Linda Sputnik. Linda Color Television. Linda Contact Lenses. Daughters of the American Revolution.

Needless to say, none of us turned out right.

At 9 A.M. on the dot, Linda W. pulls up in a borrowed pickup just as I am scooping melon balls into the fruit salad I've made to go along with the crab-and-asparagus quiche. We have delegated responsibilities so as to best utilize our talents: Linda B., the art director, made the signs. Linda W., a public relations writer, placed the ads in the newspapers. I, a chef, would provide the lunch. Linda W. sits on the counter, sucking on watermelon seeds, recounting to me her most recent dream, in which the bonsai tree Sonia gave her for her last birthday suddenly turned into a redwood overnight and punched a hole through her roof. Since Sonia abandoned her for a man, the Freudian implications seem too obvious to comment on.

The phone rings. It is Linda B. calling to say she will be a few minutes late because she's spotted a fantastic old birdbath sitting out by the curb on Crescent Heights Boulevard and has somehow managed to cart the thing back to her place.

"What the hell's she going to do with a birdbath?" Linda W. says when I hang up. "It's just another thing to move."

I shrug noncommittally, smooth Saran Wrap over the salad bowl, and put it in the refrigerator.

Linda W. shakes her head and tucks a nonexistent strand of hair behind her ear—a gesture left over from years and years of glorious waist-length hair as smooth and shiny as black lacquer. Shortly after Sonia's departure, Linda W. had shown up for brunch one Sunday morning at The Fig Tree with a brush cut. "I love it," she'd said defensively as Linda B. and I gaped at her, heartsick, envisioning this carpet of silky jet hair lying on the floor of the beauty parlor, going to waste. Linda B. had reached over with her index finger and touched the top of Linda W.'s head—gingerly—as if expecting to get pricked or shocked.

"It looks good," I managed to say. "Spunky."

"I should have done it years ago," Linda W. declared, opening her menu. But after six months she still seems to be experiencing phantom limb syndrome.

"Any word from Kelvin?" she asks suddenly, sucking carnivorously on a piece of cantaloupe rind.

Speaking of phantom limbs, I think. In the middle of the night the left side of the bed still seems to sag with his weight, and I can feel my body tilting toward the empty depression, even though I weigh two pounds more than he does.

"Nothing much," I say. "He's busy with the new restaurant."

"Not to mention the new girlfriend."

I ignore this, furiously sponging off the countertop. Linda W. is famous for her insensitive bluntness, which she inherited from her mother. "Hello," Mrs. Wu would say, all smiles, offering some delicious little oriental dumplings unlike anything you got in American restaurants. "I see you have more gray hairs. I see you've gained weight. Linda tells me you got fired. Are you still seeing that young man with the crooked teeth?"

"Let's go outside and get set up," I sigh.

*   *   *

While I am busy hanging old clothes from tree branches and Linda W. is compulsively pecking through her cartons of old paperbacks making certain that all the spines are facing up, Linda B. sails up in her magenta Le Car. Linda W. and I exchange looks.

"I thought you were borrowing Peter's van," Linda W. says. "Is he following you?" She squints into the bright sunshine and peers hopefully up the street.

"Nope. Turned out I could fit everything in here."

Her daughter, Annie, is sitting in the passenger seat, holding a jar of artichoke hearts, sucking contentedly on her oily fingers.

"What you got there?" I ask as Linda B. leans over and unbuckles her daughter's seat belt.

"My breakfast." Annie squirms her stubby fingers into the jar for another hit.

"She's really into olives and artichoke hearts these days," Linda B. informs us. "Anything marinated."

"Whatever happened to peanut butter and jelly?" Linda W. whispers to me.

Linda B. reaches into the backseat and hauls out a carton with a lidless Scrabble game on top. "The thing is once I really started sorting through stuff in earnest, I realized there wasn't that much I didn't need."

Linda W. pokes her head in the car window. "Two boxes," she says to me. "Can you believe this? Her apartment looks like a fence lives there and she shows up with two measly fucking boxes. What's this?" She pulls out a badminton racquet and rams her delicate fist through a big hole in the strings. "Don't tell me you're really going to part with such a treasure? This one-of-a-kind *objet?*"

"Okay. Knock it off." Linda B. grabs the racquet and marches up the driveway, a sudden gust of wind fluttering a couple of Scrabble letters onto the pavement behind her.

"Who does she think is going to buy a single badminton racquet with no strings?" Linda W. mutters, as if offended to be even tangentially associated with such shoddy merchandise.

I kneel down and pick up one of the fallen Scrabble letters as Annie pounces on the other. "I've got a K," I say. "How 'bout you?"

"A T." She opens her fist and shows me the little wooden square.

K. T. Kelvin's initials. What are the statistical odds? A cosmic chill shivers up my spine. I look up to comment on this to Linda W. but something about her expression stops me. I shove the letters in my shorts pocket and go back to sticking neon orange price stickers on all my clothes and costume jewelry, most of which I bought at other garage sales. Linda W. sets up some folding chairs. Linda B. sorts through my old clothes. Annie kneels on the grass petting my cat, Mr. Right, who ecstatically licks her greasy fingers.

"I'll take this scarf and kimono," Linda B. says to me, making a little pile on the ground by the hibiscus bush.

"The purpose of this sale is to get rid of stuff," Linda W. scolds. "Not accumulate new stuff."

"What's with her?" Linda B. grumbles to me as Linda W. bristles into the house for a dust cloth to wipe off the chairs. "Hey, don't do that!" she hollers at Annie, who has fastened a rhinestone necklace around the cat's neck and is intent upon trying to clip some matching earrings to his ears.

I hurry across the lawn to rescue Mr. Right.

"He's going to the Acatemy Awards," Annie giggles.

"Did you hear that?" I call out to Linda B. "A pun. That's amazing!"

Linda B. shrugs. "I tell you the kid's a genius."

"Gifted," Annie corrects her.

An old black Buick, the kind with the three holes in the side, noses up to the curb, and two round little old ladies, heavily bundled up despite the sunshine, make their way up the driveway. They are both wearing kerchiefs and look like those Russian nesting dolls. The driver, an elderly Hasid, sits behind the wheel and serenely blocks traffic on the narrow congested street. I live in the Fairfax district, one block east of Cantor's, the famous delicatessen where I once saw Bob Dylan eating a pastrami sandwich at 3 A.M.

"They're early," Linda W. grumbles. "The signs said ten o'clock."

The spryer of the two old ladies makes a beeline for the fake

leopard jacket that I had, at the last minute, after much vacilla-
tion, decided to part with even though Kelvin had spied it at Odd
Aardvark's and insisted I buy it—it was me. It wasn't. She sizes up
the three of us and then sidles over to me—the only likely fellow
Jew. "Two dollars," she says, opening her purse—the kind with
an alligator head with glass eyes. I can see Linda B. eyeing it covet-
ously.

"*Twelve* dollars." I point to the orange sticker. "I'm sorry."

She zooms the sticker up close to her bifocals and squints in
fake amazement, shaking her head and muttering. "Look at this,
Rivke," she kvetches to her friend. "Twelve dollars she wants for
no button here." She fishes out a crumpled Kleenex, spits on it,
and dabs ostentatiously at a faint lipstick stain on the lapel.

"Okay," I say. "Two dollars."

Linda W. rolls her eyes and grunts her disapproval. "You could
have got at least twenty for that coat," she announces loudly as
the old ladies make their getaway.

"She reminded me of my grandmother," I shrug. "Anyway.
What's twenty dollars?"

"Ten times two." She tugs the two limp bills out of my hand
and puts them in the shoe-box cash register, which she has neatly
divided into three compartments.

A handsome young Jeremy Irons type is pawing through my
display of costume jewelry. He clips on some large flat earrings I
bought in Tijuana under the influence of too much Carta Blanca.
They are supposed to be Aztec calendars, but they look more like
tarnished pizzas. He bends over and studies his reflection in
Linda B.'s busted toaster oven. "What do you think?" he asks
Annie. "These or the rhinestone teardrops?"

"The teardrops," she says. "Definitely."

"The teardrops it is." He walks over and hands me fifty cents,
nearly colliding with an obese priest who is buying a boxed copy
of *The Tale of Genji* and a beautiful ancient Hispanic woman who
seems interested in Linda B.'s matador lamp until she discovers
the amputated leg. She sets it back down with a slight shudder
and a sad, stricken look on her face—as if she had once been in
love with a dashing matador who had suffered an untimely end in
the bull ring.

"Why do I get the feeling I'm in a John Waters film?" Linda W. whispers.

At noon I distribute plates of quiche and fruit salad while Linda W. fidgets with the cash box.

"You've only made a buck seventy-five," Linda W. informs Linda B., frowning judgmentally.

"Whatever happened to those inscrutable Orientals?" Linda B. says to me. "Oh well, at least I'm getting a tan." She has rolled up the sleeves and legs of her jumpsuit and slathered her pale, freckled limbs with sun screen.

While we chow down, Annie minds the store. She does better than we did; nobody likes bargaining with a child. After every sale she runs over, announces the amount, and plucks a grape out of the fruit salad as her commission. The sun is getting hotter and hotter, unseasonably warm for December, and I feel like curling up on the picnic blanket and taking a little siesta in the sunshine. I close my eyes and remember lying on the beach with Kelvin before we had ever slept together, inches apart, our bodies zapping messages to each other like two powerful shortwave radios gone haywire. Like two teenagers. I was lying there wondering if it were possible for two people to electrocute each other when he suddenly reached over and grabbed my hand, as if to ground himself, and said, "Let's go to my place."

Unfortunately, as it turned out, our electricity seemed to blow a fuse after a few months, and we were thrown back onto simple companionability, mutual interests, the daily bread of relationships. He was also in the food business—an up-and-coming chef—but our philosophies of food clashed. He was a show-off. Always a dash too much of this, a weird gaudy touch of that—your poor overloaded tastebuds simply short-circuited themselves trying to process it all. His bouillabaisse, for instance, on which he prided himself, was like a novel with too many subplots. Of course, at the time, as Linda W. always points out, I was convinced he was a genius—next to him Wolfgang Puck was Colonel Sanders. Love is not only blind but tasteless. Still, he'd had a way in bed, sensitive and finely tuned, capable of the most subtle variations in rhythm, like a sixteen-speed blender: frappé, whip, mix, blend, stir, etc. I kept hoping for another power surge.

"Hey." Linda B. nudges me with her toe. "Isn't that your brother's wife?"

I open my eyes and squint toward the curb, where a tanned, aerobically fit blonde is slamming the door of a flashy white convertible. "No, that's not her," I say, relieved. My brother, the architect, married the perfect Linda—except that she is a WASP. When he announced his engagement, I had this picture of our mother dragging his betrothed Linda (Linda O'Connor) into Neiman Marcus, commandeering some poor salesclerk, and demanding, "Do you have this in Jewish?" For my brother's sake, Linda O. and I had always pretended to like each other even though at first glance we had immediately recognized each other as products of incompatible high school cliques. She, of course, having lived up to the promise of her name, was practically inseparable from her mother. At the wedding, the two of them were like those attractive, affectionate mother-and-daughter combos in the dish detergent commercials who could pass for sisters, whereas my mother and I didn't look like members of the same species, let alone generation.

Flipping through the wedding album a few weeks after the big event, my mother had paused at a shot of the bride and her mother—smiling, arms linked, identically slim and pastel-pretty. My mother sighed and seemed to deflate, and I knew that she was thinking *that's* how she thought it would be, having a daughter. A pretty girl with pretty clothes and nice manners and sensible ideas. Not some weirdo with hennaed hair and crazy clothes and crazier ideas. She had ordered a Linda and what had He sent her—a Barb maybe, or, at best, a Liz. What would you name a child with stick-straight hair who never smiled and always, from day one, thought she knew best?

"How much is this book?" A nerdy-looking teenage boy shoves a tattered copy of *The Second Sex* under my nose, obviously operating under the misconception it is some kind of kinky novel.

"I don't know," I say. "You'll have to ask her." I point to Linda W., who is french-braiding Annie's wispy white-blonde hair, a legacy from Linda B.'s second husband.

Linda W. flips open the cover and shuts it again, a stricken expression on her face. "I'm sorry. This book isn't for sale."

The boy rolls his eyes and stomps off.

"What's the deal?" Linda B. says. "You okay?"

Linda W. opens the cover again gently, as if reopening an old wound, and shows us the spiky handwriting. "Sonia's recipe for gazpacho."

Annie puts her hand over her mouth and pretends to gag.

"You *like* gazpacho," Linda B. tells her.

"No I don't. You must have me confused with some other daughter from a previous life."

"Now where did she learn that?" Linda B. marvels.

Annie tickles her mother's cheek with the tip of her braid and twists her wrist around to look at her watch. "When's Daddy coming? I'm bored."

"Five o'clock." Linda B. pushes the braid out of her face. "I told you."

Annie huffs over and plunks herself down next to me and Mr. Right, who is curled up in my lap in a rare burst of familial affection. "Are you divorced?" she says, petting the cat too hard.

"Careful," Linda B. admonishes. "Be gentle."

"No," I say.

"Why not?" Annie says.

"Because I've never been married." The cat springs off my lap and beats a hasty retreat underneath the hibiscus bushes. "You have to be married before you can get divorced. Understand?"

Annie nods. Suddenly I feel depressed and far, far behind—as if my life were some class I would never catch up with. While everyone else is moving on to long division, I am still stuck on simple subtraction.

"Hey, isn't that Kelvin over there?" Linda B. asks, pointing to a thin bearded guy lugging a large potted palm down the street.

From my angle it looks like the palm is walking on its own—an animated cartoon tree—and in the moment that the man's face is obscured behind the foliage, my heart thuds out some desperate Morse code plea or warning against my breastbone. Then the man sets the potted palm down on the sidewalk, resting for a second, and I scoff, "That's not him. Have you had your eyes examined lately?"

"I need new contacts, but I can't afford them," she says, making me feel bad.

The guy across the street, who does in fact look a bit like Kelvin, hoists the potted palm up again, bending correctly—at the knees—and as I watch him stagger across the courtyard and disappear, a little grenade of disappointment explodes inside me. All day I have been expecting Kelvin to drop by. He lives just three blocks away—on Sierra Bonita—and I know he has to drive by at least two of our signs on his way to and from work. The signs are hard to miss. Linda B. went all out. THE GARAGE SALE OF THE THREE LINDAS. The signs resemble primitive brightly colored *retablos* with the three of us hovering above a mound of miscellaneous stuff—the patron saints of discarded merchandise. I figured he'd see the signs and at least walk over to check it out. It hasn't been that long since he moved out. A couple of months. You think he'd still have at least a twinge of proprietary interest. I had purposely picked out a couple of items of sentimental value—a hideous painted coconut we'd brought back from Kauai, and a pastry tube that had once figured in a particularly ardent sexual interlude—in the hopes of making him feel bad. The coconut had sold almost immediately to a little Vietnamese boy who lived two doors up, but the pastry tube was still up for grabs.

"I think we ought to call it a day," Linda W. declares, tossing *The Second Sex* into the box of unsold books. "We haven't unloaded anything in the last half hour."

"And it's clouding over." Linda B. yawns and rolls down the legs of her jumpsuit.

"What do you say?" Linda W. asks me.

"Whatever."

The night before Kelvin moved out we prepared a special banquet just for the two of us, several of our favorite dishes. With the china and silverware my mother gave me, one setting at a time, before she came to terms with the sad fact that I might never be someone's wife. I didn't have much appetite; it was hard to slide the food past the lump in my throat. I didn't know, honestly, if I was in love with Kelvin, but I did know that I didn't want him to leave; I didn't want to be alone again. I didn't want to have to start from scratch with someone new, assuming I could even find someone new. (New-used, that is.) As we were clearing the table for dessert, I started to cry. He put his arms around me. I sat in his lap while he spoon-fed me some of his chocolate mandarin orange mousse, like baby food. His eyes misted, too. We were both getting too old to start over and too old to believe anything could last. It just seemed like, unbeknownst to us, we had passed that critical age in our lives where you could ever really convince yourself that *This was It.* "Why are we doing this?" I asked, between sobs and spoonfuls. He shook his head. "Are you sure you want this?" I asked. Meaning: "Don't want me." He shook his head again. He looked miserable. "It's okay," I said. He nodded. We washed the dishes together in silence, stopping occasionally to hug each other. I kept the leftovers in the refrigerator until they started to grow mold.

The cat yowls and we all turn just in time to see his head stuck through the hole in the badminton racquet, dragging it along behind him like some sporty Elizabethan ruff.

"Shame on you! How would you like it?" Linda B. extricates the cat and paddles Annie's behind with the racquet.

"It didn't hurt him," Annie insists. "He liked it."

The sun is sinking. I survey the yard to see what is left. The chairs and tables, backlit by the fiery glow, look surreal. "This reminds me of *Out of Africa,*" I say. "The scene where she sells off all the stuff from the farm."

No one bothers to respond. Linda W. is busy consolidating the leftovers into one carton and Linda B. has dragged Annie inside to clean up before her father arrives to take her for the night. Then, like the proverbial late guest, a battered Honda Civic pulls up and two people get out—a mother and daughter. The daughter looks to be about Annie's age. The mother circles the tiny lawn, giving the skimpy remains a quick once-over and then sighs, as if this were just one more disappointment in a long, long series. For some reason I feel a sudden need to apologize for how sad and crummy it all looks. "We were just packing up," I say. "I'm afraid there's not really much left."

"I was just curious," she says. "I saw your sign. I'm a Linda too."

"Really."

"I always hated my name." She claps a hand over her mouth. "I guess that's not very tactful."

Her little girl runs over with the lidless Scrabble game. "I want this."

The mother digs a quarter out of her pocket.

"That's okay," I say. "It's free."

"You sure?" The mother shrugs and hands the quarter to her daughter. "Well, thanks." As she is about to leave she turns back and says, "You ever hear of that Linda Convention in Iowa or Idaho or some place?"

"No," I say.

"I read about it in the paper. Some dinky town. They hold it every year. Last year there were something like a thousand Lindas. From all over the country."

"Wow," I say.

"Personally, I'd rather go to a Bob or Bill Convention myself," she winks and then laughs, embarrassed. "Come on." She tugs her little girl's hand and abruptly drags her back to the car. As the Honda clatters away from the curb, I remember the two Scrabble letters in my pocket. *K. T.*

"Hey!" I raise my arm and wave for them to stop, but they don't see me. "Shit." I toss the letters into the bushes and sink back onto my chair, suddenly exhausted and depressed.

"We took in a grand total of ninety-two dollars and fifty cents," Linda W. announces. "Anyone up for Thai food? I'm starved."

"Sure, fine, anything." I close my eyes.

"You okay?" she asks me.

I nod. But I'm not.

With my eyes closed, sitting there surrounded by cast-off junk, I can see it all with horrifying clarity. A terrible religious vision. Like something out of the Old Testament, illustrated by Hieronymus Bosch: a huge ugly ballroom festooned with crepe paper, in the middle of nowhere, surrounded by miles and miles of cornfields, crowded with hundreds and hundreds of sad, aging Lindas. Grandmothers even. From every state in the union. All wearing neatly printed name tags. Even though we could have recognized each other anywhere.

the prodigal father

The day his house burned to the ground Marshall was camping at the Russian River with his men's group. He had seen a segment about these so-called Wild Men weekends on "60 Minutes" or "20/20" and this was nothing like that. They did not beat tom-toms and there was relatively little whooping and weeping. Most of them were academics, mostly in the humanities. All the men in the group had been divorced at least once. They understood one another. They seemed, Marshall thought, like nice, intelligent, sensitive guys—easy to get along with. Sitting in the leafy, peaceful woods, earnestly telling their stories to one another, nodding in empathetic harmony, it seemed as if all those irreconcilable differences and strident custody battles had taken place on some other planet, to some other species.

In the darkness they huddled around the campfire, roasting hot dogs and drinking beer. A couple of men brought out guitars, and soon they were singing old sixties songs. *Suzanne takes you down to a place by the river . . . /She feeds you tea and oranges that come all the way from China.* Someone passed around a joint. After a couple of hits, Marshall entered a time warp. He was back in his dorm room in Madison. After a couple more hits, he was in Billy Kuka's backyard with his Boy Scout troop, encircled by pup tents, eating s'mores, pooling their erroneous and vicarious knowledge of sex. Leonard Cohen flowed into Bob Dylan. *How many roads must a man walk down/before you call him a man?* Suddenly, wordlessly, the men seemed to grasp one another's hands in unison—except for the two guitar players—and looking around the circle at their faces in the flickering firelight, Marshall saw that they were just an aging troop of battered, bewildered Boy Scouts who, despite all their merit badges, were ill prepared to deal with adult life. His heart went out to them. And then he found himself imagining Elena sitting in a similar circle of fortysomething Girl Scouts, holding hands, and his heart went out to her too, even though he knew that, in fact, she was at a conference in Chicago. The ashy bitterness that had been smoldering inside him for the past couple of months since she moved out seemed to lift and drift off in the hazy stream of smoke from the campfire. He felt both fragile and strong: tender as flesh, tough as scar tissue.

His new down sleeping bag—guaranteed to twenty degrees below—was as warm and snug as a womb. For the first time in weeks, he slept soundly.

The next morning, Sunday, he awoke rested and refreshed. They ate breakfast and went for a hike, talking quietly in small trysts of twos or threes. In the late afternoon, the men bear-hugged good-bye as they climbed into their Hondas and Mazdas and headed back to civilization. It was a beautiful warm, windy day. Marshall rolled down the window and flicked on the radio. Which is when he heard the news: the Berkeley-Oakland hills were on fire. The fire was raging out of control, whipped by the shifting, unpredictable winds. Broadway Terrace, his neighborhood, had been evacuated. He snapped off the radio, then snapped it on again, punching the buttons one after another, as if hoping to find some other frequency of reality.

During the long drive back, he pictured his house, room by room, taking mental inventory, telling himself it would be all right, even though he knew that it was all gone, like so much else in his life, up in smoke. The one stroke of luck was that on his way out of town he had dropped his golden retriever, Toynbee, off at his daughter's house in the flats. And most of his important manuscripts and notes were in his office at the university. To calm himself as the sun set and the miles passed slowly he sang to himself the songs they had sung the night before, trying to salvage the old idealistic lyrics from the cynical rubble of his memory.

*   *   *

Two weeks after the fire, Marshall paces restlessly around his new one-bedroom apartment with its bare walls and rented furniture. The place has less personality than a motel room. He feels anonymous, identityless, like someone relocated in a witness protection program, forced to make a new life from scratch. It is his first night in the apartment. It is dark already and he is hungry. His first impulse is to order a pizza, but instead he pep-talks himself into driving to the co-op, where he splurges on filet mignon, asparagus, and a twelve-dollar bottle of wine, telling himself that the homely act of cooking will make him feel less like a transient.

As he fumbles for his keys, standing in the dimly depressing hallway of his apartment building, he imagines hearing his dog's eager, impatient thumping tail on the other side of the door. He misses him. He thinks maybe if Toynbee were here, the apartment wouldn't be so bad. But he could not, on such short notice, find an apartment that would allow dogs, so he was forced to leave his dog at his daughter's house for the time being, until his house is rebuilt. Six months minimum. Six months in Motel Six. He sighs as he sets the bag of groceries down on the dinette table in the kitchen, and then it hits him that he does not have a corkscrew. Even though he spent over two hundred dollars at Payless that morning, up one aisle and down the next, tossing things into the cart, like that TV show from his childhood where the crazed contestants could keep as much as they could grab off the shelves in three minutes, he has no corkscrew. He checks all the kitchen drawers just to make sure. He supposes he could try to borrow one from a neighbor, none of whom he has yet to meet, but he just doesn't feel up to it. He is afraid he might burst into tears or stab himself with it. The thought of replacing, item by item, a lifetime's accumulation of essential and inessential stuff overwhelms him.

With his friends, he has tried to put on a good face, not wanting to appear self-absorbed and self-pitying when, after all, people were losing their jobs, dying of AIDS, being mass-murdered. "Just call me the Phoenix," he had joked to Hannah, his ex-wife, who had called from Madison to offer her condolences. "My

God," she had said, "I can't even imagine. I lose an earring in a movie theater and I'm depressed for a month." He had to restrain himself from saying that she hadn't seemed *that* upset about losing him, their marriage. "It could be worse"—he'd pontificated to his distraught long-distance mother, who presided like an anxious curator over her antique-stuffed condo in Arizona—"they're only things, right?" For a moment he had felt the old surge of antiestablishment fervor, circa 1969, Woodstock Nation—burning draft cards and self-immolating Buddhist monks. *Hell no, we won't go!* But they weren't only "things." They were *his* things. His context. His force of gravity. Acquired DNA.

The day after the fire he had bought a pocket notebook in which to jot down all the odd little items he remembered he had lost as they would suddenly flash into his consciousness. He told people it was for insurance purposes, but it wasn't. Not really. It was for something else. At night he left the notebook by his bed—a mattress on the floor at his daughter's house—and usually turned on the light two or three times in the middle of the night to jot down another item or two—a beaded offering basket that Elena and he had brought back from Bali, a clay bagel paperweight that Tilden had made for him one Father's Day, a copy of *The Little Prince* the first girl he had ever slept with had given him. The first week he went through three notebooks. He had also taped a shopping list to his refrigerator, to which he had been adding all day, at an alarming rate. Tweezers, spatula, Scotch tape. The list was endless. Maybe he should just take off for India and become one of those roving monks in a saffron robe with a little rice bowl. There was really nothing holding him here. *Freedom's just another word for nothing left to lose.* What did Kris Kristofferson know? He was just a kid back then. What did any of them know back then? What did they know now? Shit. He prints CORKSCREW in big letters at the bottom of the list, grabs the bottle of wine, and heads over to his daughter's house on Prince Street.

As usual, he has to hunt for a parking place and jog two blocks to the dilapidated three-story house with its weedy patch of front yard and sagging porch cluttered with spindly hanging plants and bicycles, but the instant he opens the front door—with the key he conveniently forgot to return—his spirits lift. The first time, last August, he had set foot in his daughter's house, a disorienting, bittersweet wave of déjà vu washed over him. He had felt that he could close his eyes and navigate from room to room without bumping into anything. Lumpy yard sale furniture covered with Indian bedspreads and Mexican blankets, an old cable table littered with a week's worth of newspapers and magazines, more listless-looking Wandering Jews and spider plants trailing from the mantel. Blindfolded, he bet he could read off half the titles of the books in the rickety brick-and-board bookshelves flanking the nonfunctioning fireplace. As he caught a glimpse of himself in the cloudy mirror over the mantelpiece, he had felt dazed, as if he were sound asleep in some crash pad back in Madison dreaming this incredibly vivid, disturbing dream in which he was a middle-aged man visiting his daughter in college.

Overhead a stereo thuds out some music he doesn't recognize and the shower clunks off. He smells sautéed garlic and onions and heads for the kitchen as Toynbee skitters down the bare wood stairs and nearly bowls him over, yelping and cringing in a gratifyingly ecstatic welcome. "Hey there!" Marshall squats down and scratches behind the dog's ears. The most poignant aftermath of the big fire is the blitz of photocopied fliers (complete with fuzzy photo) offering rewards for lost cats and dogs. The pets' names read like a cultural dictionary: Gorby, Mandela, Oprah, Madonna. The feline and canine Disappeared.

A large pot of water is boiling on the stove and the dark, blank kitchen windows are steamed up. "Smells good," Marshall says.

"Hey." Jason waves a wooden spoon by way of greeting. "My special spaghetti. You're just in time, man."

Liza leaps up and grabs another plate, still wet, from the drainer. No one in the house ever seems to get around to doing the dishes until the next meal. "How's the new apartment?" she says.

"Grim." Marshall sets the bottle of wine on the table. "I didn't have a corkscrew."

Jason fishes out a strand of spaghetti and flings it against the wall as Liza rummages in the drawers for a corkscrew. The spaghetti bounces off the wall and Toynbee makes a beeline for it. "Needs another minute," Jason says.

Liza hands Marshall a corkscrew. "Tilden's over at Kyle's. I think she's spending the night there."

"Oh," Marshall says, "that's too bad." But actually he is just as glad. He feels most at home here when his daughter is not around, a tangible reminder that a quarter of a century has passed since he last lived in a group house. Mostly, when Tilden is not around, which is most of the time, he feels as if he's gone Back to the Future. The first couple of days he stayed here after the fire they were a bit reserved and polite with him—little Eddie Haskells. But once they realized he was not Ward Cleaver, they loosened up. They seemed to forget he was Someone's Father. And so did he. A fact that his daughter seems sometimes to enjoy and other times resent. An ambivalence that he understands. He had been both pleased and nervous when she had decided to transfer from Madison to Berkeley this year. They had not lived within fifteen hundred miles of each other since she was three years old. Before the fire, they usually met once every week or so for lunch or dinner at some restaurant— his treat. There were other places he could have stayed while he was apartment hunting—friends, colleagues—but he had felt most comfortable right here. He was almost sorry when, after two weeks, he finally found an apartment. He has to admit he misses hanging out.

Jason dumps the pasta into a colander and Liza hollers upstairs to Fritz that dinner is ready. It's Saturday night. The other two housemates, Holly and Rick, must be out somewhere. Liza pulls a loaf of foil-wrapped garlic bread out of the oven. Jason sets the aluminum pot full of spaghetti on the table.

"Looks great," Marshall says, digging in. The basic no-frills spaghetti of his childhood suddenly seems like an exquisite treat after a decade of sun-dried tomatoes, fresh basil, and goat cheese.

Fritz meanders in barefoot, long hair still soaking wet from a shower, wearing a dingy, frayed cotton kimono. He spent last year in Beijing, teaching English and learning Chinese. He is reputed to be some sort of economics genius. He plans, eventually, to work for the World Bank, but in the interim he seems to spend most of his time practicing t'ai chi and calligraphy.

"The Prodigal Father returns," Fritz says, tearing off a hunk of garlic bread. "How's it going?"

"Okay." Marshall shrugs. "A little on the quiet side after this place."

Fritz nods, takes a swig of wine, and peers at the bottle label. "Wow. Pretty ritzy." He piles a heap of spaghetti on his plate. "Any Parmesan?"

"We're out, man," Jason says. "Sorry."

"Really?" Fritz says.

"Really," Jason says. "Trust me."

Fritz walks to the cupboard, takes out an imaginary can of Parmesan, and pretends to sprinkle it liberally on his pasta, and digs in. "This is great, man."

Marshall laughs. Fritz looks up at him and then says, "Oh, sorry. Where are my manners?" He passes Marshall the cheese.

After dinner, Jason and Liza rush off to a party. Marshall fills the sink with soapy water and starts washing dishes; otherwise he knows that they will still be sitting there at breakfast. Besides, he is in no hurry to return to his empty apartment. Fritz hangs out in the kitchen, talking about this article he just read in *The Atlantic* about *feng shui*, the Chinese art of placement. According to the article, Fritz says, housing contractors in California are calling in *feng shui* consultants in order to attract Asian home buyers.

"I was thinking"—Fritz extracts a thin, elegant joint from the pocket of his kimono—"you ought to hire a *feng shui* master to help you rebuild your house. Make sure everything's in the right place for the right vibes, the most auspicious flow of energy and all that jazz."

"Please." Marshall scrapes another plate into the trash bag and rinses it. "I've got enough trouble just dealing with the damn building codes, let alone some fortune cookie blueprint."

"Suit yourself," Fritz shrugs. He offers the joint to Marshall, who dries his hand on his pants and takes a toke. "Be a typical close-minded, arrogant Western chauvinist. Rots of ruck."

"Fuck you." Marshall exhales a stream of smoke and passes the joint back. During the two weeks he lived in the house, he and

Fritz had often stayed up until 1 or 2 A.M., talking and smoking dope. Before the Men's Weekend, Marshall couldn't even remember the last time he had smoked any pot; now he can't remember why he ever stopped.

"Just tell me this," Fritz says. "Did you have a beam on your bedroom ceiling?"

Marshall shuts his eyes and sighs, picturing the bedroom, which Elena had painted a deep coral that she jokingly referred to as Electric Lox. With the morning sun glowing on the walls, it was like waking up inside of some lush tropical fruit—a mango or papaya. "Yeah, there was a beam," he says. "So?"

"Did it run lengthwise over the bed?"

Marshall nods reluctantly.

"Thought so." Fritz takes his time relighting the joint. Inhaling, exhaling. "According to *feng shui*, a beam running over a bed like that increases the chances of separation."

Marshall snaps off the faucets and glances at his watch. Only eight-twenty. He thinks of his empty apartment, the long slow Saturday evening ahead. Fritz is madly in love with a woman named Ling-ling he met in Beijing who is coming to Berkeley in June, and in the meantime he is usually just hanging out in the house on weekend nights, hoarding his money for the summer. Marshall has no desire to get involved with another woman any time soon, or, for some reason, to spend time with old friends, most of whom have houses and wives and state-of-the-art corkscrews.

"Want to rent a movie?" he asks.

"Sure," Fritz says.

At the video rental store on College Avenue, all the decent new movies are already checked out, so they rent something they have both seen before, *Altered States* with William Hurt. During the short drive back, they figure out that Marshall's first acid trip occurred five years before Fritz was born. Over the years, Marshall has accustomed himself to the bizarre, depressing fact that most of his students were born ten years, twenty years, now thirty years after Kennedy's assassination, but somehow this new calculation knocks him for a loop. He keeps refiguring the math in his head thinking there must be some mistake.

"When's the *last* time you tripped?" Fritz asks as he squats down and inserts the cassette into the VCR.

"I don't know," Marshall says, remote in hand, fast-forwarding past the FBI warning. He knows perfectly well that it was in 1970, on Maui. Hannah and he and some friends had dropped acid and driven to an Eric Burden and the Animals concert and camped out in the parking lot, eavesdropping, because they didn't have the money for tickets. In the fall he started graduate school at Cal and Hannah got pregnant. "How about you?" he asks.

"Couple of weeks ago. The day of the fire, actually." Fritz settles back on the lumpy sofa and kicks off his thongs. "It was pretty weird. I was taking this walk in the hills, kind of blissed out, and suddenly there were fire sirens all over and all this smoke and everything. It was intense. Kind of a bummer, really."

"No kidding," Marshall says.

They watch the movie in silence for a few minutes and then Fritz hits the Pause button and says, "I've got some."

"Some what?" Then he realizes. "Oh." He glances at his watch. "I don't really think—"

"Why not? What's the big deal? So it's been a few years." Fritz leans forward, his eyes shining with missionary zeal. "It's like riding a bicycle."

"That's what I'm afraid of," Marshall laughs. "Elena bought me a bike for my birthday two years ago and the first day I fell and dislocated my shoulder." It suddenly occurs to him, in hindsight, that it was all downhill after that. He had not been able to drive or cook or do much of anything for five weeks and Elena had resented his helplessness, and he had resented her resentment. They had both suddenly seemed to picture a mutually incompatible old age. Now sometimes, lying alone in bed, he resents the fact that Elena had moved all her precious possessions out just one month before the fire destroyed everything he owned. Even though he knows she couldn't have known, he holds it against her. He feels twice burned.

"Okay," Marshall shrugs. "What the hell. What do I have to lose except my mind?"

*   *   *

It comes on slowly. He feels it first in the back of his teeth. His back molars vibrate and buzz, like a plane taxiing down some runway, about to lift off. He remembers this sensation as if it were yesterday. The last time he'd experienced it, he had not trusted anyone over thirty, and now, here he is, slouching toward fifty. Suddenly he does not trust his own mind. This professorial voice in his head is lecturing away at him, asking him how he could have been so stupid and irresponsible: *What are you trying to prove? To whom?* The old fart is deliberately trying to bum him out. Fritz is staring at his reflection in the dark window, practicing the same t'ai chi move over and over, like a slide stuck in a projector. Marshall would like to talk, to burn off some of this nervous energy, but Fritz has turned into some silent Buddha type, loftily ignoring all attempts at interpersonal communication. The t'ai chi move is called Parting the Mane of the Wild Horse, and as Fritz repeats it over and over and over again, it drives Marshall wild with impatience. He imagines felling Fritz with a sudden vicious karate chop. The violence of the image freaks him out. As if sensing his agitation, Toynbee sits up and rests his head on Marshall's thigh like a devoted paperweight. Marshall pats the dog's head, breathes deeply, then stands up and says, "I'm going for a walk."

Outside, he feels calmer. Overhead the stars seem to twirl and twinkle and he feels exaltedly disoriented, as if he has been transported to some celestial discotheque. He can feel the cool night air passing in and out of his lungs, his heart beating against his chest like a tom-tom, the sidewalk breathing under the thick soles of his running shoes. Everything seems subtly animated and Technicolored: Disneylike. He trails a few steps behind Toynbee, who seems as reliably straight and stolid and steady as one of those Seeing Eye dogs. In an attempt to ground himself, Marshall tries to focus on the book he is writing about the interplay between history and myth, focusing on the Kennedy assassination. He had stumbled across a line in an Alexander Theroux novel that Elena had been reading last Christmas vacation on Kauai. She had left the book lying open on the sand while she

took a quick dip in the ocean, and as if moved by the hand of
Fate, he had chanced to reach over and pick it up and skim a couple of pages until he was stopped dead by what would become
the epigraph of his new book: "Myth, after all, is what we believe
naturally; history is what we must painfully learn and struggle to
remember." He could still feel the shiver of recognition he had
felt reading that sentence as Elena stood over him, dripping cool
saltwater onto his sunburned back.

She was living in the city now, on Russian Hill. She had fallen
in love with one of her graduate students, an ex-tax attorney who
had suddenly "got literature" the way some people "get religion."
A born-again bibliophile living off the interest from his invest-
ments, writing his dissertation on Magical Realism. Her guilt had
made her more than generous. Except for her clothes and books
and a few cartons of personal treasures, she had left the house
intact. It would have been better had she carted off furniture and
paintings, so that he would have come home each evening to
gaping holes, tangible losses, rather than this externally untouched
but internally eviscerated space. She had just left him more to
lose, a bigger pile of ashes. But the odd thing was that in those
long silent nights before the fire, as he sat alone in his house taking stock of his life, like a man in a rowboat in the middle of a
small stagnant pond, it was Hannah and his long-gone marriage
that he mourned. Hannah and their baby daughter. As if this latest loss were just a tributary that flowed back to the source.

It starts to rain softly. He can hear each drop pinging against
the pavement. "Acid rain," he jokes to the dog. They are walking
south toward Telegraph Avenue. It occurs to him that this is not
a safe thing, walking around here at night, and he is glad the dog
is with him, although he cannot imagine anyone being the least
bit intimidated by Toynbee, who seems to exude goodwill indis-
criminately. The aroma of charred meat wafts from The
Smokehouse at the corner. Toynbee perks up and trots faster.
When Hannah was pregnant, she craved Smokehouse cheese-
burgers with onions and pickles. Sometimes late at night
Marshall would throw on his jeans and workshirt and jog the two
blocks to The Smokehouse to get one for her. In those days he'd
had a black Lab named Stokely who used to accompany him

everywhere. The dog eventually died of heartworms.

Some Pavlovian response propels Marshall up to the takeout window of The Smokehouse, where he orders a cheeseburger and a Diet Coke. Waiting for his order, Marshall sits down at one of the picnic tables and tries to appear calm and composed—business as usual—even though when he looks at his hands on the scarred table he can see the blood flowing through the veins, which freaks him out. He shoves his hands in his pockets and then takes them out again, suddenly worried that the two black dudes at the next table will think this is some manifestation of racist paranoia. He smiles at them. The smaller guy in the Rasta cap says, "Hey, man, how's it going?" and tosses Toynbee a french fry. "What's the dog's name?"

"Toynbee," Marshall mumbles, feeling foolishly effete, as if he has a scarlet Ph.D. stamped on his chest. Still, he supposes it's better than "Stokely." Although these guys are young—it's probably all ancient history to them.

"Got me a pit bull named Emily Post," the larger dude says, and they both crack up.

Marshall knows they are mocking him. Even his dog seems to have defected, the shameless beggar. Marshall abruptly averts his eyes from the bag of french fries, which has started to quiver and pulse, the fries writhing and slithering to escape. He closes his eyes and breathes deeply. For a moment he feels calmer and then he flashes on this lurid poster in the veterinarian's office in Madison: The Heartworm Life Cycle. A graphic horror show, like something out of *Alien*. He can still remember the text verbatim: *"The larvae enter the dog's skin through the bite wound and, within three months, begin their migration toward the heart."* Dr. Wu, the vet, said the worms could grow to be fourteen inches long. Marshall shudders. The woman behind the counter calls out, "Cheeseburger. Diet Coke." He opens his eyes. The guys at the next table have split. A couple of stray fries lie limp and still on the table. He walks over and claims his order. The thought of food makes him gag. He unwraps the burger and sets it on the ground for Toynbee, who wolfs it down in a couple of voluptuous bites.

He starts walking again. The rain has turned to a fine cool

mist. He feels surprisingly okay, wired but mellow. He can hear the coins jingling in his pocket like faint Tibetan bells. As he heads back toward the house, he observes the inside of his brain working: idling, shifting gears, accelerating. It's interesting. He remembers sitting in a vinyl booth in the old International House of Pancakes on Telegraph at 4 A.M. with his best friend, Sam, surrounded by all the other crazies intently staring into space or studying the paper place mat, which showed the locations of all the I-Hops in Amerika, and Sam saying, "You know, the great thing about tripping is it's impossible to be bored," and himself nodding in profound agreement. Sam, in fact, lives not far from here—a couple of blocks up on Benvenue—and Marshall toys with the idea of dropping in on him, but Sam is recently remarried with twin baby girls, high on belated fatherhood. Boring.

He keeps walking, past Benvenue and College Avenue, toward the hills.

He walks and walks with no conscious destination, no sense of time passing, until suddenly he finds himself there.

It smells like an old fireplace and looks like satellite photos of the moon. He walks up the fifteen concrete steps that used to lead to his front door. Beside him, Toynbee paces and paws through the rubble, anxious and agitated, expectant and disappointed. Or so it seems. He had bought the house seven years ago, after being promoted to full professor. Despite having attained this dazzling pinnacle of his career, he'd still had to borrow half the down payment from his father, a retired air force colonel who died swiftly and efficiently, true to form, the following year. The couple he had bought the house from were getting a divorce—the husband had already moved out, the small lawn looked anemic and ragged. Bad *feng shui*, clearly.

The city has already planted grass seed and spread bales of hay over the ashes. Marshall collects a bundle of hay, arranges it in front of the brick chimney, which looms like something out of Stonehenge in the darkness, and makes himself more or less comfortable. Toynbee settles himself beside him, gnawing on an old bone he has unearthed. It is unbelievably dark and quiet up here, an eerie sort of apocalyptic wilderness. Over the past couple of weeks, during his frequent visits to his insurance company, Marshall has run into several of his neighbors, all suffering from various degrees of shell shock. Most of them had been at home when the fire started and had salvaged a carload or two of their most valuable belongings, whereas Marshall has nothing, nothing left, except a brass Buddha and some half-melted opium weights from Thailand he had sifted from the rubble the first time the police had allowed him to enter the area. He has not been back since—except one time—with an architect he had met, prophetically enough, during the Men's Weekend at the Russian River.

Marshall lies down, pillowing his head against the dog's warm flank, and closes his eyes, exhausted. He's starting to come down; the jangly buzz has mellowed into a pleasant sort of hum. Peaceful yet aware, "tuned in," as they used to say back then. He opens his eyes and gazes up at the night sky, the universe, the cosmos. The house seems a small thing. Someday he will be nothing but ashes himself, and then what will it matter? The thought of getting old, of not being forever young, scares him, but the thought of dying does not. He can more easily imagine himself dead than old. Like Janis and Jimmi and Jim, whose grave he had visited in Paris with Hannah when Tilden was just a baby, learning to walk. He supposes that he is a *puer aeternus*, one of those boy-men that all the male psychology books talk about, but he feels like an old soul. An old, old soul. For the first time, he is glad it all burned up. All that petty personal history, the accumulated infrastructure of identity. He remembers telling Hannah once, in a pompous pique, that life is a process of accumulation, not substitution. But he realizes now that he was wrong; she was right. She was right to burn her bridges.

He sighs and closes his eyes and lets himself drift off.

When he wakes up, cold and damp, the sun is rising. He is starving. His brain feels hung over, tender, spent. His bones ache. Profound, shriveled insights litter the floor of his brain like so many deflated balloons. Still, in an odd way, he feels good. He stands up, stretches, brushes the hay and ash from his clothing, walks behind the chimney, unzips, and lets loose a fierce stream that sounds like a rushing waterfall in the early morning quiet. Toynbee sidles over and joins him. For an instant, Marshall imagines his penis as a magic fire hose and when he looks up and around, he sees his house standing there, the door wide open, as if he has just stepped out to pick up the Sunday newspaper. He can smell the coffee and see the flash of Elena's red silk robe, like a cardinal, as she flits past the open doorway. The mirage vanishes. He zips his pants. Everything looks normal and, at the same time, painstakingly counterfeit, like a superrealist painting.

"Hungry?" he asks Toynbee. "Come on. Breakfast time."

They set off down the road, back to civilization. As they cut across his neighbors' lifeless lawns, Marshall suddenly flashes back to a dream or vision that must have come to him during the night. He was standing in his former house with the *feng shui* master, who had just completed his methodical inspection of the place. "Yes, I see the problem," the *feng shui* master said, nodding inscrutably. He led Marshall back through the house and pointed out all the ornate footbridges that connected the rooms one to another. "All these bridges, very bad," he said, shaking his head at such naive foolishness. Marshall felt crestfallen; the bridges had been his idea, his big home improvement project. "Past time flow into present time," the *feng shui* master said. "Very bad. Big problem."

"I see," Marshall frowned. "What should I do? Will it be expensive"?

Abruptly yet unjarringly—a dream jump cut—the *feng shui* master was Dr. Wu, the veterinarian, and he was standing there in his white jacket, nodding grimly, while Stokely whimpered on the examining table. "Heartworms," he said. "Very bad."

Involuntarily, Marshall clutched a hand over his heart, as if he were about to recite the pledge of allegiance. "What can you do?" he asked.

Dr. Wu shook his head sadly.

As he opens the creaky gate and walks up the weedy flagstone pathway to his daughter's house, clutching a white paper bag full of warm bagels to his chest, his daughter flings open the front door and shouts, "Where the hell have you been? We've been looking all over for you. Are you all right?"

Marshall kisses her on the cheek and hands her the bag of bagels, smiling serenely.

"It's not funny," she snaps. "I've been going crazy, imagining what might have happened."

"So have I," Marshall says and laughs.

"What's that supposed to mean?"

He shrugs. Fritz walks downstairs, half-asleep, hair standing on end. "Hey, man," he yawns, "where you been?"

"I took a walk. Up to my old house." He opens the bag and hands a bagel to Fritz. "They're still warm."

"Must've been some walk," his daughter mutters.

"I fell asleep."

Fritz takes a bite of his bagel and chews. "I told her you were okay."

"I'm a big boy," Marshall says. He tosses a bagel to Toynbee, then chooses one for himself.

"You said it," Tilden snorts. "That was a really dumb stunt to pull. Dropping acid at your age. I even called Mom in Madison."

"You told her I dropped acid?" Marshall says, pausing midbite.

Tilden nods, arms folded across her chest, looking scarily like her mother.

"Really?" He feels his foolish smile fade away. "What did she say?"

"None of your business," Tilden says, reaching out to brush some stray hay out of his hair. "I hope you feel better than you look."

"I do," he says, echoing his long-broken marriage vows. "At least I think I do." He rubs his hand over his heart. It was Hannah who finally took Stokely in to be put to sleep. Marshall didn't have the heart to do it. Then, not long after that, they split up and she moved back to Madison and ended up marrying a cardiologist. A heart doctor a dozen years older than she. As if, the second time around, she wanted an expert, someone with skill and experience in matters of the heart. Not some bumbling amateur. Apparently she knew what she was doing. They have been married now for fifteen years.

"Come on," Marshall begs. "Tell me. What did she say?" He really wants to know. "I really want to know," he says.

Tilden takes a bite of bagel and chews deliberately, taking her time. She swallows.

Marshall waits.

"She said, and I quote, 'Good for him.'"

"Really?" Marshall bursts out laughing, surprised and inordinately pleased. "She really said that?"

Tilden rolls her eyes and nods her head. There is a sudden crash of glass in the kitchen and someone yells, "Shit!"

"You want some coffee?" Tilden asks him.

He can smell it, it smells good, but he shakes his head and gives in to a yawn. "I'm beat. I'm going home." He pats the dog on the head.

Fritz hands him the video. "Here. You can drop this off on your way."

Tilden cocks her head and reads the label upside down. "Perfect."

Marshall shrugs sheepishly and flashes her a peace sign. He opens the door. The sun is shining brightly now, the air is warm. He breathes deeply. The yard, an overgrown jungle, smells of roses. As he steps off the porch he glances down at his watch, as if synchronizing himself with something.

Then he remembers—fishing in his pants pocket. "By the way, here's your spare key back." He holds it out to her. In the early morning light the key seems to wink and glitter like gold, and suddenly Marshall wants it back. All of it.

His daughter drops the key into a cracked clay pot perched precariously on the railing, a half-dead jade plant. "Call me later," she calls out to him. "Okay?"

He turns and nods. For an instant, as he squints into the bright sun, he sees Hannah standing there, waving. They have just made love. She glistens with dew from the shower. She is smiling. He sees himself smiling back, Stokely waiting impatiently by his side. Ready to go. The picture of health. They have no idea, no idea at all. Although, even then, the larvae must have been slowly migrating, inching their way toward the heart.

the still point

Being married to T. Rex was a lesson in downward mobility and inward nobility—although I didn't see the latter until it was too late. He told me I worried too much—my whole family did—it wasn't my fault I'd inherited the worry gene, but it was up to me whether I was going to let it get me down or not. He had attended various community colleges, dropped in for a semester here and there—he had a transcript that even the FBI couldn't piece together—and during one of his tours of duty as a college student he had read a couple of books on Zen Buddhism, which he quoted frequently as a means to philosophically dignify his lack of get-up-and-go. Or so I thought.

I remember the first time I walked through the living room carrying a load of laundry and saw him sitting there in his favorite armchair with a beer in his hand and I said as sweetly as possible, "Honey, the grass needs mowing if you're not doing anything." And he said, "I *am* doing something. I'm following the breath." I looked around. "What breath?" I don't know what I expected to see—some sort of vapor trail, like an airplane leaves. "It's called *zazen*," he mumbled under his breath, "the still point."

"Don't you have to sit cross-legged or something?" I asked.

"Bodhidharma said, 'In order to see a fish, you must watch the water.' He didn't say anything about sitting cross-legged."

The stiller T. Rex got, the more I worried. Until I was in such a constant state of agitation I couldn't even sit still to watch television; I had to be doing something every minute. In the beginning when we first married and moved down to Florida, he'd been working for his father, building three small houses in the neighboring town of Wachula. His dad paid him minimum wage, but the deal was we'd get one of the three houses when they were finished. Meanwhile we were living in this sweatbox of a trailer and I was working as a waitress while I sent my résumé to all the school districts within driving distance. I never did trust Buddy Rexinger, though I tried to remain neutral and optimistic, but not long before the three houses were complete, he picked some fight and reneged on the agreement, so that was that. T. Rex had worked nearly six months for next to nothing, skilled labor, and we didn't have any money in the bank or a decent roof over our heads. The only bright point was I'd landed a teaching job for the fall in Arcadia, the same school district where someone had burned down the house of that little boy with AIDS.

After the deal with his father fell apart, T. Rex got real quiet and seemed to lose some of his spirit. You didn't have to be a Zen master to see the wind had gone out of his sails. For a while he hustled to get some construction jobs in the area. We had to buy him a new Toyota pickup so he could get to work and back—the jobs were all over the place—but it seemed that the jobs got shorter and shorter with longer dry spells in between them, and pretty soon he was spending most of his days in the mobile home we'd rented, sitting in front of the TV with the volume turned off, following his breath.

My job, although steady, didn't pay enough to cover the bills we owed. I'd fret about the truck payment and the utility bills and my student loan being overdue and get depressed, tossing and turning at night, imagining how the pickup was going to be repossessed, and then T. Rex wouldn't be able to get any work at all, and I'd wake him up and say, "We're just always struggling to play catch-up. How are we ever going to get ahead?" Then, sometimes, I would start to cry out of pure frustration and desperation, seeing that there was only more of what was behind us ahead of us, only worse probably, and what kind of life was that? And T. Rex would hold me in the crook of his huge arm and say something that was supposed to be enlightening and comforting like: "The sights we see from the train will change, but we are always running on the same track." Meaning success is just an illusion so why bother? In the end there's just the end.

"But what will happen to us in the meantime?" I would cry.

Then he'd say something like, "What we call 'I' is just a swinging door that moves when we inhale and exhale, so who is this 'we' you keep worrying about?"

Which would drive me crazy. He knew perfectly well who we were. Once I jumped out of bed in the middle of the night and grabbed his wallet off the dresser and snapped on the bright light and shoved his driver's license up in front of his nose. "This is you!" I shouted, opening the billfold. "Thomas Myron Rexinger. And you have four dollars to your name."

Squinting, he reached over calmly and turned off the light. After I had stopped sniffing and my heartbeat had returned to normal, he leaned over and kissed the back of my neck. "It will be all right," he whispered, his breath warm in my ear. "I'm working on it." He fell asleep and I lay there in the darkness until almost dawn listening to him inhaling and exhaling, watching his chest rising and falling, following his breath and wondering where it was going to lead us.

Where it led us still seems hard to believe and harder still to understand. It's hard to reconstruct these things that, at the time, just seem as random and inexorable as a series of bad storms blowing in, but in a long letter that I wrote to T. Rex explaining why I needed to sever our relationship in order to save what was left of my sanity and credit rating, I laid it all out point by point, priding myself on seeing it all so clearly, when in fact, in hindsight, I was so busy looking down, where we seemed to be heading, that I never once looked up, to see what T. Rex was staring into.

I did my best to be fair and I think I was. I conceded the fact that there was some sheer bad luck involved. Like the time he finally got it together, about six months after his father had stabbed him in the back over that house deal, to land a job building a Laundromat just down the road in Gardner, making good money. The first Friday night he brought home T-bone steaks and grilled them to perfection while I just relaxed in a chaise lounge, drinking a beer. We made love for the first time in a while and things were looking up again. We even had enough money to buy a VCR. But then, about a month into the job, he was walking out to his truck after a hard day's work and, out of nowhere—thwack!—he got slammed on the back of the head with a baseball bat. The guy stole his wallet and left him lying there by the road until his boss found him and drove him to the hospital. Turned out he had a severe concussion and for a while the doctors prepared me for the possibility of some permanent brain damage. He stayed in the hospital for ten days, without health insurance, and the doctors advised against any physical labor for at least two months. Even after that, he had problems with his balance and was prone to bad headaches, which ruled out any jobs like roofing and left him moody where he'd always been even-tempered before. They caught the lowlife who'd mugged him, and T. Rex got himself a lawyer who tried to get him some big settlement under the Victim's Assistance Act, but nothing came of it. Instead we had to contend with a $9,000 hospital bill. As I said in my letter to him, I understood that none of this was his fault—it was just sheer bad luck. It seemed that just as there were "repeat offenders," there were "repeat victims" and T. Rex was one of them. Anyway, that was the big blow—literally and figuratively—after which we never could seem to get back on our feet.

In the letter, I also told T. Rex that I understood he'd had an unfair start in life with such unsupportive parents who never lifted a finger to help him with college or anything else that might have helped him build a firmer foundation for success. His father was remarried and had a daughter, Riva, with his second wife, and that daughter could do no wrong in Buddy's eyes. He put everything he had into her and treated his only son like he was some distant unwanted relation with no potential worth paying attention to. Riva had graduated with a degree in advertising from Emory, financed by her daddy, and then through sheer pushiness and luck, managed to land a job doing PR for the Atlanta Braves. She made a big salary and had a fancy new house, which Buddy and his second wife were always going off to visit in Georgia. Once they even dropped Mee-ma, Buddy's own mother, off at our place on their way to Atlanta and said they would pick her up again in three days. Mee-ma was senile—she never once called me by the right name—and hard to get along with. But T. Rex was her favorite grandchild, and it warmed my heart to see how sweet and patient he could be with this cranky old woman who half the time didn't even know who *he* was. As it turned out, his parents didn't pick Mee-ma up again for two weeks, by which point she was a real emotional wreck wondering what had happened to her and asking where she was all the time. It was hell. And when they did finally sail up in Buddy's brand-new black and silver Voyager, all luxury-equipped for travel, they barely even apologized, just made up some lame excuse. And just a month later, at Christmas, they gave Riva a crystal chandelier (like something you'd see at Carnegie Hall) for her new house, and all they gave their son was some stupid ugly Braves sweatshirt they'd probably got for free. It hurt to see the look on T. Rex's face when he unwrapped his gift.

It was somewhat harder to be fair (nonjudgmental) about T. Rex's getting busted and charged with a felony and slapped with a $500 fine—because I had, in fact, told him I didn't think he should grow pot. There were a lot of rednecks in the area, born-again types with JESUS LOVES YOU bumper stickers, etc. One night T. Rex had come home from visiting an old friend in Naples with this bumper sticker on his truck that said JESUS LOVES YOU BUT EVERYBODY ELSE THINKS YOU'RE AN ASSHOLE, which he thought was hilarious. I thought it was pretty funny, too, but I spent the next morning with a pail of hot water and Lestoil rubbing it off his rear bumper. I didn't want him to get shot at—those same Jesus Loves You types always have NRA stickers on the other bumper—and I didn't want any flak at school from my colleagues, some of whom were your basic Jesus Loves You types. One of them, an older woman who taught the learning disabled, had complained to the principal that I didn't wear a bra to school, which was not the truth. Fortunately, the principal was a great guy who was clearly embarrassed to bring the issue up with me and apologized when I said the old biddy was dead wrong and offered to whip off my bra then and there as proof.

On T. Rex's behalf, as I acknowledged in my letter to him, who in their right mind would have imagined that anyone would have taken notice, let alone offense, at three Maxwell House cans with three spindly plants withering away right up close to the back of our mobile home? Which was on ten acres out in the middle of nowhere. T. Rex frequently forgot to water the miserable-looking plants, and they probably would have been dead long ago and none of the legal trouble would have happened if it weren't for me breaking down and watering them now and then, so I guess I was at fault too. I didn't want him spending what little money we had buying dope from friends, and to be completely truthful, I liked to take a couple of tokes at night to unwind after a day of squirming, screaming second graders. I loved teaching kids, but they could take it out of you. We never did find out who turned us in. We figure some would-be drug czar with X-ray vision riding by on a horse must have spotted the plants. All I know is one sweltering afternoon, shortly after school had let out for the year, I was lying on the sofa reading a novel when a loud pounding on the front door startled me. Turned out it was two police officers with a warrant. At first I couldn't even imagine why they were there. When they told me, I burst into tears, panicked I'd lose my job at the school, and the younger of the officers—a real good old boy—said he was sure I hadn't known anything about it and assured me they wouldn't press charges against me. So it was just T. Rex they hauled off to jail.

In jail for two days before we found a lawyer to get him out on bail (which my parents sent me under the guise of an abscessed tooth emergency), T. Rex had a lot of time to practice his *zazen*. He even got his cell mate, a check kiter, interested in practicing with him. Most people were drawn like that to T. Rex. I often tried to convince him he should get a job as a salesman and he did try a couple of times, but there weren't any openings available, or so he was told. Or so he told me. In the end, I found out there were a lot of things T. Rex had not told me. Financial indiscretions primarily. One thing I do believe, even after all this time and tragedy, is that he didn't cheat on me. I believe he loved me. He always swore he did. He just thought that love means as long as you say you're sorry, everything is okay.

One of the things that T. Rex had neglected to tell me about turned up on our doorstep a couple of days after he was released on bail. Her name was Nicole and she was fifteen and looked just like how T. Rex would look if you siphoned off the testosterone. T. Rex had told me all about his first marriage, to his high school sweetheart, and how it had gone sour the way those things do, but he had neglected to mention any offspring. The night she showed up we had a whispered argument about it in our bedroom—she was asleep on the other side of the thin drywall with her Great Dane—and T. Rex swore he had told me about her, but I wasn't buying it. "Believe me," I hissed at him, "this is not the sort of thing that would have slipped my mind." Although it seemed to have slipped his easily enough for the past dozen years. I'd seen all those exposés on "20/20" and "Prime Time Live" about deadbeat dads. Not to mention the kids in my class who were living proof of what that kind of neglect could do—both inside and out. As I told T. Rex, when he started making excuses for himself, there just wasn't any excuse for something like that. What he said was that his ex-wife had married a Cuban chiropractor and moved away, leaving no address. She called once long-distance and said she and Nicole were starting a new life and deserved a clean slate. They were doing just fine, she told him, and he didn't have to worry about them anymore. He could devote his time to worrying about his own life, she said, and he should see this as an opportunity, a second chance to start over unencumbered. "And how did that make you feel?" I shouted in a whisper, not wanting his daughter in the next room to overhear us. "Your *own* daughter."

That's when he told me about the Buddhist concept of "home-leaving": the cutting away of all attachments, both mental and physical. He said it was part of the path to enlightenment. He said he'd felt a lot of pain at first, especially that first Christmas after they'd left, when he went out and spent his paycheck on toys he had no place to send, but he tried to accept the pain as part of his growth. "To give," he said, quoting some old Zen master, "is nonattachment." I couldn't sleep that night for mulling it all over and listening to that big dog of hers shifting and scratching, his metal tags tinkling like restless wind chimes through the thin wall.

I think it was that night, as I lay awake hour after hour until dawn, so exhausted when the birds started twittering outside the window it felt as if they had been inside my head all night, that I started mentally composing my letter to T. Rex. I suppose I sensed things coming to some sort of a head, and I wanted to have thought it all through rationally when the shit hit the fan, in case there was no room for cool reflection in the heat of the moment. Even at the time, I still loved him. At least it felt like I did. It's hard to say now. Back then I had more attachments than a brand-new Hoover. Whenever T. Rex spoke of "nonattachment," I felt this bottomless vacuum yawning inside of me that made me want to reach out and hold on to him with both hands, no matter what. For richer or for poorer, for better or for worse. But once you start writing that letter in your head, you're as good as gone, off in your own private zip code. I see that now.

Once his daughter came to stay with us, I spent so much time adding postscripts to this letter in my head that I gradually stopped speaking. Except for your basic *Please pass the butter*, *Don't forget to turn down the A/C when you leave*, etc. It was not a conscious decision. I didn't even realize it until one night at dinner when T. Rex made some joke to Nicole about my having taken a vow of silence. I said I was just tired, trying to make myself heard above the din of thirty second graders all day. To be sociable I told them what Cory Clinton had said to me during recess that day: "My Daddy lost his car insurance. He drove so fast it fell right off." T. Rex laughed until tears ran down his face and Nicole looked at me expressionlessly, like always, as if she were watching "Star Trek" with the volume turned off.

It turned out she was pregnant. I thought she should get an abortion or at least put the baby up for adoption. She lay in a chaise lounge all day perfecting her tan, expecting me to wait on her hand and foot. Never washed a dish or made a sandwich once in the three weeks she lived with us. How was she going to take care of a baby? But I stayed out of it. I didn't say anything and no one seemed to notice I wasn't saying anything. They were all too busy racking up a two-hundred-dollar phone bill—Nicole, her mother, the boyfriend, and T. Rex, all arguing long-distance, with no thought of waiting until after five when the rates go down, until it was finally decided that Nicole would go back home to Harpers Ferry and marry the boyfriend and have the baby. I kept my mouth shut, but in my mental letter I went on and on for pages about the cycle of poverty, quoting facts and statistics. What I didn't know for sure I made up: *92 percent of all teenage mothers end up on welfare; 68 percent turn to drugs. Only 21 percent of babies born to teenage mothers finish high school.* Knowing T. Rex, he probably just skimmed over that section anyway. In the three years of our marriage I never once saw him read a whole book from cover to cover. He preferred magazines, where he could skip from one article to the next like a bee buzzing from flower to flower. In fact, I think part of what initially attracted him to those Zen books was all the snappy one-liners and haiku, all that white space on the page.

When I got home from work a couple of days later, there was a note on the dinette table from T. Rex saying he was driving Nicole back home to West Virginia and would be back in a couple of days, he'd call me from the road. The trailer felt eerily peaceful. Except for a half-empty bag of dog chow slumped in the corner, it was as if I'd dreamed the whole visitation. But the moment of tranquillity was just that, a moment, before it hit me that T. Rex was violating his probation. Those three half-dead marijuana plants had turned out to constitute a felony, and the lawyer had managed to cut a deal for a fine, plus court costs, plus two years probation during which T. Rex had to visit his parole officer once a month and had to apply for permission to leave the county, let alone the state.

I was beyond anger at that point, well into a deep fatalism. When the phone rang late that night I didn't answer it. Whatever it was, wherever he was, I figured I was better off not knowing. I got into bed with our wedding album and looked at the pictures for a long time. We looked happy and optimistic. In his white tux T. Rex looked handsome—tall and sturdy—yet gentle with his halo of soft brown hair and warm smile. Like a palm tree. All that hard muscle had gone soft in the past couple of years since he hadn't been doing much physical labor. He didn't believe in exercise for the sake of exercise and made tired jokes about Jane Fonda whenever he saw me doing my sit-ups and leg lifts. In the shot of us cutting the wedding cake, I was looking up at him, eyes shining, as if I really looked up to him. My gray-haired parents were sitting there in the background looking dubious, as if, in their minds, they had already fast-forwarded past the good times to what came next. My Dad, who had paid for the whole affair, was probably thinking about what a bad investment it was.

The next afternoon I was not really all that surprised when Vivian from the principal's office appeared at the door of my classroom and said I had an emergency long-distance call. I was in the middle of reading them *Koko's Kitten*, my favorite kid's book, about the gorilla at Stanford who demanded a kitten for her birthday. I handed the class over to Vivian and cut across the empty playground to the office. The sun was shining brightly and I told myself there was a faint possibility this wasn't bad news, maybe it was Ed McMahon calling to tell me I was rich and our troubles were over.

The highway patrol said it was a miracle he wasn't killed. The truck crashed through a guardrail and rolled over twice. In an effort to save money on a motel, T. Rex had driven straight through the night and fallen asleep on I-95, twenty miles or so outside of Raleigh, where he was planning on stopping for break-fast. The good news was he walked away with only a few scratches and a dislocated collarbone. The bad news was his parole officer issued a warrant for his arrest, and T. Rex was sen-tenced to ninety days in jail. While he was serving his time, what was left of the truck was repossessed.

When I hung up the phone in the principal's office after talk-ing to T. Rex that afternoon of the accident, I was still clutching *Koko's Kitten* in my hands. I looked down at the cover, a photo-graph of Koko cradling the little gray kitten in her huge leathery palm, and the more I stared at the gorilla, the more it reminded me of T. Rex: large and gentle but capable of mass destruction.

The lawyer got the ninety days reduced to forty-five. Still, that gave me plenty of time alone to think. Three weeks before T. Rex was due to be released, I wrote out the letter I had been car-rying around in my head for months. It came out to thirteen pages, single-spaced with small handwriting, on yellow lined legal paper. I had been composing and editing in my head for so long that I didn't need to copy it over; it flowed from my head to my hand clear and neat on the first try. After I had proofread the letter and sealed it in an envelope, I felt light-headed, literally light-headed, as if I'd suddenly shed a couple of pounds of gray matter. As if each of those words weighed something. The next morning on my way to school I stopped at the post office and mailed the letter to T. Rex in jail. I wanted to give him as much time as possible to make some plans, like where and how he was going to live when he was released, and to adjust to the idea of his new life without me.

A couple of days later I got a call from T. Rex in jail saying he had read my letter and wanted to talk to me. I had been staying away because I was afraid that the sight of him in his cell would cause me to break down, weaken my resolve. Because the thing about T. Rex was that he didn't have a mean bone in his body. Which was maybe why he was such a perfect victim; there wasn't an ounce of aggression in him. "T. Rex" was a misnomer. Actually he was more like one of those big, benign-looking plant eaters—brontosaurs or hadrosaurs—that my second-grade girls were always drawing pictures of while the boys went for the meat eaters every time. As a young boy he had kept bees as part of a 4-H project. And the one time we visited his real mother, in Ohio, shortly after our wedding, she showed me two grayish photographs of Tommy, as she called him, with his bees. One of him standing behind a table with some jars of honey holding a second-prize ribbon, and one of him naked to the waist, arms outstretched, his skinny arms and torso freckled with bees, smiling a gap-toothed smile. Just looking at it made my flesh crawl. In neat white ink his mother had written this corny caption that said *Suffer the little bees to come unto me*.

Sunday afternoon was visiting hours. He had asked me to bring him some books that were in a box in our bedroom closet. They were all about Buddhism—some old and yellowed from his defunct and erratic college career (*Essays in Zen Buddhism* by D. T. Suzuki, *The Lazy Man's Guide to Enlightenment*, *The Autobiography of a Yogi*) and a couple that looked newer, which he must have bought more recently. On the way there I stopped at Food Lion and picked up a bag of dried papaya, his favorite, and half a dozen candy bars. Next I drove to the drive-up window at Sun Bank, and while I was waiting in line I picked up *Zen Mind, Beginner's Mind*, flipped it open randomly, and read: "Ashes do not come back to firewood. Ash is ash." The guy in the car behind me honked and I tossed the book aside and inched up to the bank window and whizzed my check through the pneumatic tube. While I was sitting there waiting for the teller to zap it back, I thought about the lines I had read and how true they were. They seemed to be speaking about our marriage, and I thought about how if T. Rex tried to give me any shit about how we should give it another shot, I would refer him to that passage. Then I drove to the jail.

When he walked into the visiting room I might not have recognized him except for his height. He had lost a lot of weight— as if he were on a hunger strike—and shaved his head. He looked like a cross between Michael Jordan and Gandhi. His blue eyes had that super wide-awake look of a baby's, and when he looked at me it was like a beam of bright clear light. I found myself squinting and wishing I could put on my dark glasses. He thanked me for the books and the food. I asked him how he was doing and he said he was doing fine. "I hate seeing you in here," I told him.

He shrugged and said, "No snowflake falls in an inappropriate place. Right, Ed?" He smiled and winked at the guard, a young guy with huge red-tipped ears, who nodded and smiled back, as if embarrassed to be eavesdropping.

Ever since I sent it I had been worrying about what T. Rex was going to say about my letter and worrying about what I was going to say back to him, but five, ten minutes went by and he didn't even mention it. I had assumed he'd asked me to come visit so as to change my mind, to beg for a reprieve, but he seemed perfectly content to sit in silence and look at me. It made me nervous. Finally I said, "Did you read my letter?"

He nodded and took my hand. "Don't cry, honey," he said gently, enfolding me in his big arms. I glanced over at the guard, who was pretending not to notice. Another one of T. Rex's converts.

"Almost five years," I choked out. "Don't you even feel sad?" I felt as if my heart were being crushed like a walnut. He let go of me, tore open the bag of dried papaya with his teeth and offered me one, as if he were offering me some really precious gift, as if he'd completely forgotten that I was the one who had given them to him in the first place. I shook my head and waved it away. "Bottom line," he said, popping a slice into his mouth, "life is suffering."

"You don't know what suffering is," I told him, "until you've been married to you!" Then I scraped my chair against the linoleum, stood up, and stormed out.

That was the last thing I ever said to him.

The drive home took over an hour. I'd forgotten to bring my cassette carrier and there was only one loose tape lying on the floor of the car without its case. I picked it up and shoved it in the tape player. As if on cue, Van Morrison started singing about enlightenment—*Chop that wood, light that fire/Carry water/ What's the sound of one hand clapping?* T. Rex used to walk around humming the song under his breath. I snapped it off and punched all the radio buttons until I found Patsy Cline. I breathed a big sigh of relief and turned the volume up as she sang her heart out about falling to pieces every time some bastard of a former boyfriend walked by. "Time only adds to the pain," she wailed so loud the car windows rattled, and I wailed along with her. I'd always loved Patsy Cline and now I knew why: she didn't know the meaning of the word *nonattachment*.

When I got back home, the sun was setting. As I walked toward the trailer I noticed an unusual number of bees flying around the yard, and I swatted at a few with my free arm, which was not holding the bag of groceries I'd picked up at Food Lion earlier that morning. Fumbling with my keys, I opened the door, walked inside, set my purse and grocery bag on the dinette table, and then I saw them. The setting sun was illuminating the west window, where the kitchen was, and the window appeared to be *moving*. There must have been ten thousand bees crawling and buzzing against the glass, like something out of a horror movie. A shudder ran through me as I hurried over and reached for the wand to shut the miniblinds, and that's when I realized that the bees were on the *inside* of the window, trying to get out. It was a bad moment. A bad moment that got worse when I turned around and saw the other three windows in the living area similarly dark and swarming, backlit by the fiery glow of the sun's rays low in the sky. There was something surreal about it. I felt panic rising, but for some reason the bees seemed oblivious to me, so instead of running away I just forced myself to sit down on the sofa and think. I knew these bees were some sort of sign sent to tell me something I needed to know. A test. I thought about that old photograph of T. Rex and the bees at his mother's house, smiling that gap-toothed smile, as if he were too smart or too stupid to be scared.

Once the sun set, the bees stopped their agitated buzzing and seemed to fall into some sort of still, quiet trance. Cautiously, I got up off the sofa and dialed the local police department, not knowing what else to do, and asked if anyone in the vicinity had reported a similar occurrence and whether anyone could help me. I wasn't surprised when the officer said there had been no reports of any unusual bee activity in the area. I was afraid that maybe he'd think I was just some crazy lady, but he seemed courteous enough and offered to call another police officer who was a part-time beekeeper and call me right back. I thanked him and went back to the sofa to wait.

It turned out that a beekeeper in the neighboring town of Gardner had somehow allowed his swarm to escape and they had made a beeline to my place, three miles away. The beekeeper himself called to apologize. He instructed me to spray the bees with insecticide while they were dozing and promised he would be over first thing in the morning to help. I did as he said and swept up a mountain of dead bees, which I dumped in the trash out back, feeling guilty, like maybe I should bury them instead. Then I went back inside and slammed the windows shut over the old torn window screens, which I had been after T. Rex to mend ever since we moved into the place, almost three years ago.

I was tired and went to bed early. It was stuffy in the trailer with the windows closed tight and I set the fan on the dresser in our bedroom. My bedroom. For the first time it really struck me that it was over. T. Rex wouldn't be coming back and I would be all alone again. In the middle of nowhere. I decided to go to the pound on Monday after work and get myself a big calm, devoted dog. Somehow the thought of that dog, which I'd already named Koko, made me cry even harder. I could see her lying at the foot of the bed looking at me with sad brown eyes, asking me what was wrong, whimpering empathetically. I wondered if it was even fair to afflict such an emotional basket case on an animal; maybe I wasn't fit company for a dog. Finally, exhausted from the day's ordeals, I must have sunk into a deep sleep because when the phone rang sometime after midnight, I woke up disoriented—suspended in some nameless, placeless, timeless fog—and it took a moment for the vital statistics to snap into place as I fumbled for the receiver on the end table next to T. Rex's side of the bed.

When has the phone ringing in the middle of the night ever been good news? Still, there's the sort of bad news you half expect and then there's the other sort. The sort that nobody in their right mind could ever imagine, let alone expect. The sort that elevates you from nobody to somebody on the evening news.

It was the warden. T. Rex was dead, he told me in such a roundabout, euphemistic way that at first I thought he was telling me that T. Rex had been transferred to some nicer jail up north somewhere. Finally, as the terrible truth began to emerge through the fog of the warden's words, I interrupted him. "You aren't saying he's *dead?*" And as the warden reluctantly said that's in fact what he was saying, I snapped on the light and screamed when I caught sight of a dead bee lying on the pillow next to mine. I must have fainted then because when I came to, I was lying on the carpet with the phone buzzing in my hand next to my ear and someone pounding on my front door.

The facts were slow in coming, but what happened was this: T. Rex had somehow managed to get hold of a small can of lighter fluid and had sprinkled his clothes with it and used a Bic lighter to set himself on fire, sitting cross-legged on his bunk, like those Buddhist monks in Saigon back during the Vietnam War. The young guard with the big ears had smelled the smoke and rushed in and wrapped him in a blanket, but it was too late. He died in the ambulance on the way to the hospital. Later, when I went to pick up his effects, the warden gave me a scrap of paper torn out of a book that they had found taped to the cell wall next to his

bunk: *When you do something, you should do something completely,
like a good bonfire, leaving no trace of yourself. —Shunryu Suzuki*

Needless to say, I was in shock. Stunned. We all were. I think
it made us all—even T. Rex's father—see him in a new light. You
couldn't help but feel some sort of awe. Nicole, four months
pregnant, flew down for the funeral wearing a loose black sundress. In the bright sunlight, from certain angles, you could just
barely discern the pale waxing moon of her firm little belly.
Outside the chapel I overheard her telling a reporter from the
Sarasota Herald that she planned to name the baby either Rex or
Rexanna after her father, whom she now seemed to see as some
sort of saint or martyr. Inside, during the service, she held one of
the cousins' fussy infant twins in her lap, cuddling and cooing
him into a contented silence. I was surprised by how tender and
maternal she was with that baby; I wouldn't have known she had
it in her. But then, I wouldn't have known T. Rex had it in him to
do something like this. Something so breathtaking.

Among his effects that I brought home from the jail was the
small stack of books he had asked me to bring him the last time I
saw him. Feeling too fragile and distracted to deal with rowdy
and morbidly curious second graders, I took an indefinite leave
of absence from my job and sat at home reading. At first I paid
special attention to the lines he had underlined or starred, even
copying them onto a notepad, as if we were having a conversation with me asking the questions and then searching through
the marked texts for his answers. But after a while, the second or
third time through, I began to make some faint marks of my
own. Tentative questions or comments in the margins. I suppose,
at first, I was just trying to find out why he did it. But after a
while I started to forget about him and started to read for myself.
It seemed clear to me that regardless of whether or not T. Rex
had got it all wrong, there was a lot there in those books that was
worth knowing—or "unknowing," as they said. So I drove to a
spiritual bookstore in Sarasota and bought myself a round black
pillow, a *zafu*, and I started to sit. Just sit and follow my breath.
With my dog, Koko, sitting there next to me, calm and content
in her Buddha nature.

It is an amazing feeling just to sit still for once and watch my thoughts, like bees in a hive—buzzing, buzzing, buzzing. And as the days pass, there are moments now and then when the buzzing ceases and there is just the breath, the same breath I used to watch entering and leaving my husband's lungs as I lay there beside him in the thin moonlight, worrying. I still don't know what to think of what he did. And each day I think and know even less. Something I see as a good sign.

As I told my principal when he called to ask how I was doing and when I thought I might be able to start teaching again: "To know what we do not know is the beginning of wisdom" (Maha Sathavira Sangharakshita). He let that pass and said to let him know if there was anything I needed. He even offered to mow the grass. He seemed anxious to help and disappointed when I declined. There was a little silence and then a sigh on his end. "Well," he said, "I hope you'll be back soon." I thanked him and said I hoped so too. Even though I figure it will be a long time before I can see my way clear to standing at the front of a classroom, teaching anybody anything.

A month after our daughter's sudden death, I came home from work one afternoon and found the house empty. There was a one-line note from my wife on the kitchen table saying that she had decided to take a trip back to Crete, Nebraska. I was dumbfounded. Not only had she not been back to her home-town since she'd left at the age of eleven, but over the years she had steadfastly and stubbornly refused my suggestions that we return for a visit. In those early days of our marriage I'd been hell-bent on playing resident shrink and believed that it would be healthy for her to see the place again—to demythologize it, as it were. But even when we were moving from Berkeley to Madison, driving cross-country on Route 80, she had violently vetoed my suggestion that we take the twenty-minute detour. Sensing my slightly petulant disappointment, she'd said to drop her off in downtown Lincoln—she'd browse through the shops while I took a drive out to Crete and satisfied my morbid curiosity once and for all. I was tempted but shrugged off her suggestion, argu-ing that *she* was the one who should see the place, not me. In truth, I think I was a little afraid to go alone. Even though ratio-nally I knew that whatever there was to see was in the past and only my wife could see that. Still, years later, reading her brisk, businesslike note, I felt profoundly gypped. As if, after all my years of urging and waiting, she had sailed off to the lighthouse without me.

The note did not say how she was getting there. I had a sudden vivid image of her boarding the plane in the faded flannel nightgown she had worn day and night for the past month— since changing out of the black suit she'd worn to the funeral— her long hair straggling down her back uncombed, the other passengers giving her wide berth. Ophelia flies the friendly skies. Taking a few steps down the hall, I was relieved to find the familiar pink nightgown drowning in a puddle of water on the bathroom floor. She had taken a shower. I took that at least as a good sign. Then I walked back down the hallway and opened the garage door. Clutching the damp nightgown, I sat in the driver's seat of my wife's old Honda Civic like some psychic searching for telepathic clues.

That night I couldn't sleep. I went to bed early, tired from grading British Lit blue books, or perhaps I was just tired *of* grading blue books, because I lay there tossing and turning, restless in the bleak dawn, until finally I fell asleep for a few minutes and dreamed I was driving through wheat fields. Literally. There was no highway. The car just skimmed along, effortlessly ploughing through the graceful undulating wheat—the agrarian version of the parting of the Red Sea. When I woke up, the first sunlight was just trembling through the blinds and I imagined how it would be out on the interstate with the early morning sun at my back—bright and spacious and fast—and suddenly I knew it was the thing to do. It seemed that my wife had planned it this way, testing me. Together we would go back to the moment, the accursed spot, and then we would start over again, fresh. An exorcism of sorts. I leapt out of bed. It was a ten-hour drive from Madison to Crete. My classes were over for the semester, and there was nothing to prevent me from throwing a small suitcase in the car and following my wife. I could be there by suppertime.

Before I left the house, I turned down the thermostat in the hallway and then paused for a moment outside Lyddie's closed door, my hand paralyzed on the doorknob. It seemed to me I could hear her breathing in there, but I could not bring myself to open the door. As I walked outside to my car, I had the uneasy sense that I was forgetting something, something important, and as I sat in the car waiting for the motor to warm up, I thought of all the times I had complained about the hassle of finding babysitters, of being tied down and unable to take off for New York or Katmandu on the spur of the moment (as if I ever had). And as I backed out of the quiet driveway, I remembered a painful scene with a new baby-sitter—Lyddie wrapping herself like a boa constrictor around my leg, sobbing histrionically and shouting "Don't go, Daddy, don't leave me!" as I resolutely headed toward the front door, dragging her along with me. It had taken all three adults to pry her loose and carry her howling to her bedroom. I apologized to the shaken baby-sitter, raising my voice to be heard over my daughter's muffled but persistent wailing. In the car my wife, also shaken, suggested that maybe we should stay home, see the movie or play—I don't even remember now—another evening, since Lyddie seemed so distraught. I'd pounded the steering wheel and said no, she had to learn. What kind of monstrous adult would she grow into if we always gave in to her? My wife had reluctantly agreed that I was right and we had gone off to wherever we were going that night. When we got back home, the baby-sitter was peacefully watching TV and assured us that Lyddie had stopped crying as soon as we'd left and the two of them had "gotten along famously." Smiling, I had turned to my wife and said, "See?" But now, of course, these are the moments that haunt me. I wish I could run the tape backward, like a home movie. There I am walking backward toward the house. There I am lifting Lyddie up off her bed, bringing her back out to the living room, holding her in my arms.

The morning had been clear and crisp in Wisconsin, cold bright sunshine reflecting off the thin hard crust of snow, but just east of Omaha the sky bleached to bone and it began to snow lightly, a few flurries every now and then. I felt myself tensing as I fiddled with the windshield wipers and negotiated the rush hour traffic after miles and miles of open country. I suppose the tension might also have had something to do with my nearness to my destination. The questions I had been ignoring for the past ten or eleven hours seemed to be waving their hands wildly in my brain like overeager students demanding to be called on. How would I find my wife? Would she be glad to see me? Was this really such a good idea? I passed a billboard for Boys Town and remembered that old movie with Spencer Tracy as the priest and Mickey Rooney as the orphaned kid, or maybe it was Jackie Cooper. *Boys Town.* The name seemed so quaint, so wholesome and midwestern. I was surprised the place still existed. Then it occurred to me that if my wife had been a boy, maybe that's where she would have ended up. I felt a sudden coldness and moved the car heater up a notch.

My wife I will call Jane Jones. Even with a false name some readers may recognize the details of her life or at least vaguely remember having read something in the newspapers years ago. Particularly if they were in or around Nebraska in the late fifties. Which I wasn't. I was busy riding my souped-up two-wheeler in the unblinking Southern California sunshine. I had a paper route during the year that my future wife's tragedy was reported in the news, and I always get a little cosmic chill when I think of myself blissfully, ignorantly flinging those rolled-up papers, like so many diplomas, onto our neighbors' neatly tended lawns. Both my parents, high school teachers, were avid newspaper readers and sometimes I try to imagine just what I might have been doing on that early June evening while they were busy reading about the grisly fate of my future in-laws. It is the split-screen contrast that gets me: the idea that while I could have been nursing a Popsicle, watching "Dragnet," fighting with my younger brother over some minor territorial trespass or pleading with my mother to let me stay up an hour later, my future wife—age eleven, a year younger than I—was surrounded by actual homicide detectives who offered her sticks of Black Jack gum and refused to let her go inside her own house, where everyone was dead.

My wife has never shared my "morbid," as she deems it, fascination with her past. The first and most deadly fight we ever had was over this very issue. Shortly after our first anniversary, she stormed out of a party one night, leaving me to find my own ride home, and later accused me of "putting her on public display like some freak in a freak show." She had overheard me telling one of her piano students' parents about the murders, even though she had sworn me to secrecy. "You didn't marry *me*," she screamed. "You married *In Cold Blood*!" She'd had it, she swore. I was on probation. And I knew she meant it. I apologized abjectly and swore to keep my mouth shut, it would never happen again. And it never did. Even when the topic of conversation, as it not infrequently does in these times, turned to the latest sensational murder, I would look over at my wife and dutifully change the subject to something bland and boring.

In the meantime, I generously allowed my wife to commandeer my own "Leave It to Beaver" childhood. From time to time at some cocktail party or backyard barbecue, I have been startled to overhear her casually relating a small anecdote from my childhood as if it were her own. The anecdotes are usually rather dull and ordinary, which is, of course, precisely what charms her about them, and the listener usually looks mildly bored and impatient, having grown up safe and sound in the suburbs himself. I can never help imagining how his expression would change from polite boredom to impolite avid curiosity if my wife were suddenly to tell him the real story. To tell him how she'd been sleeping over at a neighbor friend's house when they heard all the commotion and saw all the police cars. How they ran out onto the front lawn in their baby doll pajamas, and the first thing my wife saw was Bobby Axelrod, her sister Marjorie's recently spurned boyfriend, seventeen, being dragged toward a squad car, all handcuffed and bloody. How she'd had a little sister's crush on Bobby who, unlike Marjorie, had always treated her nicely when their mother said, "And take your little sister along." How he'd gallantly bought her ice cream at the roller rink or popcorn at the movies while Margie alternated between yelling at her and pretending she didn't exist. So how her first thought on seeing Bobby like that was there'd been some accident and he'd hurt himself. How she shouted out his name, and as she ran across the street before the police could grab hold of her, he sort of smiled and winked at her and tried to wave, just as if nothing special had gone on in there. How they could all hear the dog, Taffy, barking shrilly in the backyard, hurtling itself against the chain-link fence, and hearing the dog, how she suddenly started to cry. And best of all, how as Bobby passed her, flanked by two policemen twice his size, he twisted his head back in her direction and said, "I'm real glad you weren't home."

*   *   *

It was dark by the time I reached Lincoln. Somewhere on the open, rolling stretch of highway between Omaha and Lincoln, I got cold feet; I decided to postpone my arrival in Crete until the following morning. The snow was starting to fall more heavily and steadily, sticking to the asphalt. The radio weatherman was predicting a foot or more before morning. I was tired now from all the driving and didn't know if there was even a motel in Crete. The car slid and fishtailed at the red light, jolting me into wide-awakeness. In the distance, through the lace curtain of snow, I could see the capitol building, beckoning like a lighthouse to a weary sailor. Cautiously, I headed downtown in search of food and shelter. I checked into the Cornhusker Hotel, took a long hot shower, and then made my way down to the dining room for dinner. As I passed the reservations desk, I noticed that a small crowd had gathered, dripping snow onto the carpet and talking among themselves about the blizzard. Seated at a quiet corner table for two next to the window, I looked out onto the deserted street and watched the sudden gusts of snow shivering against the plate glass. As I watched the parked cars vanish under a blanket of white, I wondered where my wife was and what she was doing at that moment. In my split-screen imagination, I saw her sitting at another table in another restaurant not far away, watching the snow, slowly sipping a single glass of red wine. And as I picked up my glass of house burgundy, I had the eerie sensation that our movements were synchronized.

After dinner, I headed moodily back up to my room. On the elevator with me were a husband and wife and their small blonde daughter. The sleeping girl, swaddled in a fuzzy pink blanket, was slung over the man's shoulder limp as a large rag doll. The wife reached over with a crumpled Kleenex from her coat pocket and wiped something red and sticky off a strand of her daughter's pale hair. The elevator doors opened and the family got off on the third floor. I could hear them arguing about which direction their room was in as the doors slid shut again, and I continued my ascent alone. Back in my room, changing into my pajamas, I was suddenly seized by a terrible jealous rage toward the man in the elevator—as if this man had butted in front of me in line and managed to finagle something that should, by all rights, have been mine—and I wanted to protest bitterly, to complain to whomever was in charge. I wanted to pick up the phone and dial the manager and through the sheer logic and poetry of my justifiable complaint, get the whole sorry mess straightened out. I imagined handing over Lyddie, still wrapped in that fuzzy pink cocoon, to my wife, who always cringed whenever I complained about poor service. "See?" I would say. "You have to speak up. You can't take these things lying down."

The next morning, after a quick cup of coffee and bowl of cornflakes, I checked out of the hotel. Snowplows had been working through the night. As I headed out of town toward Route 77 South, the sun was glittering off the powdery snow, the sky was baby-blanket blue, and for entire seconds I would experience a sort of false happiness, a mirage of happiness brought on by the perfect day and the exhilarating motion. For a moment, I would hum to myself, forgetting who I was and where I was going. For a moment I was a college kid, one of my students, en route to Aspen or Sun Valley for a ski trip. Then I would remember, I would remind myself. And if I didn't remind myself, something else would. On the outskirts of Lincoln, I passed by the Nebraska State Penitentiary. A concrete wall with guard towers surrounded the stark brick building. I looked for guards armed with rifles, but the towers appeared to be empty. Even though last we heard Bobby Axelrod had been transferred to some prison in Iowa, I imagined him right here. The car seemed to slow down of its own volition as I watched the penitentiary recede in the rearview mirror and pictured Axelrod sitting at a long cafeteria table or doing calisthenics in the yard like movie prisoners. My mental picture was clear even though I'd never actually seen a picture of Bobby Axelrod. If there'd been any in the three family albums my wife had inherited, they had been removed. I suspected that her Aunt Rosemary had gone through and plucked out any disturbing photos before handing the albums over to her niece, but, unlike my own Kodak-mad family, the "Joneses" weren't much for photography and it's entirely possible there never were any snapshots of Margie and Bobby.

From Route 77, I took 33 west to Crete. I had forgotten how flat it was out here, flat as a dinner table covered with a snowy white linen tablecloth, or a vast empty stage. This road was not so well cleared. I slowed to well below the speed limit, following a safe distance behind a battered pickup. After miles of white nothing, we passed a GM dealership and a big furniture store. Out there in the middle of that lunar landscape, they seemed like relics from some defunct civilization. But shortly thereafter, things picked up. An Alpo plant, a small boarded-up motel, houses. CRETE, population 4,872. Two intersecting blocks of small shops and restaurants, a couple of banks, the library, the newspaper office, Heidi and Harold's Cafe, the Alibi Lounge—all laid out as neat and square as a Monopoly board. At the end of Main Street I could see the Crete Mills and what I took to be silos towering over the prevailing flatness. No sign of the Maidenform bra factory where my wife's father had been a super-intendent. One of the few facts my wife freely offered about her childhood. Imagine, she'd say, how warping for a young girl to have to say out loud in public that her father worked at a brassiere factory.

I didn't have much of a game plan, I now realized. I suppose I'd imagined simply bumping into my wife on the street or find-ing her registered at some cozy little bed-and-breakfast, although it now seemed apparent that there was no such place. But, still, the town was no bigger than the town I had imagined, and I had every faith that I would find her because I knew that she was waiting for me to find her. We had been married for nearly fif-teen years. I had the sense that she knew exactly what I was going to do, was orchestrating my movements just as surely as if she'd drawn me a map.

My first destination was the house. No doubt almost anyone on the street could have pointed me to my wife's family's house— even kids too young to have been alive when it happened—but I preferred to find it myself. I remembered the name of the street, Forest Avenue, because a realtor in Madison had once taken my wife and me to look at a beautiful old house on Forest Avenue, just the sort of house we'd always wanted, but my wife had refused to get out of the car when she saw the street sign. The older residential section of Crete seemed to be back out in the direction I'd come from. I drove methodically—up each street and down the next—Juniper, Ivy, Oak—solid old two-story houses with a few newer fifties-style bungalows mixed in, neatly shoveled walkways, an occasional Santa's sleigh or makeshift nativity scene, white wood churches, brick churches, an elementary school with no kids in sight. The streets widened, the terrain sloped upward, the houses grew larger, and suddenly there it was—on the corner. I recognized it immediately from the photographs in my wife's albums. The house had been painted yellow instead of white, but it was otherwise the same. The same shutters, the same wraparound porch, the same chain-link fence erected to keep the dog, Taffy, from being run over. Only superimposed over the bare trees and snow-shrouded shrubs was a picture of green leaves and grass and vivid flowerbeds, the way I remembered it from the photo albums. In the albums, it was eternal summertime in the exterior shots; the winter snapshots, the annual Christmas gift-opening scenes, were always indoors, shot with a cheap flash camera that made everyone's eyes glow red, like demons in a horror film. I parked across the street and sat there staring, waiting for it to hit me—this was it, the cursed spot—but it looked so unremarkable, so snug and well tended. Bright curtains on all the windows, a wisp of smoke drifting from the chimney, a holly wreath hanging on the front door. I felt disappointed, let down. I suppose I had expected to see peeling paint, sagging steps, broken glass, doors banging in the wind, cobwebs and bats—a haunted house. The Bates Motel. As I sat there watching, a large orange cat leapt on top of the sofa and stared out at me, blinking in the bright sunshine. My wife was allergic to cats.

The next stop on my mental itinerary was Aunt Rosemary's place in Beatrice (pronounced Bee-at-trice), which, according to the map I'd checked at breakfast that morning, was only twenty or so miles south on 103. I looked at my watch and decided to grab a quick lunch before heading back out onto the highway. It had begun to snow again, a light confectioner's dusting. With the perfect snow and the chamber of commerce Christmas decorations suspended like tinsel tightropes across Main Street, downtown Crete looked like the set of *It's a Wonderful Life*.

It was early for the lunch crowd and the Sportsman's Grill was nearly empty except for a few old-timers sitting in the booths, hunched over cups of Sanka. I slid into a booth about midway down the dusky aisle. When the waitress appeared, I ordered a cheeseburger and a Coke. To pass the time until my food arrived, I was skimming through the song titles on the tabletop jukebox when two women and a man bustled past, their winter coats emitting clouds of cold air, and settled in the booth across from mine and up one. The two women slid into opposite sides of the booth while the man hung their coats on some pegs. Then the man slid in next to the woman with her back toward me. All three ordered black coffee. The waitress brought my food and I eavesdropped as I ate. The couple was buying a house—apparently they'd just put in a bid on some place that morning—and the other woman was their realtor. She reminded me of someone, someone whose face I couldn't place, but then the older I got everyone looked familiar; a truly original face was as rare as a truly original idea; every semester I seemed to be lecturing to the same impervious faces. The man was a nervous wreck—tapping his silverware and twitching around in his chair like some hyperactive child. The real estate agent noticed me staring and flashed me a big smile, as if to assure me that everything was perfectly all right, couldn't in fact be any better. The moment she smiled, I recognized her. Some shutter clicked and I could visualize the wavy-edged snapshots in my wife's photo albums with the neat, cramped captions: *Janie and Betsy, First Communion, 1955. Janie and Betsy, Bathing Beauties, 1956.* And so on. The two of them seemingly inseparable. In the last snapshot—*Chang and Eng, Halloween, 1958*—they had actually bound their arms and legs together with twine and, an inspired touch, braided their long hair into a single thick plait, an exotic copper and platinum snake. The one time I'd asked my wife whatever happened to Betsy, she'd shrugged and said they'd lost touch when she—my wife—left Nebraska.

Stunned, I sat there mute and motionless as my wife's childhood friend swooped up the bill and the man retrieved their coats. She was coming toward me, still talking, not even seeing me, and then just as she passed by my booth, my hand shot out and I cleared my throat. She paused, startled, with a half-friendly smile on her face. "Excuse me," I said, "but I couldn't help over-hearing you. I'm new here and might be interested in some prop-erty. I was wondering if you've got a card you could give me."

"No card," she said, smiling more broadly. "But the name's Betsy Beemis and I'm with Ace Realty, just a couple doors down. You interested in residential or commercial?"

"Residential."

The couple with her shuffled impatiently.

"I got to run, I'm afraid, but give me a call later on"—she paused as if mentally flipping through an appointment book— "say about four, four-thirty—and I'll be happy to help you. Your name's?"

"Jones," I said. "Paul Jones."

She reached out and shook my hand. "Welcome to Crete, Mr. Jones. Crete's a nice friendly little town. Safe, quiet. You got kids?"

I gripped my coffee cup and shook my head no. "Just my wife and me."

Her smile faded a little, as if she sensed she'd somehow hit the wrong note. "Well, see you later then, I hope?"

"Definitely."

I turned to watch her leave and then turned back to my lunch. My half-eaten cheeseburger was floating in a pool of rusty blood, already half congealed. I shoved the plate aside and tossed my napkin over it, repulsed, wishing I'd ordered the grilled cheese instead. I rarely ate meat. My wife was a strict vegetarian. When I met her, she shopped only at health food co-ops and her kitchen cupboards were full of strange-smelling bags of unfamil-iar teas, spices, and grains. She seemed to subsist on handfuls of raw crunchy stuff. I kidded her about her Squirrel Diet and she kidded me about my Elementary School Lunch Diet—Kraft macaroni and cheese, hot dogs, canned chili. But even though I teased her about it, I was attracted by her idiosyncratic purity. When we met I saw right away that she was not like the other young women I'd known: she was stripped clean of all the baser emotions, like bone purified by fire, all the fat and gristle singed away. Before I ever managed to maneuver my way inside, I knew just what her apartment would look like: spare, modest, bare white walls, a single mattress on the floor. The mattress, as it turned out, was covered in crisp white sheets the likes of which I had not seen since leaving my parents' house. After we started sleeping together, I took to calling her "Saint Jane."

The waitress sidled over, refilled my coffee cup, and slid my plate away. "How was everything?" she asked a bit aggressively, eyeing my half-eaten sandwich.

"Fine," I assured her. "Guess I wasn't as hungry as I thought."

Mollified, she smiled and wagged a flirtatious finger at me. "You're a bad boy."

The waitress's facetious remark seemed to hang in the air after she'd gone, like some Delphic insight into my essential, unalterable nature. And she was right: I was a bad boy. I had thought at first that my wife's goodness would rub off on me and I would become a better, more generous and compassionate individual, but in fact the opposite had occurred. Balanced precariously on the edge of that single mattress covered with those chaste and snowy percales, I would try to lead her into temptation, try to make her say something petty and catty about some mutual acquaintance—a former lover, say—but she would only look uncomfortable and retreat into a noble silence. It was as if she, with her stubborn goodness, had created a deficit of spite that I was forced to balance out. It all backfired. None of it worked out the way I'd hoped. My original hazy intention was that I, a callow catastrophe-less child of the suburbs, would marry into this tragedy of my wife's and thus attain the status of tragic hero—like a foreigner marrying to achieve American citizenship—and all without actually having to shed any tears or break any skin, so to speak. I guess you could say I wanted *to have suffered* but I did not actually want *to suffer.* The actual suffering itself I would just as soon skip. I was no masochist. I just wanted—I don't know what precisely—something she seemed to have that I didn't. Some charisma possessed by the extraordinarily fortunate and unfortunate of this world.

The coffee had swelled my bladder. I got up and walked back

to the men's room. On the way back out, I caught sight of a pay
phone. I dug a fistful of change out of my pocket and dialed our
number in Madison, just in case she'd already done whatever it
was she'd come to do and gone back home, expecting to find me
there waiting for her. I let it ring and ring, picturing first the wall
phone in the kitchen and then the princess phone on the night
table by our bed. When I hung up finally, a sudden strong gust of
depression hit me. Maybe she didn't want me to find her after all.
Maybe I had it all wrong. I thought about going to the police station, filing a missing persons report, but somehow it seemed like
a mistake. I knew my wife wouldn't like it. I could see the
reproach in her eyes, as if she were sitting across the table from
me. *But what was I supposed to do?* I'd say. *I was worried about you.*
Tomorrow morning, I told myself. If I haven't found her by
tomorrow morning, I'll go to the police. On that decisive note, I
walked back up front to the cashier. Sitting next to some miniature peppermint patties on the counter was one of those dona-
tion cans for Muscular Dystrophy with a glossy picture of Jerry
Lewis and some little girl all dressed to kill in pink ruffles and leg
braces. I'd always hated Jerry Lewis, thought he was a real
unfunny idiot, but when the cashier handed me back my change,
I stuffed it into the can, almost five dollars. For no good reason.
My little girl had died of something else—spinal meningitis—a
disease that didn't even have its own movie star.

At four o'clock I was standing on the street in front of Ace
Realty, pacing. I had spent an unproductive afternoon driving out
to Beatrice only to discover, from a neighbor lady, that Aunt
Rosemary was now living in a nursing home outside of Denver
near one of her sons. Then I'd driven back to Crete and spent a
couple of hours hunched over a microfiche machine at the public
library, reading and rereading the newspaper accounts of the
murders, glancing guiltily over my shoulder to make sure my
wife wasn't watching. There was a prom photo of Margie and
Bobby Axelrod so close to the one I'd always imagined that it
gave me the chills: Bobby in a white tux, smiling self-consciously,
like a bad actor, standing at attention next to Marjorie in her stiff

full-skirted dress, a crushed gardenia drooping from the thin
shoulder strap. But the only new detail I gleaned was that
Marjorie had not died in the house, as I had always assumed, but
had in fact been rushed to the hospital where she'd died the following day, having regained consciousness just long enough to
say, "Tell Bobby I forgive him." A detail that I found highly suspect, like a false note in an otherwise gripping novel.

It was cold—the digital clock on the bank said ten degrees—
and finally, when she still hadn't appeared by four-fifteen, I got
back in my car parked a few feet away and turned on the heater.
Every five minutes or so I'd get out and peer in the plate glass
window to make sure she hadn't entered by some back door, but I
could see the empty desk with her nameplate facing me. At a
quarter to five, as I was peering intently in the window, she
tapped me on the shoulder. "I'm so sorry," she apologized
breathlessly as I followed her inside. "The escrow officer was late
and there was nothing I could do." Sighing, she slipped off her
coat and stamped her boots. "It's really snowing out there." She
sat down behind her desk and I sat down in the chair opposite
her. Her cheeks glowed a rosy pink from the cold and with her
bright windblown red hair she seemed altogether too vivid for
such drab and businesslike surroundings. "Now, why don't you
tell me what sort of thing you're looking for, Mr. Jones." Behind
her easy smile, her voice sounded a little stiff, rehearsed, almost
apologetic, and it occurred to me that she was new at this.

"Actually it's not Jones. It's Vilmore, Paul Vilmore." I paused,
waiting to see if the name struck a chord. It did. As her smile
flickered, I rushed on. "I'm looking for my wife. I thought maybe
you'd seen her."

"No." She shuffled some papers around on her desk. "I'm
afraid not. We lost touch years ago."

I didn't believe her. She was too unsurprised. After all these
years she should have been astonished, astounded at the very
mention of Janie.

She glanced up nervously and must have seen that I knew she
way lying. "Well, actually, she did stop in here for a couple of
minutes yesterday." She looked down at the papers again. "She
asked me not to tell anyone."

"And?"

"And nothing. I was on my way out the door with a client. We hardly had time to exchange two words. She said she'd give me a call." Flustered, she looked pointedly at her watch and stood up. "I'm afraid I have to pick my son up from day care. He's five and this is his first month in day care full-time. He carries on like he's dying if I'm a minute late." She inhaled sharply and looked away, and I knew that Janie had told her about Lyddie.

"Look," I said, touching her arm lightly, beseechingly. "I'm worried about her. She hasn't been herself since our daughter died." I took my hand away. I could see her hesitating, mentally weighing something, sizing me up. I stood there embarrassed by what she must be thinking, resisting the urge to defend myself, to protest that I did not drink or gamble, that I had never laid a hand on my wife, that I had never even been unfaithful. As she pulled her gloves out of her coat pocket, her car keys jangled to the floor. "Please." I bent down and held them out to her. "If you know anything—"

"Look," she said briskly, taking the keys from me. "I really do have to run." Then something in my expression must have caused her to relent. She sighed. "Why don't you drop by the house around seven, after I've fed Ryan. We can talk then." I nodded as she scribbled the address on a While You Were Out memo. "Thanks. I'll be there." As I followed her out of the office, I glanced down at the address and was surprised to see that she still lived on Forest Avenue, the house she grew up in, across the street from my wife's. "I really appreciate this," I told her.

"You seem like a nice guy." She shrugged.

Watching her pick her way carefully down the icy sidewalk in her high-heeled boots, I felt a huge lump of gratitude lodge itself like a snowball in my throat. At that moment, standing there in the freezing darkness in the middle of nowhere, it seemed like the nicest thing anyone had ever said about me, the highest possible accolade.

It was snowing hard as I drove back in the direction of Forest Avenue after killing a couple of hours over a bean burrito at El

Toro. I was beginning to feel like Dr. Zhivago, trudging through the Siberian steppes, weary and heartsick. The house numbers were impossible to read in the dark through the thick, wet swirl of snow, so I just parked across the street from my wife's old house and trudged up the block until I came to a modest aluminum-sided cube with a screen porch tacked on one side. It was the only house on the block that was not outlined in colored lights and the only one whose walkway was not neatly shoveled. As I ploughed my way through the ankle-deep snow, it seemed to me I suddenly knew how Betsy's life had gone: like something out of a Bruce Springsteen song.

When I rang the doorbell, she opened the door right away. Trusting. As if she'd never heard of crime. Her hair flamed in the bright overhead light of the foyer. I had always assumed the snapshots in my wife's albums must have exaggerated the shade, but if anything, they'd muted it.

"Come on in," she said, leading me into the living room. She was one of those petite perky women, high school pretty. In the snapshots Betsy is cute and sexy, smiling confidently at the camera, while my wife is gawky and thin-faced, self-consciously scowling, her future beauty a well-kept secret. The photographs always break my heart. I wish I could have been there, standing off to the side, whispering in my future wife's ear, "Relax. Smile. You're going to be gorgeous," just as the camera shutter clicked. Dressed in jeans and a baggy plaid flannel shirt, Betsy had not changed much in the twenty-five years since those photographs. She seemed to have shed twenty years along with her business suit and high heels. Suddenly it was not at all difficult to imagine her standing out on the front lawn on a warm summer's evening in baby doll pajamas.

As I was thanking her for agreeing to see me, a child's voice whined, "Mommy, Mommy, come up here. I *need* you!"

"That's Ryan." Betsy smiled. "I better go see what he 'needs.' Make yourself at home."

The living room looked like a set from "Father Knows Best"— the sort of vinyl couches and waxy chartreuse lamp shades that would sell for a small fortune in the trendy shops in Chicago or LA. A small cluster of photographs in lacy gilt frames huddled

together on the mantel making a united stand against the
encroaching army of bric-a-brac. I walked to the fireplace to take
a closer look, thinking that perhaps I might find my wife's face
smiling at me from one of the group photos. But up closer I
could see at a glance that all the children were of a younger generation. As I stood there at the mantel, I suddenly had the odd
certainty that my wife had stood very recently where I was now
standing looking at these same pictures. I could feel her lingering
presence in the room like a ghostly trace of perfume. On the
mantelpiece, as in time-lapse photography of a rose blooming, a
red-haired baby developed from cuddly infant in playpen to cute,
grinning toddler on tricycle, to surly sneaky-faced punk on dirt
bike. For a moment, I was almost relieved that Lyddie would
never grow up.

"That's Dale, my older boy," Betsy said, walking up behind
me. "He lives with his father." She let out a sigh that seemed to
sum up years of heartache. "You want coffee?"

"That would be very nice, if it's no trouble." I followed her
into the kitchen, which was messy but cozy and smelled good. A
pot of chili was congealing on a cold stove burner. Crayoned
drawings were stuck to the refrigerator with alphabet magnets. I
remembered the look on my wife's face the day after the funeral
as she peeled our daughter's last masterpiece—a gaudy tempera
self-portrait with two hamsters—off of our refrigerator, painstakingly easing the Scotch tape loose so as not to tear the fragile
edges, and put it away in the filing cabinet. My hand shook as I
took the coffee mug from Betsy.

We returned to the living room with our coffee and a plate of
cookies.

"Nice place," I said after the first scalding sip of instant coffee.
"Homey."

"I moved back in when Mother had her stroke. She died last
year."

"I'm sorry." I sighed, waiting for her to bring up the subject of
my wife.

"She was old," she said, shrugging, "but your little girl"—she
shook her head—"I'm so sorry." She looked truly sympathetic as
she held out the plate of cookies toward me, then hurriedly set it

down again, as if suddenly realizing the poverty of the offering in contrast to the richness of my loss. To be polite I took a Fig Newton.

"Do you know where my wife is?" I asked softly.

"Not really. As I said, we really didn't get much of a chance to talk." She looked down and busied herself rearranging the cookies more symmetrically on the saucer.

"After our daughter died, she didn't leave the house for a month. I couldn't get her to go to a movie or restaurant or even to the grocery store. Then suddenly I come home and find she's taken off for Nebraska." I leaned forward in my chair. "You sure she didn't say anything? No hint?"

Nervously she reached across the coffee table and snatched an Oreo off the little saucer like a guilty kid expecting to get her wrist smacked. She twisted the cookie into two halves, the way Lyddie used to do, and nibbled around the edges of the frosted half. I sighed again more loudly.

"She told me not to say anything," Betsy said with apologetic stubbornness. "I promised."

"But *why?*" I exploded, then took a moment to calm myself as I saw Betsy retreat slightly in her chair. "I don't get it." My voice was soft, sad, bewildered. I held my head in my hands and pressed the heels of my palms against my eyelids, as if to force some sudden insight. "Did she say why?"

Betsy suddenly leaned over and put her hand on my shoulder, the kind of warm, spontaneous demonstrative gesture that my wife and I had always been incapable of but always affected me deeply. I fought against the urge to bury my head in her lap and bawl like a wounded, outraged baby.

"She probably just needs some time alone," Betsy said soothingly. "To get herself together. She was always that way. She never liked people fussing over her." Absentmindedly she picked up another cookie then set it back down. "I'm on a diet." She smiled a self-deprecating little smile and waved her baggy flannel shirt. "Summer's coming."

"It's only December."

"Thank you." She picked up the cookie again and took a bite. "You're a college professor, aren't you?" she said shyly, with a tinge of old-fashioned deference I hadn't heard in decades. "Janie was always smart, too. Straight A's. I was never much of a student myself." She took another bite of cookie. "You know I tried to keep in touch with her after"—she paused delicately, apparently reluctant to speak of such tragedy aloud—"after she moved away. I wrote to her but she never answered my letters. Once I even called her long-distance, when Gary and I got married. Her aunt back east gave me her number at college. Her roommate answered and took a message, but she never called me back. Or sent a card or anything. I was always sort of hurt. But I under-stood," she added quickly, lest I think she was blaming my wife for any petty little lapses in etiquette after the terrible thing that she'd been through.

"She doesn't like to talk about the past," I said. "She doesn't even like to think about it. You shouldn't take it personally."

"Oh, I didn't. I mean I tried not to."

"She's talked about you a lot," I lied.

"Really?" She brightened. "I figured she'd forgot all about me. With her college friends and all."

I stood up. "I better get going. Thank you for the coffee. It was a pleasure meeting you," I said with a sort of formal awkwardness that I tried to offset with a quick clumsy hug. "I'd have recognized you anywhere, from the pictures. You've hardly changed."

"Not like Janie anyway. God, I didn't even recognize her. She's beautiful."

I nodded. "She doesn't believe it though. She still thinks of herself as a beanpole with braces."

"Yeah, and I still think of myself as head cheerleader." She gave a funny little varsity leap, and we laughed for the first time. As I was pulling on a glove, she reached a hand out and took hold of my arm—our little outburst of silliness suddenly seeming to break through her solemn resolve. "Look, I know where you can find her. But you're not going to like it." She paused as if to give me time to stop her. I pulled on my other glove and remained silent, afraid to say anything—just generally afraid—and after a moment she went on. "She's rented a house. That's why she came to see me yesterday—she'd heard I was in real estate. And she said she figured she could trust me to keep it quiet."

"A house," I repeated blankly.

"A small one-bedroom place on Ivy. Kind of run-down really, but she said she didn't care," Betsy rushed on, anxious to fill in the details now that the dam had broken. "It was the first place I showed her. She hardly even looked at it. I told her I thought she could do better if she looked around more—there's some nice new townhouses over near the college, but she didn't even want to take a look." Betsy shrugged. "She said she wanted a house with a garage, nothing fancy."

"I can't believe it." I stood there staring at the front door, seeing my motionless hand reaching for the doorknob. Half of me wanted to drive right over to Ivy Street and force a confrontation, to have it out once and for all. The other half wanted to get in my car and just keep going, to California maybe, or New Mexico. Get a new driver's license, a new life. I took a step toward the door.

"Where are you going?" Betsy said, worried and protective, as if I were her responsibility now, as if it were all somehow her fault. I could tell she was the sort of woman who blamed herself for everything, took it all on herself, no matter what—the shiftless husbands, the delinquent son, the invalid mother, now me. "She's not there. She didn't take the place 'til Friday afternoon and there's no way she could've got the utilities hooked up. She's not going to sit around some empty house in the freezing dark."

"I just want to see the place," I said, but I wasn't so sure.

"It's a blizzard out there. You can't drive back to Lincoln in that. Why don't you at least stay and have a drink, figure out what to do." Before I could answer, she was off to the kitchen.

She had reminded me that it was Saturday night. When she came back with a bottle of Jack Daniel's and two glasses, I said, "I'm not keeping you from anything?"

She shook her head and splashed a couple of inches of bourbon into the glasses.

"Cheers." Our glasses made an ironic clink. I eased back on the sofa and looked around the room, imagining myself living there. Betsy sat down on the sofa next to me but a safe and respectable distance apart. I sighed and she reached out and squeezed my hand. We sat there holding hands like a couple in a doctor's waiting room, waiting to be summoned for some bad news. But what bad news was left? My daughter was dead. My wife was leaving me. I reached out and touched Betsy's red hair, imagining my wife's pale straight locks interwoven with Betsy's, moonlight and sunlight. "Chang and Eng," I mumbled and held out my glass for a refill.

"How're you doing?" She tapped her stockinged foot lightly against my shoe as she poured me another shot.

"Couldn't be better."

"That's the spirit." She looked relieved. I looked away. Just like my students, I marveled, no sense of irony.

She shivered. "I'm going to build a fire."

"I'll help."

She scrunched newspaper while I took a couple of logs from a crate by the fireplace and stacked them with extreme precision, absurdly anxious to impress her with my manly fire-building prowess, to show her that I was not just some effete intellectual. That wasn't why my wife was leaving me. Pleased when the fire caught easily, I sank back onto the sofa feeling a kind of simple domestic contentment I had not felt in weeks, since before Lyddie suddenly woke us up in the middle of the night, feverish and crying. It seemed more like years than weeks. I could feel myself melting. The bourbon was like a low-banked fire glowing inside me and the fire was like a warm soft blanket someone had tucked over me. Betsy leaned forward and unearthed a large photo album from a messy pile of magazines underneath the coffee table.

"I thought you might like to see these." She flipped through the plastic-coated pages. "See." She pointed. "There's Janie and me naked. A little kiddie porn for you."

I slid closer and adjusted the lamp shade. There they were, huddled together in one of those inflatable backyard wading pools. Just out of frame someone was holding a garden hose. Water arced through the air, splashing them. Betsy was laughing. My wife's expression was more tentative, a mixed grill of emotions. I knew that expression all too well. "Turn the page," I said.

As I sat there looking at the snapshots, listening to Betsy's easy, open narration, I felt a growing excitement, the kind of excitement I felt when I was working with a text, making discoveries, solving the mysteries, almost as if the characters were confiding in me their hidden secrets. For fifteen years my wife had been guarding her past like a jealous dog with a bone, snarling at me whenever I ventured too close, and now it was as if Betsy had suddenly rewarded me out of the blue with a whole treasure trove of buried bones. She flipped the page and a loose snapshot fluttered into my lap. I turned it over: my wife with her normally lank corn silk hair all tortured and sprayed into a droopy confection of curls holding an older boy's hand, gazing up at him with a lovesick smile. I knew even before Betsy whispered, "That's her with Bobby Axelrod."

We both sat there staring at the photograph in silence, searching for some sign of destiny, some visible portent, but there didn't appear to be any. He was just a nice-looking boy with a sweet smile. She shut the covers of the album. "I guess that's it."

Overcome by the warmth from the fire and the bourbon and Betsy's extravagant generosity with the past, I leaned over and kissed her. "You don't know what this means to me," I whispered, "thank you."

She nestled over against me, and the album slid off her lap with a heavy clunk. As I bent down to pick it up, she wrapped her arms around me and we sat there necking in the firelight, tasting the bourbon on each other's lips, like two crazed high school kids until a charred chunk of log split off and landed with a small shower of sparks on the hearth perilously close to the gold shag carpeting. Betsy leapt up, grabbed the poker, and swept the sputtering log back toward the fireplace. Then she sat back on her heels, looking up at me with a dazed and unfocused expression. "Did you hear something?" she said, poking at the ashy wood in the grate.

I shook my head and struggled to sit upright.

"I thought maybe I heard Ryan. But I guess not." Her voice sounded small and forlorn. "Fire's about dead. What should we do?"

"Got any more logs?" I smoothed my hair down.

"In the garage," she said, pointing vaguely.

I stood up abruptly, glad to be given a task. I walked purposefully if a bit unsteadily toward the garage. In the five seconds it took to navigate myself through the kitchen to the back door, the hot liquid passion was already starting to cool off, as if I'd suddenly swallowed an ice cube of guilt that was spreading through my bloodstream. *Jesus*, I thought. This was crazy, sick. I paused and tucked my shirt firmly back into the waistband of my slacks. The instant I opened the garage door a blast of arctic air hit me. I fumbled around for the light switch. The cold air slapped my brain awake—alert, bracing. As the overhead light blinked on, I spied the logs stacked haphazardly against the far wall, next to Betsy's beat-up Chevette. Seeing the Chevette, I flashed on Janie's old Honda parked in our garage back home and I heard Betsy's voice saying, "*She said she wanted a house with a garage. Nothing fancy,*" and I froze. Scared stiff. I don't know how long I stood there like that staring at the car before Betsy appeared in the doorway and said, "What's wrong? Don't you see it?"

"Get your coat," I said. "Hurry."

When we drove up, I could see the ghostly trail of exhaust drifting out from under the garage door. The car engine reverberating in the empty garage sounded so loud I was amazed that it had not roused the neighbors, but the houses on either side were dark, oblivious, muffled in snow. I insisted on sitting in the car with my wife's body while Betsy ran next door to call the ambulance and the police. When she returned, she knelt by the passenger's side where I was sitting and tried to coax me out of the car, treating me with a tender and delicate deference, as if I were some sort of celebrity invalid. She was talking softly, her face close to mine, and I was startled all of a sudden by what I saw there. I recognized the expression in her eyes when she looked at me and the tone of her voice when she spoke to me. It was like looking at myself all those years ago. And I knew, I knew precisely what it was she wanted from me and what she would have to pay to get it. She reached for my hand. I pushed her away. "Leave us alone," I growled. She snatched her hand back as if I'd bitten it. In the distance we heard the faint wail of a siren speeding closer. Betsy walked down to the end of the driveway, glaring back at me reproachfully, as if I were some mean-tempered, old jealous dog with a bone.

As I lie in bed night after night in the dark, I see it all on the split-screen, over and over again, the midnight show: while Betsy and I are toasting by the fire, my wife is sitting in the rented Chrysler LeBaron in the cold dark garage, running the car heater to keep warm. For a while she just thinks, plays the radio, eats some candy. (There were two Milky Way wrappers lying on the seat next to her.) About the time Betsy and I are looking through the old photographs, she flicks off the car radio, having decided what she wants to say, and turns on the battery-operated cassette player she uses with her piano students. She records her message, which is short and businesslike: *I should have been home that day Bobby shot everyone else. I should have been there. I always knew that down deep. I can't live knowing that my daughter paid for my not being there.* Her voice sounds nervous and self-conscious, thinner and higher and more midwestern than her usual voice, and when I hear the tape, it strikes me that it is the voice of an eleven-year-old. She turns off the recorder. The garage door is already shut. About the time that Betsy pours us more bourbon, my wife turns the ignition key and rolls down the car windows. As Betsy and I grope each other on the couch, my wife bunches up her coat to make a pillow and stretches out on the front seat. Her pulse slows as ours quickens.

I remained in the car with my wife. I couldn't move. The blank white garage wall was like a movie screen, and as we sat there in the front seat holding hands in some grisly parody of a couple at a drive-in, the story of our whole marriage flickered across the screen accompanied by a babbling soundtrack inside my head that made no sense, as incomprehensible as Chinese. I reached over and turned on the radio. Classical music, measured and civilized, filled the small car. The Chinese babble quieted. I closed my eyes and felt something pass from her to me in the darkness, some intangible inheritance, and in those few oddly peaceful moments before the ambulance wailed and screeched into the driveway, red lights flashing, rousing the neighbors from their innocent dreams and guilty nightmares, I felt that we were more in tune, in harmony, than we had ever been before—as if some slight but persistent foreignness had disappeared, some long process of naturalization had finally been completed, and, after all these years, my wife and I suddenly found ourselves citizens of the same country.